BREWED AWAKENING

CHARM CITY CONNECTIONS
BOOK THREE

ROXANNE BLACKHALL

BLACK LABEL PRESS

For all the folks who like their bad boys secretly squishy, but still beasts in the bedroom.

For all the folks who like their bad boys secretly squishy, but still beasts in the bedroom.

CONTENT NOTES

This book is intended for adults and contains content that may be upsetting for some readers. Detailed information can be found on the author's website.

www.RoxanneBlackhall.com/content

BREWED AWAKENING

Sam is a bookshop owner rebuilding her life after a "safe" relationship that left her numb. Zach is a charming brewmaster who keeps things casual—and keeps his heart locked down after a betrayal that cut too deep.

They're wrong for each other in every way.

But when business turns into banter and sparks fly, their tension explodes into heat that's raw, intense, and a little rough around the edges.

She wants honesty. He wants to stay guarded. But real love? It doesn't play by the rules.

CHAPTER 1

SAM—FRIDAY, APRIL 17

The door latch clicked into place and Sam Crowley flipped the sign to say 'closed', then turned to face the shop. A flower garden with legs came in from the back and Sam rushed to help. She took an armload of roses and laughed as a stem caught in Carla's almost black curls.

"Hold still. Let me just..." Sam disentangled the wayward bud, then the two of them got to work arranging flowers. Carla Pérez, Sam's best friend and business partner, had wanted to put up streamers and other spring-theme decor for their grand opening, but Sam had convinced her lots of flowers and a balloon bouquet for the front door were enough decoration.

"What did you do? Buy out the entire florist shop?" Sam surveyed the assortment of roses, carnations, lilies, and who knew what all else, as well as piles of greenery and filler.

"You said abundant." Carla shrugged as she stuck a handful of eucalyptus in a waiting vase. "I figure we can get the flowers done and have time to grab a late lunch before the team from Cold Bottom gets here to set up the beer station."

The flowers took longer than Carla had planned and they wound up ordering takeout to save time. Sam dropped their leftovers in the fridge while Carla went to answer the back door. Voices carried from the hall as Carla showed the brewery team through to the front. Sam settled at her desk, figuring she had time to get a little work done, but before she could turn on her laptop, Carla was back and looking like she was up to something.

"C'mon. You need to meet the crew. Especially the brewmaster." Carla dragged Sam to the shop floor, where a small team in pristine Cold Bottom tees bustled around setting up a bar. *Wow. They're going all out.*

"Coming through." The deep voice rumbled through the air and Sam hurried out of the way as a giant Viking wheeled a cart laden with kegs toward the front corner. Lines of ink traced biceps that bulged under the pushed-up sleeves of his T-shirt. His arms were a display of corded muscles that flexed and moved as he shifted kegs into place behind the bar.

A sharp poke in her own biceps broke whatever strange thing had taken over Sam's brain and brought her back to the present. Carla smirked and said something. At least Sam assumed she said something. Her friend's mouth moved, but all Sam heard was the gravelly voice near the bar talking about tasting order.

"I'm sorry, what was that?" She forced herself to focus on Carla.

"You were right. I was wrong. Zach agrees the food station should go in the reading area."

Who's Zach? Is that the Viking?

"Oh? Sure. That makes sense. I uh..." Weeks ago, when they'd planned the layout, Sam had suggested that very thing, but Carla proposed that having the food up front by the bar would be better for visibility.

"Been a minute since I've seen that look on your face. Wow." Carla tipped her head and looked over Sam's shoulder toward the team finishing the bar set up. "He is totally your type. Or at least your type before the stick in the mud. Also, about time you came out of that shell."

Carla angled around Sam and waved an arm in the air. "Hey, Zach. Come meet my business partner."

Sure enough, the Viking lifted his head and nodded. He said something to the rest of the crew, then straightened, pulled off his gloves and swiped a hand through the sandy hair that had fallen over his forehead. He crossed to them and Sam sucked in a sharp breath.

Her best friend was right. Pre-Preston, she'd have been all over this guy, but she had no interest in repeating her early college mistakes.

And what was Preston, if not a seven-year-long mistake?

The Viking's hand swallowed hers as he gave a firm, but somehow gentle, handshake and he introduced himself as Zach Muir, Cold Bottom's brewmaster and the tasting guide for tonight.

"Nice to meet you, Sam." A perfectly groomed beard covered the lower half of a face that looked as if it could have been chiseled by the gods. Then he broke into a dazzling smile and Sam smiled right back. "Carla said you'd know where to set up the food station. We passed an open space near the back."

Oh. Yeah. The event. Pull it together.

"Perfect. Follow me." She led the way to the back of the shop. "We designed this as a reading area that could be configured for classes, or book signings. It's flexible and we have stackable chairs we can put out."

Zach paced along the borders of the space, then stood in the middle, arms crossed and eyes narrowed as he looked around. As if Sam needed more opportunities to admire the man. He looked exactly like what you'd expect of the brewmaster at a craft brewery. A heady combination of Viking mixed with lumberjack, biker, and bad boy all rolled into one package.

Catnip.

And not at all what Sam wanted, or needed, in her life.

"Show me where you keep chairs. I think we've got extra tables in the truck. If not, someone can run back for them. I'll get the staff setting everything up."

She led him to the small storeroom and sucked in a breath as Zach braced a hand on the doorjamb, then leaned past her to peer into the space. Sam bit her tongue to keep from asking what cologne he was wearing. He smelled like a bonfire on the beach at sunset—smoke and warm skin mixed with a salty ocean breeze.

"I'm guessing those right there." He hooked his finger toward the stacks of chairs wedged in the corner, then straightened. "Catering should arrive any minute. We've got the food and beverages handled. You and Carla can focus on running the rest of the event, and if you need anything, I'll be at the bar all night."

He headed back into the shop, and Sam leaned against the wall, trying to catch her breath. She hadn't looked twice at a man since the breakup with Preston. First, because she was too busy figuring out how to rebuild her life. Then came the move to Baltimore, and then the shop.

This place had become everything to her. She didn't have time for men.

When she left Preston, she'd felt directionless. The only thing she knew was she wouldn't, couldn't, keep going the way she had been. She'd bet on herself and Carla, sinking her savings into the dream they'd had since college. This wasn't just a business, it was her lifeline.

Besides, she had toys, and they didn't come with the problems men brought.

"Why are you hiding back here?" Carla grabbed Sam's elbow and steered them to the office, where she shut the door, then crossed her arms and fixed Sam with a look that said she was up to no good.

"That man is gorgeous." Carla waved one hand toward the front of the shop. "It's time to get out and do something. I know you haven't dated in what? Two years?"

It had been twenty-one months, not that Sam was counting. She didn't bother answering Carla's question. It wasn't necessary. She'd been there for all of it.

"Even if I were interested, he's at work. It would be inappropriate to flirt." Sam reached past her friend and unlocked the door. "I'll get the swag bags if you'll check with the Cold Bottom crew. We've got about fifteen minutes till the event starts."

Sam didn't wait for Carla's response. She marched from the office, dodged around a pair of catering staff carrying insulated containers down the hall, and picked up the bundle of balloons and the bin of goody bags she and Carla had assembled.

There was a quiet hum of energy in the shop as she passed the catering set up, that shifted to a more festive feel in the front where the bar sat across from the register.

Aw, man. I'm going to be looking at him all night.

Sam shook her head and focused on storing the goody bags. She could avoid the register tonight. They had staff coming in for that, so Sam and Carla would be free to mingle. Sam checked the till and double checked the VIP list. Then detoured to the counter to run a systems check on the coffee and tea machine.

They'd invested in some sleek, automatic, capable of delivering near-barista-quality coffee machine that could also do custom tea steeping. It was a splurge, but worth it as far as she was concerned. Sam tapped through the menu, checking that it was stocked and ready to go.

All good. One more to-do item crossed off.

She'd promised herself that no matter what, Shelf Indulgence wouldn't just exist, it would thrive. Books and Brews was just the start.

So ignore the hot Viking, suck it up, and smile.

She grabbed the clipboard and marched across the shop to where Zach was laying out what looked like drink menus while the rest of the staff assembled small bar-height tables. Zach looked up as Sam laid the clipboard on the bar.

"That the VIP list?" He picked it up and scanned the single page before bringing his eyes back to hers and Sam couldn't look away from those sparkling blues. "Just a reminder, you don't need to worry about checking IDs. That's on us. And confirming, the VIP list gets a purple wristband and open bar. Everyone else gets an orange band and they pay for their drinks. Food is on the house. I get that right?"

"Yes. Perfect." Sam tried to breathe, or look away, or something. She wasn't sure she was capable of blinking.

"Kinda going all out. What's the occasion?"

"Grand opening," Sam replied. "Shelf Indulgence soft opened two weeks ago, but the Books and Brews event was always part of the plan. Something fun. Different. Unexpected."

Zach leaned down, elbows on the bar and getting eye level with Sam. "You can always tell when someone loves what they do. Their passion shows. Cool shop name, by the way. Really clever. Sounds a bit naughty."

He winked and straightened. Sam tried to tell herself that wasn't real flirting. It was the type of friendly, mildly flirty banter people in customer-facing jobs often employed. Nothing more. She was sure of it. None of that changed the fact that his wink sent her thoughts careening into places she had no desire to go. No matter how hard she tried, she couldn't think of an appropriate response. She wasn't prissy or prudish, but she didn't want to seem like she was misinterpreting friendly as something more.

"Thanks." Sam tore her eyes away from him and hurried to get the balloons to the front door. She was saved from dwelling on it too much when she found a line of about a dozen people waiting outside. She pushed open the heavy glass door, propped up the A-frame sign and anchored the balloons to it, then gave the group her best smile and stepped out of their way.

"Welcome to Books and Brews at Shelf Indulgence! Thank you for coming."

ZACH

Books and beer were never a combination Zach expected. Wine? Sure. Hell, even whisky. He'd never imagined bookish people to be into beer. The event had been packed from the moment the doors opened and it had stayed steady for three solid hours. Things hadn't slowed down yet, and with an hour left, he surveyed the crowd.

"I'm gonna take a break." Zach whipped off his apron and hung it on a hook under the collapsible bar. "Text if you need me."

The crew waved him away and Zach eased through the

clusters of people happily drinking, munching on food, and talking books. From the covers, it looked like mostly romance and fantasy. Stuff Deke's sister Sarah liked.

"Zach? Since when did you go back to working events?"

Speaking of. He turned around and gave her a big hug. "You just get here? Hubby got the twins?"

She tipped her head toward the bar where Chris stood chatting with one of the crew. "They're with my folks for the weekend. I twisted his arm into coming with me to this. We've got concert tickets tomorrow night. I plan to take full advantage of a child-free weekend."

Zach tried to ignore the wink she sent him. There was a time when he had a thing for Sarah, back in his freshman year of college, but Deke had threatened him within an inch of his life. In hindsight, that was probably a good thing. Chris came over with two drinks, handed one to Sarah, then shook Zach's hand. "Good to see you. Been a while. Thought you were strictly in the brewhouse these days."

Zach hooked a thumb toward the back. "There're still some munchies, if you're hungry. And yeah. I usually am, but Ryan couldn't be here tonight, and Mom insisted I'd be a better choice than Reg. She talked me into it."

Looking around, he got her reasoning. Lynn Abell was an award-winning brewmaster, and she also knew business. Like any good bartender, Reg had the gift of gab, but he gave off dad vibes, and not the hot kind. Great for a bar setting. Maybe not so great at an event that seemed to cater to women. They'd given out more discount cards tonight than usual.

Correction: I've given out more cards than usual.

"Oh, yeah, I'm sure working this event was a tremendous burden to you. How many numbers have you gotten tonight?" Sarah jabbed an elbow into his ribs and Chris laughed along.

Zach took it in stride. He was an only child, but then he'd met Deke his first week of college and gotten to know his family, and suddenly he had three older sisters.

"Believe it or not, none. A little flirting goes with the territory, but even I understand professional boundaries."

He would not discuss the disaster that was his January. He'd tried going out a time or two since, but the mindless conversations left him flat. Never mind that he never wanted to wake up next to someone who couldn't remember they'd been fucking for three weeks.

"Seriously? Wow. Who the hell are you and what did you do with the real Zach?"

He flipped his middle finger up, then grabbed Sarah's shoulders and steered her toward the food. "Hey, Chris. Feed her before she gets hangry or something."

Sarah shot him a dirty look, but thankfully went along with Chris to find the food. Leaving Zach stuck in the middle of the shop, unwilling to go to the front where the bar was, and not wanting to keep hanging around with Sarah and Chris in the back.

"This shop is designed to get lost in." Sam crooked her finger and beckoned him between the bookshelves before disappearing. He'd caught her staring at him a few times through the night, but then she'd look quickly away. Behavior that often said a woman was interested, but shy or uncertain. He stepped between the shelves and realized there was a gap about halfway down the aisle. He turned and there she stood in a small area ringed with bookshelves. Two cushy looking chairs filled most of the hidden room.

"You looked like you needed a quiet moment." Sam stepped sideways, giving him room to get to the chairs.

"More like a break from being on." Zach suspected she'd understand that feeling. Socially, he was the life of the party,

9

but work was a different game. She tossed her head back and let out a soft laugh.

"Grab a seat. Pick up a book if you want. That's what this spot is for." She slipped between the bookshelves, leaving Zach alone.

He stuck his head out, but she'd disappeared. *Weird.* The hum of conversation seemed distant. Quieter. Maybe all the books muffled sound, or the event was winding down. He'd forgotten how draining working a bar could be. Especially doing guided tastings. Zach eyed the chairs; in his experience, furniture like that wasn't meant to accommodate his height. The crew would text if they needed him. He settled carefully, then leaned back with a smile, surprised at how comfortable he was.

Sam must look like a kid in these. She's tiny. She was also not his usual type, but there was no denying she was cute, in a hot librarian kind of way. Fuck. He needed to get out more if he was thinking shit like that.

"I don't know if you're a tea drinker, but this is one of my favorites when I've had a stressful day." Sam placed a steaming mug on the little table next to him. "If you don't want it, or don't like it, that's fine."

Zach caught her hand before she could turn away. "Thank you. There's a sort of... I dunno... weird sound distortion happening here or something."

Sam smiled and slid into the other chair. He'd been wrong. She didn't look like a kid. The hot librarian part? That he'd gotten right.

"We wanted the shop to feel a little magical. Like something outside of time. Some of the shelves can be moved to change the flow of how folks move through the space. When I left earlier, I moved the shelf at the end of the row. Makes this space harder to find. I'm sure that dampened sounds."

At least he hadn't been imagining that shit seemed quiet. He picked up the tea and took a cautious sip, afraid it would be too hot. It wasn't, and it was delicious.

"I'm dying to know. Why beer?" Zach took another sip of tea. "Not wine? Or I dunno, brandy?"

Another soft laugh whispered in the cozy space, and Sam shrugged. "Carla and I both like beer." She shifted sideways, leaning one elbow on the back of the seat so she was looking directly at him.

"You think bookish folks are pretentious." It was a statement, not a question.

"No, I don't... well, maybe?" This wasn't the usual type of conversation he had with attractive women. *And maybe that's a good thing.* "Would it surprise you to know I have a dual degree in chemistry and brewing microbiology, plus a graduate degree in brewing science and operations?"

Most people didn't think about the science behind a successful beer, and trotting out his CV wasn't in his typical flirting tactics. Sam didn't look surprised.

"And you're asking me why beer? Let's do a tasting." Her head tipped at an angle and her lips curled into a smile that kept his attention riveted on her face.

"What? Now?" He checked his watch. They had time. "Okay. Let's go. Lead the way."

Sam rose and led him out of the reading nook, taking a different path than how they'd entered, so they came out next to the bar.

"How did you..." Zach shook his head. She wasn't kidding about the shop feeling a little magical. He pointed her to a stool at the end of the bar, then grabbed his apron. He looped it over his head and tied it behind his back with practiced ease. It had been a while since he'd worked the bar. Brewhouse duties rarely included front-of-house charm, but he'd gotten back in the swing of things quickly. Like riding a motorcycle after a long winter. A little stiff at first, but then the engine purred, and every part of him remembered exactly what to do.

His hands knew where the tasting cups were without him having to look. Muscle memory took over as he popped the cooler, lined everything up, checked the tap. The shift of his weight behind the bar, the lean-in, the pour. It was all choreography. A slow, confident dance that invited people to lean closer. Add some easy banter and good to go.

Then he almost dropped a glass doing the spin before he set it on the bar, but the rhythm was already humming under his skin. He'd been coasting most of the night, but for Sam, he pulled out all the old tricks. The teasing patter, the slide of the glass, the low rumble of his voice when he asked what someone liked. It wasn't just service; it was seduction. Not in a sleazy way. More like the bar itself was an extension of him, and tonight he let it speak.

And with Sam watching him like that, eyes curious, lips slightly parted, Zach didn't mind putting on a show.

"You've done a tasting with us before?"

"Of course. With Lynn Abell before we contracted for this series of events."

No pressure then. Great. His mother knew every brew inside and out. She'd created most of them. His were the newer ones. He removed three of the tasting glasses, and Sam raised an eyebrow.

"You'll know all about the colors, the flavors, the nose. So let's deep dive on three of my favorites. Two are from kegs— the pilsner and the amber you included in your selection for tonight. The other is from a can. We bring a selection to events to pad out the choices, but they're not available for the tasting flight. For you, I'll make an exception."

He winked at her, easily flowing into the banter and routine of being behind the bar. Sam rolled her eyes but propped her chin on her hands as he pulled a can from the cooler.

"We'll do one at a time so you can savor each taste." He filled the first glass with the classic pilsner from the keg and placed it in front of her.

"Looks like your typical beer, but this is better. And I'm not just bragging. I never brag without reason."

That earned him another eye roll, bigger this time, but her smile grew.

"The pilsner is our best seller and has won several awards."

Zach leaned down and braced his elbows on the bar so he could see her face better. "Pick up the glass and close your eyes, then tell me what you smell."

Her eyes narrowed, but she smiled and lifted her chin from her hands then scooped up the glass. Her gaze shot back to him and held as she brought the glass to her chin level. *Hazel. Her eyes are hazel.* No. They were a starburst with spikes of green and gold and brown. Her lids closed and Zach felt like he could breathe again.

What the fuck was that?

"Citrus." The single word pulled his attention to her lips. Pink and plump. "Toast! It smells like toast."

"Don't open your eyes." He wasn't sure what had just happened between them but he knew if she looked at him like that right now, he'd have a hard time not kissing her. *Not on the clock. Nope.* "Take a slow sip. Take your time before swallowing then breathe out through your nose."

"You talk to all the girls like this?"

She tipped the glass and drank then made a little humming sound. It was barely noticeable in the still busy room, but Zach heard it clear as day. *What was in that tea?*

Sam sat the glass down and opened her eyes. Whatever the weird thing was from before was gone. *No. Still there. Just mellowed. Huh.*

"Amazing. And I don't usually care for lighter beers. So, why is this one of your favorites?"

"So glad you asked." Zach shifted the glass to the side and filled the next glass with the amber lager. "You can pair beer with food, just like you do wine. And that one is what you reach for when you're having a burger. Or a steak. Or it goes really great with a grilled cheese, bacon, and tomato sandwich."

"Because it's crisp and would cut the fattiness, but it's not too much if you're having a rich meal. I get it. And for the record, that sandwich sounds delicious."

"It is and it's on the menu." He slid the glass of red over to her and she leaned in, chin in her hands again and her gaze fixed on him. The rest of the world disappeared as Zach explained the flavors of the new beer.

Sam laughed at the usual jokes he peppered into any tasting, her smile wide and bright and her laugh soft. He was mesmerized by her every move as she tucked a strand of blond hair behind her ear, or tapped a short, pink nail against the beer menu in front of her. When she licked her lips after tasting the second beer, the urge to kiss her reared up again and Zach shook himself.

"That one is more my style," she said. "I like the flavors and it's not too heavy. The hint of cardamom is nice."

That wasn't something most people picked up, and it wasn't in the tasting notes. "Last one, and it may be a bit adventurous. Did you try the stout during your tasting?"

"No. We stuck to the most popular selections."

He opened the can and poured the dark brew into the last

glass then reached for a second glass and poured one for himself.

"I wondered when you'd join me."

"I avoid drinking when working, but it's the end of the night, I'm not driving, and I'm a little fond of this one."

He raised his glass and tapped it against hers, but didn't drink. He watched as she closed her eyes and inhaled. Her eyebrows lifted and she inhaled again, then her eyes opened wide and she looked up at him.

"Coffee and something smoky."

"You have a remarkable nose. Taste and tell me what else there is."

Sam took a slow slip and Zach nearly dropped the glass in his hand as her lips parted on a sigh before she took another taste.

"It's woody, and there's another layer to the bitter. Something a little sweet. Is it chocolate?"

Zach swallowed hard then tipped his glass back, finishing in one swallow. Anything to get his brain on a more normal path. Something about her flipped his world into an alternate reality. Maybe it was the shop, but Zach suspected it was her. He took a deep breath and forced himself back to his routine.

"Great palette. Most people catch the bitter, but can't identify it. You're right. Coffee and cocoa." He topped off her glass before she said anything. It was the only one she'd taken a second drink of and that was a good sign someone liked the brew.

"Over the Barrel generates a lot of interest, even though it's not to everyone's taste. Aged in bourbon barrels. That's the smoky and woody you picked up."

Sam closed her eyes as she took another drink and Zach was struck by how immersed in the sensual she was.

"That last one was your creation."

"Yep. Launched at Christmas. The amber is also mine, but it came out about a year and a half ago."

She finished her glass and Zach offered to pour more but she shook her head. He tipped the rest of the can into his glass then leaned back down. Maybe he'd get her number. Sam was easy to talk to and there was chemistry or something between them.

"Hey Zach, time for last call. You want me to handle the till?"

Shit.

"Guess it's back to work." Zach straightened and shoved a hand through his hair. Flirting was one thing, but pursuing when he was supposed to be working was stepping into a gray area. He'd blurred those lines in the past, but she was one of the shop owners. That wouldn't go over well.

Sam leaned in and placed a hand on his arm. The contact brought his swirling thoughts to a single point of focus—her.

"Duty calls for me, too." She shifted off the stool and her hand slid away. "I get the feeling you're not normally on this side of things. At least, not anymore. Thank you. That was a remarkable experience."

She turned away and disappeared behind the small crowd that clustered around the bar to get another drink. Zach cleared their glasses and wiped the counter, throwing himself into the rhythm of end of night tasks and trying not to dwell on whatever had happened between them, or how she'd seen him like no one else ever had. Not just once, but twice.

I need to get laid. Been a while. That's gotta be it. This is what happens when I'm fucking horny.

CHAPTER 2

SAM—SATURDAY, APRIL 18

Sam stepped through the nondescript door into a small room that looked like it belonged in another time. A handful of people, mostly couples, sat around compact tables in a space that felt like a basement speakeasy in the twenties—from the distressed wallpaper to the framed art on the walls. She made her way to a seat at the bar and ordered a drink.

Books and Brews had been wildly successful, but she'd been swamped in the weeks leading up to it and was ready for some downtime.

Carla had been nagging her to get out, but before last night, Sam had no interest. Then Zach came along, tripping all of her happy buttons and all of her danger buttons at the same time. He was hot, and the spark between them had been amazing, but she knew better than to fall into that trap. Hot and off the charts chemistry equaled toxic. Last night, she'd gotten carried away by it, but the cold light of morning brought her to her senses. She'd given up the bad boys. They were not good for her.

So the alternative is boring?

"Excuse me, mind if I sit here?"

Oh no. That is not him.

She turned, crossing her fingers the low, rumbly voice belonged to anyone but him. Any other man she could handle. Those hopes were dashed when she found herself eye level with the broad chest of the Viking. A battered leather jacket hung open over a shirt of some chunky-looking knit and worn jeans. Heavy silver rings sat on long, tapered fingers and when she looked back up, his blue eyes danced with amusement.

Zach.

He pointed at the empty stool next to her and raised his eyebrows. Hugely tall and even hotter than she remembered. Sam clutched her glass in both hands and blew out a breath. She could do this. They had a professional connection. It was fine.

"Nope, I don't mind at all." Sam put on her best smile as Zach settled onto the open seat. *I'm gonna throttle Carla.* All her chatter that Sam was turning into a hermit had worked its way into Sam's brain. After so many years with Preston, Sam had forgotten what it felt like to flirt. It was heady.

A slow grin spread on his face, lifting the corners of his lips and crinkling his eyes. Sandy hair swept back from his forehead and his beard looked like he'd just stepped out of the barbershop, the edges were so crisp and perfect. The bartender came over and the Viking hadn't even looked at the menu.

"The honey old fashioned, and open a tab, please." He handed the bartender a card, then turned toward Sam and tapped the glass she still gripped in her left hand. "One of my favorites. Not to be cheesy, but... come here often?"

His lopsided smile and eye roll turned the trite line into a fun joke. Instead of laughing, Sam summoned her best teacher-scowl and stared at him until his smile started to fade.

"That your best line?" She tried to keep a straight face, but her lips twitched and just her luck, he caught it. His smile bloomed again and he shook a finger at her like you would a misbehaving child.

"Not even close." The look he gave her was pure smolder. "Lemme try that again. Is this your first time here?"

"It is. Heard about it from one of the guests last night." Crap. She'd meant to avoid bringing up last night. Zach nodded and looked around the bar before leaning closer to her.

"Seems like your kinda place. Quiet and unexpected."

She wasn't so out of practice that she didn't recognize flirting, and this she couldn't blow off as him doing his job. No matter how much she tried to convince herself last night's banter was Zach being a good bartender and knowing how to make a customer feel at ease, it had seemed like more.

Yeah, like "how quickly can I get in your pants."

"You a bourbon fan?"

His drink arrived and somehow that broke the spell. Sam sipped hers, then set the glass down, determined to not be reduced to mush just because some hot bad boy flashed her a wicked smile.

"I am," she replied.

"So what brought you to a speakeasy alone on a Saturday night?"

That was definitely flirting. Sam toyed with the swizzle stick in her drink, trying to buy some time. Maybe Carla was right about Sam needing to get out and have some fun. Still, despite their apparent connection last night, or because of it, she wasn't sure the walking mountain next to her was the kind of fun she was looking for.

"I'm learning to live a little," she replied. He braced his elbow on the bar and cocked his head to the side as if she'd said something fascinating. "I moved here in January and I've been so focused on work I haven't had time to think about much else. And I'm sure you don't want to hear all of that."

She took a hurried sip of her drink. Anything to look away from his piercing blue eyes.

"There's a table open. Why don't we grab it?" Zach stood and pointed toward the back. When Sam slid off her stool right next to him, she had to look up, way up, to see his face. She'd forgotten just how tall he was. *Great night to choose flats. Not that a few inches of heel would help here.*

He gestured for her to go ahead of him, so she scooped up her glass and maneuvered through the small room to a cozy table for two in the far corner. She eyed the tight space, then looked back at Zach and tried not to laugh at the mental image of him squeezing his large frame into one of the seats.

"Hold this, please." Zach handed her his glass, then shifted the table closer to the wall before sliding into the chair in the corner and gestured for her to sit opposite him.

"I don't mean to be rude, but... Oh, never mind." She handed him his drink then sat. Zach's lips curled into a smile that looked like he was holding in a laugh.

"I'm six foot six," he said. "Been this tall since somewhere in high school. The world isn't designed for tall people in general, let alone for someone this size. So, I got really good at fitting into tight spaces."

Was that an innuendo? I really am out of practice.

Flirting with Zach was a dangerous thing, though. Carla had been right about Zach being the kind of man that turned Sam's head. Sexy. Edgy. Hot. And unbelievable sex. The trouble was that the amazing packaging was all surface.

Underneath every guy like that she'd known, all she'd found was insecurity, toxic traits, and the inability to commit.

No thank you.

"I'm sorry. You probably hear stupid questions all the time. I know I do, just the other direction. I should know better."

Zach leaned forward, his elbows on the table, and a sinful smile on his face. "I shared. Your turn."

It took a moment for his meaning to sink in. His eyes were mesmerizing. So were his lips—full and pouty and framed by his neatly groomed beard and mustache.

"Five foot one," she replied. Zach's eyebrows went up and his lips pursed for a moment, then broke into a wide grin. "Oh, go ahead, I've probably heard it all."

"I'm sure you have, but like you, I should know better. So I'll behave." He stroked the back of her hand gently with one long finger and her skin puckered into goosebumps. "For now."

That one gesture put a crack in Sam's already shaky resolve. He worked at the brewery she and Carla were partnering with for events. He was undoubtedly every bit the hot and dangerous playboy type. Sam needed to focus on making good business decisions, and if she was ever going to have a relationship again, she was determined to not settle.

But a little flirting isn't a bad thing.

"Do you want another?" Zach tapped her empty glass.

"Oh, yeah. Hang on. I didn't open a tab." Sam reached for her purse, but Zach laid a hand on her arm, sending another wave of goosebumps that reached the back of her neck.

"I got it. Be right back."

Somehow, he slid out from behind the table and scooped up both of their glasses before heading to the bar. Sam had the perfect opportunity to admire the man from behind. He'd taken off his jacket and his shirt pulled tight across wide shoulders and a broad back. Her breath caught when she got to his ass. His faded jeans clung in all the right ways, emphasizing powerful legs and an ass that made her want to grab it.

She wasn't the only one admiring. Zach's height would guarantee attention in any room, but he was also a level of handsome that bordered on unreal. He turned back around and Sam quickly looked away, embarrassed to be caught staring. She didn't look back up until he put their drinks down in front of her.

There were those chunky silver rings again. He'd pushed his sleeves up, revealing a dusting of fine, golden hair over forearms corded with muscle, and the edges of the tattoos she'd noticed last night. Without thinking, Sam grabbed his wrist before he could wedge himself behind the table again. She snatched her hand away and kept her eyes focused somewhere around his chest—not daring to look up into his face, and definitely not looking straight ahead where his belt buckle sat at her eye level.

"Hey um, would it be easier if I took the corner?"

Zach's chest lifted with laughter, then he twisted and slid into the corner seat without so much as bumping the table. "This is actually better. If I were in that seat, I'd be more in the way."

He pointed under the table until Sam leaned down to see he was almost sprawled in the chair; his shoulders braced on one wall and his long legs stretched out along the other.

"You said you'd moved here in January. What brought you to Baltimore?"

Sam straightened up to find Zach looking at her with an expression of deep interest. That question cemented it. He was flirting. Still, maybe there was more to him than the bad boy image implied.

Yeah, right. Keep your head on straight, Sam. Dating with purpose.

"The bookshop mostly." She could tell him she was trying to rebuild after a disastrous and soul-sucking relationship. Or that she felt like she was spinning her wheels, following dreams that were not hers. None of it mattered. Zach was hot and fun to flirt with but this wasn't going anywhere.

"Way back when, my college roommate and I had a dream. The kind of thing you imagine when you're young, but somehow never pursue. Then her wife got a job here, and next thing I know, she's calling me about making the bookshop happen."

The call had come at the ideal moment for Sam. Her teaching contract had ended, along with her apartment lease. She'd moved back in with her parents and started substitute teaching in her hometown. She had options but wasn't thrilled with any of them.

The best part, Baltimore got her away from memories of seven years of everything in her life revolving around Preston. His likes, his wants, his expectations.

"The timing was right," she continued. "It's been hard work, but so far, things have fallen into place like they were meant to be."

Even Cold Bottom. Maybe I was meant to meet Zach. That could explain last night. And running into him here. Okay, universe, what's going on here?

She needed to stop that train of thought right now. "I guess you grew up here?"

"Pretty much," he replied. "Born in Colorado, moved around a lot as a kid. Came here when I was five and been here ever since."

His response had the feeling of something rehearsed, or repeated so often he didn't have to think about it. Zach sat up straighter and looked toward the bar, then a big smile crossed his face. "They don't usually do food here, but every now and then you get lucky. Tonight, you got lucky, and by extension, so did I. You okay with spicy?"

Before she could do more than nod, he slid out of his seat. A few steps away he stopped and turned back.

"I suppose I should ask if you eat meat."

"Probably easier to list the things I don't eat." Sam had always been an adventurous eater and liked finding new places or trying different things. A fact that had rubbed Preston wrong. He had his favorites and never wanted anything else.

"Cool. Same." Zach headed to the end of the bar where several other people had crowded around. The small room was packed now, but still felt like a quiet, intimate space.

The whole vibe appealed to her bookish side—it was easy to imagine someone like Mary Shelley, or, considering this was Baltimore, Edgar Allen Poe sitting at a table. She fished her phone out, snapped a picture, then sent it to Carla.

> This is the kind of vibe I imagine for a bookish speakeasy.

Carla's response came back in seconds.

> Oh yeah! Been there. Awesome space and you're right. Hey. Is that the guy from the brewery? Are you on a date? You two were kinda in your own world last night.

> Yes it is. No I'm not. We bumped into each other here. He's cool, but no. Don't go there.

She tucked her phone away as Zach returned with a tray

filled with something that smelled of fried heaven with a spicy undercurrent and had her stomach grumbling. In a flash, he set out two beers, water glasses, a basket of wings, another of sweet potato fries, and enough napkins to mop up a disaster, then settled into his seat.

"Bella runs a restaurant up the street and sometimes they do a collab here. Her wings are to die for, but they've got some heat. Hence the beers. Dig in."

Sam raised her glass. "To heat."

Zach clinked it with his. "And to unexpected delights."

ZACH

Zach had no clue why that had slipped out of his mouth. Sam seemed determined to ignore it. He grabbed the little cups of extra barbecue sauce and honey mustard out of the basket and set them to the side, then waited while Sam unwrapped plastic utensils and transferred a few wings to her plate. Her eyes closed as she inhaled deeply and Zach's brain went straight to the gutter. Again.

He was normally good at reading people, but Sam had him stumped. Just like last night, she seemed to waver between flirty and almost timid. He wasn't sure how to deal with that. He gravitated toward women who made their interest clear and didn't dance around what they wanted.

And look where that landed me.

Which was why he was changing things up. His first couple of attempts at going out after the January disaster were dismal failures and he'd given up. Figured it was time to take a break. Tonight, instead of going to a busy club where finding a hookup was almost guaranteed, he'd chosen the small, relatively obscure speakeasy. Quiet. Chill. No pressure.

Then he'd spotted Sam. Her blond hair caught what little

light there was, making it look like she had a halo. He remembered she was petite, but somehow had forgotten how small until she hopped off the barstool and shrank a few inches. But damn, she was sexy as fuck. He'd sure as shit enjoyed the view when she'd walked in front of him—the fuzzy sweater nipped in at her waist and her dark, fitted pants hugged her ass like they'd been sewn on.

She was tiny, but built just right. And too damn tempting.

Keyword: tiny.

"These smell amazing. Aren't you eating?" Sam pointed at the empty plate in his hand then scooped some of the sweet potato fries next to her wings.

Zach filled his plate, then nearly dropped it as she popped a flat in her mouth and extracted clean bones like it was nothing. He waited for the tears or coughing to start, ghost peppers were no joke, but she swallowed and let out a low moan of appreciation.

"Oh, those are good." She picked up a drum and Zach forgot about his own food. Watching her eat with such uninhibited pleasure short circuited his brain. If she enjoyed food with that much passion....

"Something wrong?"

Sam had a fry pinched between her fingers and her eyes squinting in concern. Zach shook himself and smiled as he picked up a wing.

"Not a thing. Just uh..." God, what could he say? He relied on his charm in most situations, and it had taken a nosedive the second she smiled at him.

"I'm a little surprised is all. I've watched more than a few folks get red and sweaty eating these things and you're acting like they're mild. Where'd you grow up?"

"Connecticut." She winked and bit into another drum.

He waited for her to elaborate, but she just reached for her beer like that was explanation enough.

"Oh, brown ale. Nice."

She sat back and studied him with a look so direct it made him self-conscious. Zach picked up his own beer.

"I'm impressed."

"By what?" He grabbed another wing and dunked it in more sauce. He didn't know what to make of this woman and that was a new feeling.

"There's not a speck of sauce on your beard. That takes skill."

"Yeah, well, you learn to be careful so you're not gross or having to go wash your face all the time. Besides, you're one to talk. You got what—three fingers messy? On one hand, no less."

She'd somehow eaten wings drowning in sauce with a single hand, keeping the other free for her drink. It was weirdly precise. Polished and prim. But the way she enjoyed them? That was pure hedonism.

And skill. Maybe she's got a wild side under that tidy exterior.

"Okay. What just went through your head?"

He'd never been so glad to have a mouthful of food as he was in that moment. He offered a shrug and a wink, but inside, the war was real. The logistics alone should have been a turnoff. She was so petite, and he'd been in enough situations to know sometimes things just didn't fit. Then his brain conjured her moaning around that wing and imagined what else she'd sound like, and...

She has to have an amazing tongue.

"There it is again." Sam circled her finger around, gesturing at his face. "I'm convinced that was some not safe for work level daydreaming."

Fuck it.

"Maybe a little," he admitted, licking sauce from his thumb. He grabbed a napkin and wiped his fingers down. "But let's be honest. You were checking me out earlier."

Sam laughed and even the dim lighting couldn't hide the way her cheeks flushed.

"Yes, I was. You're a good-looking man, and I'm sure you're used to being checked out."

She said it like it wasn't a compliment. Mater-of-fact. Observational. That alone threw him off.

"There's nothing wrong with looking," she added. "Or a little flirting."

"I'm sensing a 'but' in there."

No matter what she said in response, he knew damn well there was a 'but' in there. His gut twisted, part of him hopeful, part already disappointed.

What the hell is up with that?

"Well, let's start with the fact that there's a professional connection here."

Right. That.

"Never mix business and pleasure," he said with a nod.

She gave him a sad smile, and damn if he didn't want to kiss it off her lips.

"If we'd met when I was in college," she said, "I'd have been one of the girls trying to get your attention. Now?"

He wasn't sure if the shrug and hand waving she did was a gesture of frustration or something else, so he waited.

"I suspect we want different things. My best friend jokes that I'm looking for a unicorn. You know, a totally mythical creature. Maybe she's right, but I'm at a point where I'm only interested in dating with purpose, and I'm okay being picky about that."

There it was. The thing that should have been a flashing

red light for him. Relationships weren't his thing, though he respected how up front she was about it. Now was his chance to tell her that. If he was smart, he would. Especially since the brewery was going to be stocking her bookstore's next three events.

"There's nothing wrong with a little banter between friends," she continued. "I'm enjoying your company. So long as we both understand the boundaries, I don't see a problem. Do you?"

Zach could see several. Starting with the fact that he wanted her in ways that were neither platonic, nor professional. Followed by the fact that he was seeing her as a challenge, and imagining how her laugh would sound in his bed. And that he was considering dodging a few truths to get what he wanted. All red flags of his own.

He didn't want to say anything that would stop their playful banter, either.

"Nope. No problem here."

The lie slid out, but it didn't feel good.

"So, friend," he said, trying to redirect. "How much have you explored the city since you got here?"

Sam had just stuck another wing in her mouth and made a so-so gesture with her free hand. All while Zach was spellbound by her pouty lips. He waited while she finished and took a swallow of beer.

"I really haven't. I've renovated and stocked a storefront and been hustling to get an indie bookshop off the ground. My best friend is my business partner. And her wife is in her orthopedic residency at Hopkins. What's free time?"

He leaned in a little, not missing the way she mirrored the movement. "I'm enjoying your company too. Normally, I'd be angling for more, but you said it—boundaries. Still, you haven't had the chance to explore the city. I think I can help there."

She raised an eyebrow, but didn't object. *Encouraging.*

He crossed his fingers they had some common interests or this was going to get awkward, and boring, really fast.

"We've established you like spicy food. Someday you'll have to explain how a Connecticut girl can handle ghost pepper barbecue. Musical tastes? Baltimore's got a pretty good music scene." Zach braced himself to hear she was a Swiftie, or listened to classical, or something like that.

"I'm all over the place." Sam stacked their trash into the empty wings basket and tucked it to the side. "I like more indie than anything, not a country girl unless it's crossover. Blues, jazz, soul, singer-songwriter stuff. You name it."

Huh. Cool.

"Yeah, same. There're a few venues I think you'll enjoy. We should hit 'em up."

She didn't balk at the suggestion. Just nodded and asked more about his favorites, where to find the best sushi, good spots for dancing. Her curiosity was genuine and infectious.

He couldn't remember the last time he'd spent this long with a woman just talking.

"You never did answer my question. Why beer for Books and Brews?"

Zach was an avid reader and always had been, but he'd never been into the bookish crowd. They were either too nerdy or too pretentious, or both. Sure, there were some craft beer folks who took pretentious to whole new levels, but they were the minority. Books and beer seemed like an odd combination.

She hesitated, then smiled. "Why not?"

Sam pulled up the store's Instagram page and handed him

her phone. "You've seen the shop. Our goal was to make it a place where people were comfortable."

The vibe came through even in photos. Warm. Relaxed. Welcoming. What the pictures didn't capture was the sense of magic he'd felt in the shop. He suspected that was all Sam.

Her passion was clear. So was her ambition.

This wasn't a woman looking to fit into anyone else's story. She was writing her own.

He liked that.

And it scared the shit out of him.

Somehow, they'd transitioned from flirting to friendly banter. Talking to Sam was smooth and easy. Anyone other time, he'd have bounced the second he realized a woman wasn't on the same page about sex, but he had no desire to stop their conversation.

And who knows where things might go.

He walked to the bar to grab their next round mostly because he needed a second to breathe and figure out what the hell he was doing. He was spending hours in a low-key bar just talking. And enjoying it.

That wasn't him. That wasn't how this worked.

He made no promises. Let things flow. Made a hasty exit when things got dull, or obvious the night wasn't going anywhere exciting.

Sam wasn't offering that kind of opening. And yet, here he was. Still here. Still hungry for more than just wings.

He brought the drinks to their table.

What the fuck am I doing?

He didn't know. What's more, he didn't care. Sam intrigued him and if he had to play a long game to figure that out, then that's what he'd do. Even if she was playing a different game.

He sat back down with a smile that she returned.

Hell, I'm playing a different game here.

When the bartender shouted for last call, Zach flicked his wrist to check the time. Quarter to one. Fifteen minutes to closing. Sam flipped her phone over and her eyebrows raised.

"Wow. We've been sitting here for hours." She sounded as surprised as he was.

"Time flies." Zach rose with a smile. "I need to close out. How are you getting home?"

"Probably same as you. I ubered."

He might be known to have a beer or two and drive, but tonight he'd done the smart thing and called a car.

"Yeah. Want me to wait with you?"

Sam dropped cash on the table. "That would be nice, thank you."

Zach scooped the cash to drop in the tip jar and nodded. "Go ahead and call the car, I'll get one after you. Be right back."

At the bar, he paid his tab, then grabbed a paper coaster and scrawled his number on it before heading back to their table. Old school but it felt right.

"Text me that you're home safe, please." He handed the coaster over. Sam nodded and pocketed it, then showed him her phone. Her ride was a minute away.

"You got lucky."

The urge to ask if he could kiss her rose up as they walked out the door. *More like your place or mine.* That wouldn't fly with Sam. No, if he wanted anything to happen with her, he'd have to play things her way. Except putting in that kind of effort wasn't his thing. Neither was outright lying. Being evasive? Sure. Noncommittal was his specialty.

"Thanks for a terrific evening." Sam bit her lip as if pondering some complicated thing, then she looked up at him with a smile. "Are you a hugger?"

What? What kind of question was that? Sam kept surprising him. Instead of answering, he spread his legs wide to get closer to her level, then opened his arms in invitation and Sam stepped in.

And his body reacted instantly.

A sweet, feminine perfume. Firm, athletic body that felt soft in all the right places. Her cheek against his chest. Her hair, ruffled by the breeze and tickling his chin.

He didn't groan. Barely. He wrapped his arms around her and squeezed. Firm, lingering half a breath longer than a just-friends hug. Then he let go.

Sam stepped back and smiled as her car pulled up. She waved, slid into the back seat and Zach lifted a hand in response.

Guess it's time to learn a new game.

CHAPTER 3

SAM—WEDNESDAY, APRIL 22

Carla shot a look over her glasses. "Tell me there's a return policy on all these books in case they don't sell."

"I would, but I'd be lying." Sam hefted the first box off the cart. "Custom order special editions with sprayed edges. Kayla's dropping by any minute to check them out, and Jen's coming tomorrow."

"Six boxes. How much of our profit from last week is this going to eat up?"

"These are both super buzzy. The next event will have a big crowd." She moved another box and shot Carla a glare. "Okay, I'll quit torturing you. Are you forgetting these were all pre-ordered and pre-paid?"

Carla brightened, then came over and helped clear the rest of the cart. "By the time we hit our one-year mark, I don't ever want to have to touch another invoice again."

The numbers didn't lie. Even after everything they'd spent to make the first event spectacular, the sales from the night meant they more than broke even. They had been prepared to go in the red for it, but the opposite happened.

"Call me a cynic." Carla eyed the book boxes again, then sank back into her chair. "So many indie shops crash and burn and this whole thing still feels like a dream and I'm just waiting for the rude wake up."

Sam grabbed her friend by the shoulders and bent enough to stare straight into her deep brown eyes.

"It's not like it's been easy or all smooth sailing. We put in the hard work and did all the planning. Sure, we've gotten lucky with a few things, like finding this space, but I feel like that's all just a sign that we're on the right path."

Last month, it had been Carla giving Sam the pep talk, and Carla's wife, Emmy, had been cheerleading for both of them in the weeks leading up to the shop opening.

"The whole point of Books and Brews is to bring more people in and change the way folks view a bookshop. If you're done with accounting, help me get these sorted." Sam grabbed two Sharpies and handed one to Carla. "Let's get these labeled before Kayla gets here. Four are hers, two are Jen's."

"And we know which is which how?"

"Two separate POs." Sam scrawled a name on the first box. "Trust me, I checked three times."

Carla snorted but followed her lead. "Hey, remember when delivery guys would haul these in for you?"

"Put that in a romance novel and it'd get a cliché warning." Sam slid a box to the side and checked the next label. "Still, it'd be a great meet cute."

"Speaking of clichés..." Carla arched an eyebrow. "You've been real quiet about that hot brewmaster. The Viking."

Sam didn't take the bait. "His name is Zach. And it was a chance encounter."

"And he's sex on legs. Don't think I didn't notice you

avoiding eye contact when he dropped off paperwork Tuesday."

Sam rolled her eyes. "We talked. It's friendly. Professional."

Carla leaned on the table, grinning. "You need a distraction. Just one nice, no-strings night."

"Except he works at Cold Bottom, and we're partnering with them. It'd be messy."

"So's your romantic track record," Carla said, not unkindly. "Maybe messy's your thing. At least he looks like he'd be more fun than the stick in the mud."

Sam laughed despite herself. "That's fair. But I'm not looking to relive my early college years."

"You never did casual right, even back then. You were always looking for forever."

"Is it so bad to want a storybook romance?" Sam looked at her cozy, carefully curated desk—dried roses in a vase, vintage copies of Austen and Brontë stacked on the worn wood.

"It's not bad," Carla said gently. "It's just... you also want wild sex. So, maybe be open to other stories, too."

Before Sam could reply, the front bell jingled.

Kayla burst into the office, eyes wide. "Becca said I'd find you back here. Are those...?"

Sam beamed. "Let's open them up. I'll grab some video for socials, if that's okay."

"Absolutely."

Carla adjusted a lamp for better lighting. Sam filmed while Kayla sliced into the first box.

"Oh my god." Kayla gasped as she pulled out a rich, jewel-toned hardcover.

"Let's take a few in the fantasy section," Carla suggested, already in motion.

They set up a few shots and Sam captured enough video

and photos for promo posts and some behind-the-scenes clips that she was sure could be used for something.

"We need that bartender from Cold Bottom here," Kayla said, scrolling through the images. "If he had darker hair and eyes, he'd be the perfect Zephyr Vaelmont."

"Right?" Carla lit up. "Shadow daddy vibes, all day."

Sam raised her eyebrows. "Shadow what now?"

"Oh hush, I'm pretty sure the concept exists in the historical romances you read. Minus the magic elements, maybe, but it's a thing," Carla replied.

Sam wasn't sure Heathcliff from Wuthering Heights was quite the same thing, or even close. Besides, she'd always preferred Mr. Darcy.

"A shadow daddy is a morally gray love interest. Powerful. A little possessive and protective. Brooding. Mysterious. Their magic is on the darker side," Kayla added.

Well, that makes sense. And characters like that existed almost across the board in romance.

"So, classic tortured, emotionally repressed, questionable hero who may be incapable of a healthy relationship, but loves the heroine. Plus magic. Shadow magic. Got it." Sam nodded. Carla had her hand over her mouth and looked like she was trying not to laugh.

"That's pretty accurate." Kayla flipped one of the books open to show off the character art on the inside flap and Sam caught her breath. An imposing-looking man with jet-black hair and beard and smoldering eyes. Other than the coloring, the resemblance to Zach was striking.

"Zephyr's a former warlord and tortured soul. And all sexy. In a dangerous kind of way. It's my favorite type of character to write, and readers love them."

Sounds about like Zach. Except for the warlord part.

Sam tried not to think about his voice in her ear or the memory of his hand briefly brushing hers at the speakeasy.

She failed.

Kayla left soon after, buzzing with excitement.

Carla shut her laptop with a satisfied sigh. "On to Cold Bottom?"

Sam stretched. She'd forgotten their afternoon meeting with the Abells. "Yeah, let me just finish putting all these in the shared drive, then check with Becca to see if she can get something up on social media tonight."

Becca was the first person they'd hired for the bookshop. In her early twenties, a social media genius, and an all-around indispensable asset. Sam and Carla were both tech savvy, but Becca was in a whole different class.

Sam popped into the front of the shop. "Hey, Becca..."

"I already saw the notification of the new pictures."

And this is why I like her so much.

Sam leaned her elbows on the front counter. "You're awesome. If you can get something up today, that would be great. And also, can you share the images with Kayla?"

Becca swung her screen around and gave a nod of approval to the behind-the-scenes video. "This is perfect for TikTok."

Sam thanked her, went back to the office, grabbed her jacket and purse then gave Carla a 'hurry up' look.

"Let's do this. Just, enough with the Zach talk."

Carla mimed zipping her lips, but the sparkle in her eyes promised nothing

Jon Abell met them by the hostess stand at the brewery, then led them upstairs to a cavernous hall where Lynn sat perched at a table near a sunny window. The smell of fresh pretzels and beer hit Sam immediately, conjuring up childhood memories of going to the Oktoberfest with her parents.

"We're so glad you want to extend the contract," Jon said as they sat down. "The first event sounded like a huge success."

"Everyone on staff raved," Lynn added. "You brought a great crowd."

Carla smiled. "We'd love to keep that momentum going past this grand opening month. We're planning to host Books and Brews on the first Friday of each month, starting in June, and we'd love to continue working with Cold Bottom."

Jon nodded as he set up a tablet and pulled out a folder emblazoned with Cold Bottom's logo. "That's definitely doable on our end. Fridays are busy nights, but we've got the staff to manage it. Will you be continuing with catering, or just the bar?"

"Just the bar," Sam said. "We might think about something light that doesn't require a full catering set up."

Lynn nodded and slid the folder across the table. "I thought you might say that. We have some proposals and pricing. We can customize however you'd like and adjust staff accordingly."

Carla leaned forward. "Speaking of staffing, can we make a request?"

Sam shot her a side-eye. Carla ignored it.

"We'd love to keep Zach on as our event bartender, especially for this week's. One of the featured authors has a romantasy book out, and I swear, if we were casting the movie? Zach would be the perfect shadow daddy. Her readers will love it."

Jon coughed into his hand. Lynn raised an eyebrow, but her lips twitched.

"I'll ask," she said smoothly. "But I won't force anyone to work events they haven't signed up for."

"Totally understand," Sam said quickly, then delivered a kick to Carla's shin. "We just wanted to float the idea."

The conversation shifted to beer choices and signage. Cold Bottom would include any seasonal specials and Sam and Carla would handle decor, ticketing, and social promo.

"This feels like a great partnership," Jon said, tapping at his screen.

"It is," Sam agreed. "We're building something really special."

When the meeting wrapped, Sam and Carla stepped out into the sunshine. The wind tugged at Sam's hair and she shook her head.

"What is it with you and the shadow daddy thing?"

"You saw Kayla's reaction. This is why we make a good team," Carla replied. "I read the genres you don't, and vice versa. Trust me, it's not just Kayla's readers."

"You're right on the team part." Sam stared ahead at the brewery's loading dock, where Zach was laughing, clipboard in hand, as he bent over a large wooden crate. "And you're right about that man."

Zach turned. Saw her. His grin widened.

Sam's stomach flipped and twisted. God help her, she wished she could believe in casual. In fun. In letting go of the past and just seeing where things led.

But she knew herself, and the real risk wasn't falling too fast.

It was falling for someone she knew wouldn't return her feelings, and doing it anyway.

CHAPTER 4

ZACH—THURSDAY, APRIL 23

S parks flew as Zach dropped a log into the outdoor firepit and quickly swung the screen closed before the flames could snap at him.

"Amateur." The firelight gleamed off Ty's grin before he lifted his beer and took a lazy swig.

Zach flipped him off. "Remind me again why I put up with you?"

"I'm the voice of reason," Ty said, his tone smug.

He's not wrong.

It had been too long since the three of them had hung out like this. Sure, they saw each other during their weekly basketball games with their old fraternity brothers, but it wasn't the same. Not like sitting around a fire, letting the evening stretch, with no one needing to be anywhere else. Never mind that it used to be them clubbing together. That felt like ancient history.

"How in the hell did you both score a night off?" Zach

glanced between Ty and Deke. "Same night even. Middle of the damn week."

"Wedding planning." Deke and Ty replied in perfect unison.

Fuck. Right. Ty and Nicky had set the date—October 31 —and Charlie, Deke's fiancée, was their wedding planner. Necessary, considering Nicky was a certified chaos gremlin. Awesome. But a chaos gremlin none the less. His two best friends were settling down.

And what the fuck am I doing? Haven't been on a date or gotten laid since January.

Ty leaned forward, setting his beer on the low table in front of them and spreading his hands. "Which is why I suggested tonight. Just us guys. No partners. No checklists. Just a fire, beer, and the three of us."

Zach tipped his bottle in agreement. "Can't argue with that."

"But..." Ty looked a little sheepish. "I do have to ask one thing."

"Oh, hell." Zach groaned. "Don't start with the sentimental shit."

"You know what this is about," Ty continued. "Nicky wants to shake things up a little. She's not into the typical best man, maid of honor, bridesmaids, groomsmen setup. And I'm right there with her."

Deke's shoulders relaxed visibly, and Zach got it. Ty's girl wasn't about to follow some wedding playbook. Nicky was a creative hurricane in combat boots, and those boots were often bright yellow, or glittery, or covered in paint.

"She doesn't want the his-n-hers lineup," Ty added. "Or the matchy-matchy bullshit."

Deke barked out a laugh. "I'm in. Whatever you call it, doesn't matter."

They both turned toward Zach.

He stared back. "We've been friends how long? Is that really in doubt?"

"No," Ty said, shrugging. "But I have to ask."

"Fuck you," Zach said, flipping him off again. "Ride or die, man. Besides, Nicky's cool as hell and I know she's not gonna make us wear pastels or some shit."

"She mentioned deep purple velvet with sparkles." Ty's voice was so serious, Zach almost believed him. Almost.

"I will kill you where you sit."

They all laughed, the tension easing. Zach was happy for them. He really was. But it didn't mean he didn't miss how things used to be—impromptu hangouts, pickup games, bar crawls. Not vision boards and talk about guest lists and matching outfits.

Though it sounds like I'll be spared the tuxedo hell.

"Oh, hey, been meaning to ask. How was that speakeasy over on 29th?" Deke raised his eyebrows and looked like he was trying to seem innocent.

"How the fuck..." Zach spread his hands and stared at Deke.

"Office gossip. Complicated office gossip," Deke replied.

Zach tried to rewind the mental tape. He hadn't seen anyone he knew that night, but he'd been laser-focused on Sam. Her eyes, her laugh, the way she'd asked questions like she actually cared about the answers.

"Someone from the office was at Books and Brews," Deke said, watching him closely. "Recognized you from seeing us at the basketball courts."

"That's a convoluted path, and what does either have to do with The Corner?" Ty asked, clearly lost.

"I'm getting there." Deke's gaze stayed locked on Zach. "That is the place, right?"

Zach sighed and scrubbed a hand over his face. He had a sinking feeling he knew where this was going. "Yeah. That's the place."

"According to the office gossip," Deke said, dragging the word out, "Zach was there with one of the bookstore owners the night after Books and Brews."

Ty leaned forward, grinning like a wolf. "Oh yeah? No shit?"

"It's a cool spot," Zach muttered. "Sometimes I like a mellower vibe. What, that a crime now?"

"Since when?" Ty snorted. "You hate hipster joints."

"They had Bella's ghost pepper wings."

"Still sounds like a date," Deke said. "And not a casual one."

Zach rolled his eyes. "Jesus, you two are worse than my mom."

"Your mom likes us better," Deke said.

"Only because she didn't have to raise you."

They let it go for a minute, the crackling fire filling the silence. Zach hoped they'd move on, but he wasn't holding his breath. He sure as hell wouldn't give up so easily if he were in their shoes.

"When was the last time you actually went out with someone?" Ty asked, tone light but eyes sharp.

Zach hesitated. He could claim he'd gone out, and he had. If going into one of his favorite clubs, sitting at the bar having one drink, then leaving without talking to anyone who didn't work there counted as going out.

"Wait," Deke said slowly. "It was January, wasn't it?"

"Fuck," Zach muttered. Like he hadn't been counting the time himself. He took a long swallow of beer. "Yeah. January was fucked up."

He hadn't told them the full story. Hadn't wanted to. But maybe it was time.

"The hookup on New Year's Eve? Got a little outta hand. I figured it was New Year's Eve, y'know. Next weekend, we go out again and it's okay, so I think we're good. Next date we hit a hell no. Third time's the charm. I'm out."

Ty laughed and scratched the side of his head, then looked over at Deke. "Are you going to call him on that bullshit, or am I?"

"On it." Deke crossed his arms and glared over the firepit.

"Yeah, whatever. Fine. Fuck it." Zach reached into the cooler for a fresh beer.

"We hooked up after the thing at the American Visionary Art Museum. Headed to a house party. Yeah, okay, there was some sex in a laundry room. Followed by a lotta drinking. Hindsight? Not the smartest move. Then we head back to her place. Except she's puking in the bushes on the way there. So I figure I'm making sure she gets home safe and calling it a night, except we both pass out in her living room. Total college-level disaster."

"Wow, yeah, that's classic," Ty said, grimacing.

"Second time we go out, it's fine. Chill. We laugh about the first night and blow it off as New Year's Eve stupidity. Cool. We have a good time. Nobody gets toasted, and I think, okay, this is salvageable."

He rubbed the back of his neck.

"Third date, we start the night with sex, because we're planning to go dancing and have a few drinks. Better safe than sorry, right? Go out. She gets blasted. Like, stumbling, falling down level trashed. There is no way I'm doing anything at that point. I get her home, she passes out. I crash on the sofa 'cause she's got some fancy-ass door alarm that auto locks and I don't know the code."

Deke winced, but didn't say anything.

"The next morning, she looks at me like I'm a fucking stranger. Asks who I am. Then wants to know if we had sex. Tells me to get out."

"Oh, that's concerning," Ty said quietly.

Zach swallowed. His throat felt dry, even with the beer.

"Tell me about it. Look, I've done some questionable shit, but never anything that would land me in that kind of ugliness. That morning? It shook me."

Zach shoved a hand through his hair. He'd been kicking himself over the whole mess for months. Saying it out loud somehow made it worse. Still, he felt better talking about it.

"I could take it as a blow to my ego. Like, you don't remember that we've had three dates and had some pretty hot sex every time?"

He swiped a hand over his face. Bravado was easy. Talking about sexual exploits? No problem. This shit was different.

"I'd had a couple drinks the first time, but wasn't drunk and I didn't think she was either. As far as I know, we were both sober before sex the second and third times."

It had been tough to pick everything apart and try to figure out just how badly he'd fucked up.

"Not gonna lie, I got freaked. I started questioning everything. Had she been drinking before I got there? Had she had more to drink on New Year's Eve than I thought? Was there more than alcohol involved? Did I miss something? Should I have known?"

He stared into the fire. Ty and Deke both sat leaning forward, elbows on their knees. And silent.

"I know being drunk's no excuse. I always get consent. No matter what. A woman could be sitting bare ass on my lap grinding away and I'm not doing shit unless I make damn sure it's okay. Just like I'm not doing shit if I think she's too far gone to actually consent. Fuck. I feel like a shithead."

Even in college, he'd been careful about how far he'd go if a woman had been drinking. A little tipsy was one thing. Go grab a late-night bite. Take a walk. Dance. Give it some time before hitting the sheets and it was all good. He had never been in a situation where a woman didn't recall they'd been together.

"The worst part? It was the way she looked at me like I was a threat. Like she'd never seen me before. And yeah, I get it, people drink and forget shit. But man, it rattled me hard."

Ty and Deke stayed silent. Not passing judgment, just letting their friend talk. Zach had spent the first few weeks hating himself for the whole thing. This was the first time he'd talked to anyone about it.

"Have you talked to her since?" Ty asked softly.

"She texted me a couple days later, like nothing had happened. Wanted to meet up. I said I was busy. A week later, I called. Tried asking her about shit. She told me to fuck off and to forget her number."

"Are you worried about anything?" There was Ty and his voice of reason thing.

"I mean..." Zach shrugged. "Condoms. Always. Still, I got an STI test done right away, and another a month later. All negative. Beyond that? I don't know. So, I've just been..." Zach threw his hands up in the air, then took another drink. "I've been laying low."

Deke exhaled. "I get it. You were trying to do the right thing. That shit's scary."

"I haven't told anyone about it," Zach admitted.

"Well, now you have," Ty said. "And for the record, you're an asshole, but not that kind of an asshole. Shit's complicated. I'm not judging. Hell, been there, but it was back in college."

Zach ignored that last dig. "Thanks. Not looking for absolution. Just looking to never fucking have that experience again."

Deke stretched and leaned back in his chair. "I mean, yeah, you could've handled things better maybe, but fuck, that's rough. And I'm not judging either. Charlie passed out the night we met. That could've gone all kinds of sideways. I get it. You did what you could. That doesn't mean you're off the hook for the other shit."

Zach raised an eyebrow.

"You think that mess is gonna distract from the fact you were hanging at some speakeasy with a bookstore owner?"

"Jesus Christ," Zach muttered. "I worked that Books and Brews event, then ran into her at the speakeasy. That's it."

"Bullshit," Ty said. "You're working the next one, too, aren't you?"

Zach didn't answer. He didn't need to.

"Holy shit," Deke said, eyes wide. "You don't work brewery events anymore."

"What's her name?" Ty asked, grinning.

Zach sighed. "Sam."

Both of them leaned in like sharks smelling blood.

"She's cute. We talked. It was nice. She's also not into casual. And she's tiny."

"Everyone's tiny to you," Deke said.

"Fuck off." Zach held his hand to mid-chest. "Like she's right here. I'd break her."

Maybe not. When she'd hugged him, Zach had carefully kept his hands in safe places, but there had been nothing fragile feeling about the body that pressed against him.

Ty laughed so hard he almost dropped his beer. "Deke's got a point. Not like you haven't slept with small women before."

That didn't change sheer physics. *Like how would things even fit?*

"Yeah, but not like this. She's pocket-sized."

He'd replayed that hug in his head like a fucking teenage boy. He hadn't wanted to let go.

"And it's work," he added. "I don't screw around with partners or hosts."

"Since when?" Deke asked, choking on a sip of beer.

"That was college."

"The Driscoll wedding," Ty reminded him.

Of course Ty would bring that up. Zach had been twenty-one, on summer break from college and his mother had pressed him to tend the bar at a wedding Cold Bottom was doing. He'd wound up fucking the bride's mother—a gorgeous woman in her forties—in a storage closet after she'd flirted with him all night, then made it very clear what she wanted. He'd felt guilty about it until he learned she was divorced.

"First? College. Second? Zero regrets. She was divorced and a consenting adult."

"Uh-huh," Deke said. "You dated her all summer."

"And had a great time. I repeat: zero regrets. Still friends, too. She's remarried and moved to California."

Ty shook his head. "Back to the subject. Sam's off-limits because she's small and wants commitment?"

"It's the way she said it," Zach replied. "Like, matter-of-fact. She knows what she wants. And I respect that."

These were his best friends. Men who knew him better than anyone else. They'd all give each other shit, but when it came down to it, he'd trust either of them with his life.

"I can be indirect, or noncommittal and avoid talking about stuff, but I try not to lie outright. I won't do something like say 'yeah, let's be exclusive' or 'I'm looking to get married' or shit like that. And I get the sense that's what she's looking for."

"Huh. Who knew you had scruples." Deke raised his eyebrows and smiled.

"Maybe you're growing up," Ty added.

"Nah. I'm not that guy."

"Maybe you could be," Deke said quietly.

Zach looked up. "What?"

"Maybe you're not that guy yet."

Zach stared at the fire again. He didn't have an answer for that.

"You like her," Ty said.

"She's cool," Zach admitted. "Funny. Sharp. Passionate about her work. And she smells good."

"She smells good?" Ty started laughing.

"Oh, he's a goner," Deke said with a grin.

"Fuck you both." But Zach was smiling now, even if his gut was still twisted.

Because this was different, and deep down, he knew it.

This wasn't just about Sam. It was about who he'd have to become, or pretend to be, if he wanted a shot with her. The thought sat heavy in his chest, restless and unfamiliar. Something had shifted. Like the axis of his world had tilted, and he wasn't sure he liked it.

CHAPTER 5

"Take a break." Becca stepped behind the register and took the next customer in line before Sam could respond. She'd been on her feet all night without a break. Sam patted Becca's shoulder then cast a glance to the bar set up on the other side of the shop.

The Viking.

Deke was in a long-sleeve shirt tonight, and had cuffed the sleeves to the elbows, displaying corded muscles and a hint of his tattoos. She'd been on a phone call when the Cold Bottom crew arrived and hadn't had a chance to say hello. The line of women waiting at the bar said she wouldn't get a chance now.

He looked up and those full lips split into a wide grin. Then he winked before turning back to his next customer. That little gesture sent flutters of anticipation through Sam's entire body.

Oh, stop it. She wasn't some hormonal teenager for heavens' sake. She was nearly thirty, had two degrees, six years of teaching high school English, and now co-owned a new business. Sam stopped at the author tables, where Carla had set up a laptop so customers could place orders after both authors had sold out of their entire inventory.

"You doing okay here?" Sam peered over Carla's shoulder at the growing list of orders. This was going to be a good week. Beyond a good week.

"Hey, I've been sitting. This is nothing. You're the one who's been juggling everything else. Have you eaten anything?"

Have I? Sam could barely remember. "I've had coffee."

The coffee machine was a definite plus for their customers, but on days like today, Sam wasn't sure it was a good idea. She was practically vibrating.

"Oh my god. Get some food. If the line's too long, grab something from the fridge, but get out of here for a few minutes and eat."

She gave Sam a playful shove away from the table. Sam wove her way through the crowded shop, bypassing the line for food. She skipped the office in favor of heading straight for the back door and the hope of fresh air and relative quiet.

Sam grabbed one of the fold-up chairs they kept in the corner and set it up in the cool calm of the tiny loading area currently filled by a Cold Bottom truck. The spring air was a little chilly, but it was a welcome relief from the crowd inside. She tipped her head back and let the sounds of the city wash over her.

"Carla said you hadn't eaten."

Sam sat up to see Zach with a chair in one huge hand and two plates balanced in the other. He popped open the chair, handed her a plate, then put his own in the empty seat.

"Didn't know what you'd want, so I got a bit of everything. Hope you don't mind if I join you. I haven't eaten since breakfast."

The smell of food had her mouth watering and her stomach grumbled as if telling her to hurry up, but even hunger couldn't distract her from the sight of Zach fishing in his apron pocket. He pulled out plastic utensils, then two cans of beer. He stuck one can in her drink holder, then retrieved his plate and folded himself into the chair.

"Thank you." She didn't know what else to say. Her brain couldn't process whatever chain of events must've happened for him to be out here with food. He pointed at her plate; his face knit into a stern scowl.

"Eat." Zach shoved his own fork into his food and his eyes nearly rolled back as he chewed. Sam surveyed her choices and settled on what looked like a mini sausage wrapped in a bun. It was delicious and she polished it off in two bites, then wiped her hands and cracked open the beer.

Zach eyed her over his own can and laughed. "Figured you'd enjoy the cheesy brat bites. I thought the first event was the big one and the rest were going to be smaller. This is... uhh..."

His eyebrows went up and he nodded his head toward the closed door.

Sam shrugged and stuffed another brat bite in her mouth. She'd answer that after she'd dealt with her complaining stomach. He seemed to get the idea and went back to his own food.

The air smelled faintly of yeast from the nearby bakery, with a hint of hops from the Cold Bottom truck and old paper from the bookstore's cardboard bins. Cool air brushed her skin, and Zach's presence, solid and warm and far too attractive for her peace of mind, was oddly comforting.

"It's the book signings," Sam replied, once she'd eaten enough to satisfy her immediate needs. "We'd planned on the bar and just snacks for the rest of the first four events. Then we had so many RSVPs for tonight, and realized how many books the authors had pre-sold, so we figured we needed more. We were lucky your catering was able to handle a large to-go order."

He should know this stuff. Maybe he didn't work that side of the business. He was their brewmaster, so it would make sense.

"I'm surprised you're doing this again. I imagine it's not your normal." Maybe Lynn had asked him to, after Carla's weird request.

Zach leaned to the side and stuck his empty plate on the truck's bumper then shrugged as he sat back. "It's not."

"That doesn't explain why you're here." She didn't mean to sound rude or confrontational. Part of her was very happy to see Zach again. *A big part. And that needs to stop.*

"The bar order increased. That means more staff." He leaned forward, his elbows braced on his knees, and smiled. The look he gave her could melt ice in a blizzard. "Are you complaining? I kinda thought we got on pretty well."

Like at the speakeasy last week. He'd been flirting then. She was sure of it. So sure that she'd been blunt about her relationship goals. So maybe this wasn't flirting. Maybe this was just more banter.

"We did." She couldn't keep from smiling if she tried. "And no, I'm not complaining. I'm sorry, the question came out wrong. I was curious. That's all."

Zach plucked the empty plate from her fingers and set it next to his on the tailgate. "No need to apologize. And to answer your question—it was short notice on needing more staff. Also, I gather Carla asked if I could be here. There was something about a shadow daddy?"

Oh my god. Sam closed her eyes. "Yeah. I was hoping the Abells wouldn't repeat that part." When she looked back at

Zach, his eyes danced with humor. "Did anyone happen to explain it?"

"No, but one of my crew read the book and she did."

"I haven't read it," Sam admitted. "But I gather it's a popular trope, and every romance genre has its bad boys."

She'd certainly been attracted to the tragic and misunderstood types who just needed the love of the right woman to turn them around. Then discovered that while they made for great reading material, the reality was not so great.

No, Sam wanted her Mr. Darcy, who was problematic in his own way. Not that she'd had luck on that front either. Preston certainly wasn't it. He had all of the problems and none of the benefits or charm.

"You do have the look," Sam ventured. Why not? He'd opened that door. She crossed her arms and regarded him as critically as she could. Zach leaned back in the seat, stretched his long legs out and laughed. *Oh, he knows exactly how good he looks.*

"The apron kind of detracts from it a bit." She wished she could take the words back the moment they were out of her mouth.

"I'll take that as a challenge." He stood, whisked off the apron and tossed it over the back of his chair. Once again, she found herself eye level with his belt buckle—some complicated silver thing with a skull. Except this time, she let her gaze wander.

The rest of the crew were all in black pants but Zach wore jeans that looked soft and supple. They hugged his thighs and practically cradled a prominent bulge that strained the button fly. Above the skull buckle, flat abs pulled her attention up over a powerful-looking chest. The Cold Bottom shirt fit him like a glove.

Sam leaned forward and stopped short of tracing the line

of ink peeking out from under the rolled sleeve cuff. It looked like a hexagon with random lines coming off of it.

"What is this?"

Zach turned his arm and pulled his sleeve higher, revealing something between a T and a Y shape on the inside of his forearm.

"It's the humulone molecule. A major component in hopped beer. I've got a few others—beta acids, esters, essential oils, plus some hops and barley."

He tugged his sleeve down and returned to his seat. "My undergrad was in chemistry. Then I went on to study brewing and fermentation."

"You mentioned that. I'd never realized you could go to school for that. I guess I assumed it was something you learned on the job. Like an apprenticeship or something."

"Some people do," he replied. "That's how it was for years. It's always been both a science and an art. Back to the original topic—did taking off the apron help?"

His voice had dipped down even lower and his lips curled into a one-sided smirk that was entirely too sexy. Somehow, she summoned the courage to smile back.

"It did, thank you. But on that note, I need to get back inside."

She stood and folded up her chair. When she turned to grab her plate, she found Zach's eyes glued on her and she sighed. She needed to learn to ignore whatever this silly attraction to him was.

"Thank you for bringing food. And for the company."

Zach stood and stretched, pulling the shirt tighter across his chest. Sam sucked in a breath at the telltale imprint of nipple piercings. He caught her looking and winked, then gathered up their trash and carried it to the can, giving Sam a reminder that his backside was as spectacular as his front—

from broad shoulders to his narrow waist, and that butt begging to be grabbed.

He folded his chair, then took hers and tucked them both under one arm. At the back door, he laid his hand on the knob but didn't pull it open. He leaned against the building and dipped his head down.

"I'd say you've earned a break after all of this. Why not take me up on the offer to show you around the city a little? There's an event at the Metro Gallery... wait, they changed their name. It's Metro Baltimore and the thing is tomorrow night. I think you'd enjoy it. Lemme know what you think. Still got my number?"

He tugged the door open, waited for her to enter then followed, stopping to deposit the chairs in their spot in the corner. From the sounds coming through the interior shop door, the event was still in full swing, despite being almost time to wrap it up.

Sam didn't want to go in. She wanted to go back outside and sit with Zach, enjoying their banter and flirty teasing. She'd known he was trouble from day one, and she was right. He'd woken something up in her and she'd gone from no way to maybe Carla's right.

She hadn't put his number in her phone, but she had tucked the paper coaster into her desk drawer, telling herself it was strictly for professional purposes.

Zach turned in the narrow hall. He braced his forearm against the ladder that led to the overhead storage area and bent down.

"Well? Yes, or no?"

The beachy-bonfire scent of him surrounded her and Sam breathed it in. She tipped her head back to see his face. The dim light of the back corridor cast his features in shadow and light. A lock of sandy hair had fallen over his forehead and bright blue eyes glimmered from under straight brows. His lips, impossibly full, were framed in a beard that looked so soft she wanted to reach up and stroke it.

"Yes," she replied. "To both. I still have your number and tomorrow night sounds fun. But it's not a date. Just friends going out."

She had to tell herself that. Otherwise, she risked falling into her old habits. When his lips curled into a smile, and his eyes crinkled up as he bent over her, the temptation to do just that was almost overwhelming.

"If that's what you want." He brought his other arm up and held on to the ladder as he leaned closer. His voice was soft, with a hint of gravel, and it slid over her skin like a caress. "Is that what you want, Sam?"

Her mouth went dry and her entire body tensed at his question. She'd told herself that keeping it platonic was what she wanted. She was only dating with intention. With purpose. To find her storybook romance. She wouldn't succumb to the charms of... *Oh, who am I kidding?*

Whatever she'd told herself, her body and subconscious were in rebellion against that logic.

"I can behave," he continued. "You set the boundaries. I'll stay within them. So, just friends is what you want?"

If she took a deep breath, she'd be in danger of bumping into him.

When did we get so close?

Zach hadn't moved. He was still braced against the ladder. She was the one who'd stepped closer. Proof her body was a traitor.

"I don't know." She whispered the words, afraid to give them full voice. Zach let out a breath that sounded more like a growl and Sam leaned into him. Her body brushed against his and shivers traveled down her spine. "Maybe a date is okay."

ZACH

It took everything Zach had to not wrap her in his arms, lift her off her feet, and pin her to the wall before kissing her.

Behave.

Last week, he'd been conflicted. Despite all his big talk to Ty and Deke, he was interested. Maybe it was the challenge Sam presented—it had been a long time since he'd had to work at getting laid. Most times, the flirtation came easy; the invitation was obvious, and the payoff immediate. There was no game to it, no friction. Just bodies and needs and forgetting.

Sam was different.

At first, he chalked up the fascination to the thrill of the chase. That was safer. Simpler. What else could explain the fact that he couldn't get her out of his head? That every time she spoke, his pulse kicked up, like he was seventeen and trying to hide a hard on in gym class?

But even as he tried to file her away as a temporary distraction, he knew he was full of shit.

He liked her.

And worse, he respected her.

Which made the way his thoughts kept drifting toward getting her naked feel all kinds of messed up. He told himself it was fine and that it didn't mean anything. There was no need to act like a fool just because a smart, sexy woman with a killer smile and librarian vibes had made him wait longer than a night to get laid.

Only an asshole saw a woman like Sam and turned her into a goal to achieve. A box to check. Fuck if that wasn't the kind of shit that got him into the mess back in January. And here he was fighting the urge to push Sam up against a ladder in a dim hallway and make her come her brains out.

She hadn't moved away. Every breath either of them took brought their bodies closer together until her chest brushed against him. If he played it right, he'd get her into his bed. It might take a while, but they'd get there. Something shifted in her tonight, and he'd watched it happen, watched her guard lower and her eyes linger, her fingers drift to her lips like she wasn't sure what to do with them.

It was going to take time. Sam would be a delicate dance. Especially considering her stance on relationships. She had her sights set on something serious. Shit he did not do.

And what kind of asshole does that make me?

Sam let out a soft sigh then bit her lower lip. She tipped her head back, her eyes on his mouth. Zach knew an invitation when he saw it. He brought his hand down, fingers curving into the soft silk of her hair, cradling the back of her head in his palm. Her lips curled into a soft smile and she made a humming sound before closing her eyes.

His cock took that as a cue to come to full attention. Not a comfortable situation in the pants he was wearing. He could kiss her now. Every bit of her body language was screaming yes.

Instead, he leaned closer, letting his lips hover just above her ear. Inhaled her scent, the same soft powdery floral he'd noticed before, and exhaled slowly. His breath lifted the hair on her neck, and she shivered against him.

"I would love to kiss you, but not here," he whispered. "Here it would have to be quick and I don't want to rush. I want to savor every moment."

He straightened, releasing her hair with a slow drag of his fingers. Sam's lips parted on a gasp, her eyelids fluttering open to meet his gaze. Her look, flushed and heavy lidded with desire, nearly undid him.

He could have her up against the wall in two seconds flat.

Her skirt bunched around her waist and her thighs around his hips. His name on her lips.

Instead he gritted his teeth and braced his arms against the ladder again, forcing himself to put some space between them.

Sam had other ideas. She reached up, hooked a finger between the buttons of his shirt, and gave a firm tug.

The door at the end of the hall burst open and the sounds of kegs clattering on a cart and chairs scraping on the floor flooded in. Sam dropped her hand and Zach let go of the ladder. They moved forward by some unspoken agreement, side stepping to let one of the Cold Bottom crew go past with a dolly full of gear.

Shit. Must be later than I thought if they're already breaking down.

"I'll text you," Sam said as they reached the door to the shop. Her voice was casual, as if they hadn't just been on the verge of combusting. She stepped into the shop like nothing had happened and vanished into the still crowded space. Zach retrieved his apron from where he'd let it drop. He'd need it if he wanted to hide the raging hard on he had going.

He paused to catch his breath before opening the door to the main shop. Inside, the event was winding down. Patrons were trickling out with shopping bags and tipsy grins, and Zach threw himself into teardown mode. Tap lines disconnected, bins carried out, everything wiped down. Anything to stay busy. To burn off the tension still clinging to his skin like sweat.

He caught glimpses of Sam—laughing with Carla, adjusting a display, pointing out forgotten swag bags—and felt something unfamiliar twist in his chest. It wasn't just lust. That was part of it, sure, but it was more than that. He liked the way she looked when she was focused. Liked that she could crack a joke and then drop a business directive in the next breath.

By the time the Cold Bottom team was packed and climbing into the truck, he was kicking himself for not getting her number.

Then his phone pinged as he was locking up the brewery.

> This is Sam. Let me know details about tomorrow.

He read it twice, trying to decide if she was being cold, or if she was embarrassed, or what. *Stop overthinking.*

> I'll send a link in the morning, but if you want to do dinner, I'll pick you up at 7.

He hit send before he could psych himself out, then pocketed his phone and climbed onto his bike, hoping the cool night air would dull the arousal still riding him hard.

It didn't.

> Sounds good. See you then. Good night.

An address followed and Zach clicked it to open the map, then laughed. She lived a few blocks from the bookshop. *Makes sense.* He sent a quick good night and set his phone aside. Thinking about seeing Sam tomorrow, away from work, had him rock hard again.

He stripped and headed for the shower. Steam filled the small room in minutes, but the heat didn't help. Cranking the water cold didn't dull the memory of how she'd looked up at him. How her finger had toyed with his shirt, as if she was going to kiss him. How close they'd come to losing control.

He'd had his eyes on her all night. It was hard not to. She'd been wearing a pink pencil skirt and what looked like a men's dress shirt, only fitted to her body. Every bit the librarian vibe, and then those hints at a more sensual side.

Fuuuuck.

He turned the temperature back up, then grabbed his soap and washcloth. Halfway through, he knew it was a lost cause. If he wanted to have any control over himself tomorrow, he'd damn well better take care of things tonight.

He wrapped his hand around his cock, already hard and pulsing, and closed his eyes.

Sam, bent over the registration table. Tapping one toe on the floor. Ass swaying side to side.

The vision was burned into his brain. It was not what he needed to be thinking, but his cock felt otherwise. It throbbed in his hand as if demanding more.

Her skirt riding up when she squatted to retrieve a dropped receipt. A flash of pink. Panties. Maybe lace. Maybe satin.

He groaned, bracing a hand on the tile and stroking harder. That little sigh she'd made when he touched her neck. The way her body had responded to the simplest whisper of breath.

I should have kissed her.

He wanted her on his bed. Flushed and breathing hard. Her thighs spread. Pussy wet. His mouth teasing her clit with slow, maddening strokes. He wanted her taste in his mouth. Her moans of pleasure in his ears.

"Oh fuck." Zach tightened his grip, jerking faster.

The way her skin prickled at my touch.

After the little taste of her in the back hallway, he could imagine how she'd respond to his hands on her body. Or his lips and tongue.

He leaned forward, letting his head rest against the shower wall as the hot water cascaded down his back. Sam was so tiny, he could hold her with one arm. Or grab her hips in his hands and lift her to his mouth, then fill himself with her taste.

"God yes."

A moan slipped out of his lips and Zach squeezed his hand on his cock. Once she was wet and ready, he'd lay her back on his bed. Go slow to start. He wanted to watch Sam opening for him as his cock slid into her pussy.

"Just like that. Nice and easy."

He'd have to be gentle. Take his time. Let her be in control, but he wanted to make her come over and over again. As many times as she could take it. Then, once she was satisfied, he'd allow himself to come.

"Fuck yes. Such a good girl." His cock twitched as a spasm rocked through his body. Zach let out a deep groan as he came, then thumped his head against the wall. He still didn't know how sex was going to work between them. After tonight, he was certain he could find out, and as much as he wanted Sam, he wasn't sure how he felt about going in knowing she wanted more than he was ever going to give.

That thought should have been a buzz kill, but his cock was still hard as a rock. He finished his shower, toweled off, grabbed a bottle of oil and dropped into his desk chair. Twenty minutes of looking at porn later and he still hadn't come a second time, even though his body ached with need. Sam was still in his head. Vivid. Unrelenting.

He'd bend her over the bench in his living room and slide her skirt up her legs, exposing the pink panties she wore underneath. Then tug her panties off and press her thighs apart before kneeling behind her and burying his face between her asscheeks.

He loved eating a woman from behind, and Sam had a perfect ass. He'd have to spread his legs wide to fuck her that way, but the view would be worth it.

Sam's round ass up in the air. Wet pussy stretching around his cock. Her asscheeks bouncing with every thrust. His thumb teasing her ass, making her gasp and arch into him.

"That's it, baby." Zach let out a harsh breath. "You can take it."

Would he have to stay gentle with Sam? Or could he go hard? Tangle his fingers into her hair, or wrap his hand around her throat. Whisper all the things he was going to do to her in her ear.

Hold her hands behind her and pull her up so her back arched and he could play with her nipples or clit while he fucked her from behind. Could she take him in the ass? Would she?

The image of his cock filling Sam's ass sent Zach over the edge. He came again with a shout, then sank back into his chair, breathing hard.

Tomorrow night was going to be interesting. He had no illusions of them having sex after their date, but he was hoping to get started on that path.

CHAPTER 6

SAM—SATURDAY, APRIL 25

Early morning light filtered through the front windows, casting flickering rainbows around the shop thanks to the suncatchers Carla had insisted on when they first opened Shelf Indulgence. Sam loved the whimsy of them, and the way they brightened even a dreary day. On sunny days like this, they were pure magic.

She took a deep breath, hands on her hips, and surveyed the store. Just last night, it had been a buzzing hive of readers, book stacks, laughter, and the smell of beer and savory foods. Now it was restored to quiet calm. Tables were back in place. Books re-shelved.

She'd been bone-tired when she got home, but sleep had refused to come. Her brain kept replaying moments from the event—specifically, him. The way Zach had looked at her over the tops of pint glasses. The feel of his hand on her back. The near-kiss in the back hallway that she'd practically initiated, like she'd grabbed the lead in her own rom-com.

Sam let out a sharp breath. "What was I thinking?"

She needed a coffee. She needed to cancel their date tonight. Or at least hit the brakes, rein it in, put everything into a neat, platonic box where it belonged. But the memory of his fingers brushing hers lingered like heat on her skin. She clenched her hands into fists then stretched her fingers wide, trying to shake the feeling, then pushed the button on the coffee machine.

Caffeine delivery mechanism in hand, she shouldered the door to the back hall open, and stopped short.

There it was. The wood ladder leading up to the loft storage. Innocuous. Familiar. And now? A whole scene flashed through her mind. His hands braced over her head, the warmth of his body, the deep timber of his voice. Her grabbing his shirt and pulling him closer.

Her stomach flip-flopped.

"I don't have time for this." She spoke directly to the ladder, because it had to be the problem. Not her, and not the Viking who had taken up residence in her subconscious. She shook herself and unlocked the office door.

Focus. She had numbers to run. Orders to finalize. Schedules to coordinate before the shop opened in two hours. She slid into her desk chair, grabbed her earbuds, and tapped on her favorite playlist—an instrumental lo-fi mix with a solid groove to help keep her on task. The Viking could go live in the dusty back corner of her brain where inconvenient feelings went to die.

She opened her laptop and tapped in her password. "Okay. Let's see how we did last night."

By the time Carla came breezing in thirty minutes before opening, bakery box in hand, Sam had almost convinced herself she was fine.

"Morning, sunshine," Carla said, setting a cherry turnover next to Sam's coffee like an offering. "I texted but you didn't answer. Emmy says she saw you leave bright and early, so... what gives?"

Sam finished typing a final purchase order, took a sip of coffee, and turned toward her friend with narrowed eyes. Carla was giving her that look. The 'I'm not leaving until you spill' look.

"Thanks for the pastry," Sam said, deliberately ignoring the interrogation attempt. Never mind that she knew what it was about. She was trying not to think about him.

"Oh, no no no. You do not get to dodge me." Carla leaned forward, dark eyes gleaming with mischief. "You and Zach disappeared for a while last night. Then I saw you two making eyes at each other over the bar. So? Details. Now."

So much for that dusty back corner.

"Like you didn't send him to bring me food?" Deflecting would only work for so long, but Sam had to try. Carla's wry expression and crossed arms were enough to know she'd failed. "We're going to some event at Metro Baltimore tonight." She needed to check her phone. Zach had said he'd send info and she'd turned her ringer off to focus on work. "Just friends."

Except that's not what we said last night.

"I love you, but you are a terrible liar. You do not blush like a kid when a just friend winks at you."

Sam could try to deny it all she liked, but Carla was right. Even their banter at the speakeasy last week had been flirty. Last night? That was more. Sam groaned and buried her face in her hands.

"There's a vibe."

"A vibe?" Carla's tone was filled with laughter. "Who are you and what did you do with Sam? Girl, you looked like you wanted to eat him with a spoon. What happened?"

Sam dropped her hands. "We flirted. A lot. We almost kissed. Maybe would've if the hallway hadn't gotten busy."

"Ooh, hallway kiss. Ten out of ten on the micro-trope meter. He had his sleeves cuffed up last night. That's another one for sure. Did he lean in a doorway, too?"

"It was against the ladder," Sam said with a groan. "I'm serious. This could be a mess. He works at Cold Bottom. If something goes sideways with him, it could screw up everything."

"Or," Carla said, unwrapping her own pastry, "you could have a great time with a ridiculously hot man and not overthink it for once in your goddamn life."

Sam gave her a narrow-eyed glare.

"I'm not saying go get married and make baby Vikings, though wow, you two having kids? I can only imagine how gorgeous they'd be. All I'm saying is, have fun. You deserve that. You spent years setting yourself aside for a man who thought orgasms were an optional courtesy."

Sam nearly choked on her coffee. "First, ew on kids. That's a you thing, not a me thing. And seriously? That is not what I said about sex with Preston."

"No? Okay, you strongly implied it. We both know Preston thought foreplay was overrated and anything outside of missionary was 'spicy.' He didn't even like it when you were on top. Plus, any man who doesn't go down on the regular is a lost cause."

Sam couldn't help it—she laughed. "Okay," she admitted. "You're not wrong there."

Carla stood and tossed her pastry wrapper. "So let Zach take you out. Wear something sexy. Let him look at you like you're his favorite book. Nothing ventured, nothing gained."

Sam leaned back in her chair. "Maybe this is a rebound

thing after Preston. Like, I'm attracted to a man who is the exact opposite of my ex."

Carla paused by the door and broke into a laugh. "You forgetting that I'm bi? Even if I weren't, that man is hot as fuck and looks like he could deliver a very good time. Who said anything about getting over the stick in the mud. You've closed that chapter and it's time to move forward."

The words echoed through the quiet after Carla left.

Sam wasn't sure what forward meant anymore. But the flutter in her chest said some part of her wasn't entirely opposed to finding out.

She pulled out her phone. A text from Zach had come through with a link and a promo image emblazoned with text. 'Tropical Disco. Come dressed for the vibes.' The flyer looked like a club on a cruise ship exploded in glitter and palm fronds.

Sam smirked.

> How exactly do you dress "tropical disco"?

A beat later, another message came through.

> I'm kind of minimalist.

Minimalist. Right. She could picture him in low-slung linen pants and nothing else. She shoved the phone back in her pocket and tried to focus.

Ten minutes later, she was changing the décor on the themed table up front. Taking down the crystal balls and dragons from the fantasy and romantasy theme and replacing them with small floral arrangements and books grouped by trope. Carla wandered over, picked a glitter globe from the box and gave it a shake.

"I'll never understand how you do this," she said, watching Sam balance a framed trope on its easel. Carla bent down and read the sign. "'Second Chance.' You make this look like magic."

"It's just pattern and balance. And a little sparkle." She clicked the switch to turn on the twinkle lights and Carla shook her head.

Sam's phone buzzed again.

> I can picture you in something slinky. See you later.

Oh boy.

Carla smirked. "That him?"

"I'm not showing you," Sam said, pocketing the phone.

"I don't need to see it. Your whole face lit up. That's all the answer I need." Carla tapped her temple. "Psychic best friend powers."

"I'll believe it when you find me something to wear for a tropical disco."

That perked Carla right up. "Say no more. Come over this afternoon and raid my closet. We'll turn you into a disco goddess."

Sam couldn't help smiling. It felt absurd.

And it felt kind of exciting.

"What's gotten into me?"

"After tonight? Hopefully Zach." Carla crossed to the door and flipped the sign. "You deserve it. You should leave early. We've got staff coming in. Go pamper yourself. Paint your toes. And don't forget to shave." She winked before she unlocked the door. "You never know."

Sam threw up her hands and retreated to the office. Maybe Carla was right. At least about pampering herself. She gathered her things and headed home. She had hours to kill, but there was no way she wanted to stay at the office where Carla could keep pestering her.

Or worse, diving into ancient history. The problem was, Carla had nailed it. The years with Preston had changed Sam, and not entirely for the better. She'd lost herself to the point of not knowing who she was anymore.

Fine. I'll primp for a date with the Viking.

Sam dropped her things inside the door and headed straight for the bathroom. If she was going to pamper herself, she might as well do it right. She lit a candle, queued up a playlist, and poured herself a fizzy water while waiting for the tub to fill. She draped a towel within reach and put her phone face down on the counter. For once, she didn't feel the need to check her email or calendar.

Sam sank into the foamy water with a sigh, then leaned her head back and closed her eyes. Maybe she was ready to move forward. Not because she needed Zach. Not even because she wanted to prove anything to herself or Preston or the universe.

All of that might be part of it, but deep down, it was that she wanted to say yes to something that felt good.

She smiled, eyes still closed.

I wonder what kissing him is like with that beard.

ZACH

A set of stone steps led from the road to the little gray house perched above. Ivy trailed along the rock wall and planters hung from the fence. The whole thing screamed English garden, right down to the vintage-looking ceramic house numbers on the gate. Which shouldn't have been surprising, considering Sam lived here.

Zach took the steps two at a time, heart thudding in a way it hadn't since his first real high school date, with the keys to his mom's old car in his pocket, and a condom burning a hole in his wallet. He followed Sam's directions, taking the right-hand path to a small porch where a pair of rain boots sat tucked beneath a bench and flowers bloomed in baskets like they knew someone cared about them.

What the hell was he doing here like this? A pre-event quickie was more his speed, but that wasn't what Sam was looking for. It didn't take a genius to figure out that she was looking for romance, and if that's what it took, well, that's what he'd deliver.

He raised his hand to knock, but the door swung open and Sam greeted him with a shaky smile and a cloud of golden fringe around her.

"That is pretty minimalist." Sam stepped out and eyed him up and down. He'd added some old wood bead bracelets to go with the white linen pants he wore on vacation, and a Hawaiian shirt from an event at the brewery. It worked well enough. "You look like a sexy vacation brochure."

Zach laughed and tugged at the shirt collar. "I'll take that as a compliment."

"It is. You pull it off." She stepped onto the porch, twirling once in her own ensemble.

Her entire torso shimmered in gold fringe that danced with every movement. It stopped just below her ass, and he sincerely hoped she hadn't paired it with shorts. The idea of dancing with Sam while she was wearing such a short skirt was intoxicating.

"Vintage romper I borrowed from Carla."

Romper? Damn. That means shorts.

"The matching go-go boots were too big so..." She held up a foot clad in a white platform sandal. "I wore these for college graduation so I could see over the podium."

Zach offered his arm. "You could wear anything and still steal the whole damn room."

She tucked her hand into the crook of his elbow, her skin warm against his. "Flattery already? You know that's not going to help you get lucky?"

That had him grinning ear to ear. "I mean, I showed up in linen pants looking like some cheesy eighties cop. I think that says all you need to know about my intentions."

She barked out a laugh and slid into the passenger seat. Once on the road, Sam chatted easily, telling him about her week and squirrels in the garden. At a stoplight, she tilted her head. "What made you decide to pursue beer?"

Zach exhaled slowly and turned onto Falls Road. That question always tripped him up. Most people just accepted "I work at a brewery" and assumed he was an overgrown dude-bro who liked beer. Which wasn't entirely inaccurate.

But Sam wasn't most people.

After too many bad experiences in high school and college, he avoided telling people his parents owned Cold Bottom. People learned that and friendships changed. His fraternity brothers were the exceptions. Especially Ty and Deke. He was more open about it now, but still never discussed it with women. That was an instant vibe change. Suddenly, he wasn't a guy. He was an opportunity.

"I grew up around it," he said, noncommittal but true. "Not your uncle's basement homebrew setup, but around people who studied it. Built a life on it. The science of it stuck with me."

Sam nodded slowly. "That tracks. Kind of like how I wound up teaching. The path was always there."

He glanced over. "Really? My buddy Deke's a teacher and I swear, it's a calling. What did you teach?"

He couldn't recall the last time he'd cared about what a

woman did for a living, or why. He'd make polite responses, and register enough to sound interested, but that was as far as it went.

She looked out the window for a beat, then back at him. "High school English."

Why am I not surprised?

"I should've guessed. You've got that whole studious-brainy thing going on. Like, glasses and poetry readings and telling teenage boys to shut the hell up when they interrupt a Shakespearean monologue."

"Wow," she said. "That is disturbingly accurate."

He smirked. "I aim to please. And hey, not to disappoint you or anything, but I was a teenage boy once."

At least she's got a sense of humor about it.

He pulled into the lot on the corner and came around to let her out. Despite what friends, and numerous exes might think, he wasn't a total slug.

Yeah? So why am I pursuing a woman I know wants something I'm not gonna give?

They got a few appreciative looks as they crossed the street. Zach imagined they made an interesting sight. Even in the chunky platforms, she was a foot shorter than him. The skimpy romper revealed a body that said she worked out. *Maybe she was a cheerleader.* That image of her didn't sit right for some reason.

The bar was already packed and the music hit them in a wave as soon as they stepped inside, like walking into a disco-themed beach party. Neon lights blinked, and the air smelled like lime, coconut, and sweat.

Zach snagged a spot at the bar and leaned close. "What're you drinking?"

"Something tropical and ridiculous," Sam said. "Preferably with a tiny umbrella."

She ended up with some neon orange frozen thing in a pineapple-shaped cup, and the requisite tiny umbrella. He grabbed a local IPA and they clinked glasses. The driving beat made conversation almost impossible, but he didn't care. Sam swayed to the rhythm, somehow never spilling a drop of her drink. When he tossed his empty bottle, she grabbed his hand and dragged him to the dance floor.

Sam could move. The fringe glinted in time with every shimmy and twist of her hips. Zach wasn't intimidated by dancing. He could hold his own, and look good doing it, but Sam moved like sex and joy rolled into one, and all he wanted to do was watch the show.

She caught his shirt collar and reeled him in like a fish. When their bodies met, she set a slow, rolling grind to the beat, somehow making the height difference no big deal. Zach's hands found her hips, her waist, the small of her back. He let the rhythm take over, and for a while, there was no crowd, just heat and skin and glittering gold against his chest.

He could feel her laugh as much as hear it. A soft and breathless thing, like she wasn't taking any of this too seriously. And made it feel dangerous, because she'd made it clear she didn't do casual. Zach was playing with fire, and he knew it.

"Another drink?" she shouted in his ear when the music softened as the DJ changed tracks.

"Yeah. Lead the way," he called back.

At the bar, they grabbed another round and knocked back half while they waited for a gap in the crowd. Sam pointed to a barstool tucked against the wall and darted toward it. When Zach caught up, she was already mid-conversation with the guy beside her, shaking her head with a dry smile and gesturing toward Zach.

He didn't have to guess what was happening. The guy

gave Zach a once-over and immediately turned back to his drink.

Happy to cockblock you, man. Zach leaned in and braced one hand on the bar behind her. She tilted her head, angling her face up like she had in the hallway after Books and Brews. He set his beer down, took her plastic cup and placed it next to his, then plunged his fingers into the wild mass of her hair.

Sam's lips parted on a gasp and she sat up straighter, sending the sparkly fringe dancing. Everything in him wanted to kiss her hard and deep, declaring to anyone watching that she was his. And where the fuck did that thought come from? Instead, he leaned closer and spoke into her ear.

"You're gorgeous," he said.

A flush rose on her cheeks as she slid a hand behind his neck. He didn't know who moved first, but the next thing he knew, her thighs were open, he was between them, and her arms were curled around his shoulders.

The hand he'd braced on the bar dropped, cupping her ass until she slid to the edge of the stool. She threw her head back and laughed, then let go of his neck to grab her drink and finish it before tipping her head toward the dance floor. Zach didn't think twice. He scooped her off the stool, one arm around her back and the other under her ass.

Sam yelped and braced her arms against his chest, her legs tightening around him. "You are a menace."

"You love it."

He didn't set her down until they were back on the dancefloor. Sam stepped close, moving with a liquid confidence that made his brain short circuit. This kind of dancing was easy. It was sex standing up. A slow, pulsing rhythm of hips grinding and bodies swaying together.

"You're a good dancer," she shouted near his ear.

"Is that a euphemism?"

She grinned wickedly. "In my experience? There are correlations."

She turned so her back was pressed against him, grinding in a way that had him biting back a groan. With her in front of him like that, the height difference made itself known. She arched her back and tilted her head against his chest. His hands dropped to her hips, guiding the rhythm, holding her close.

This was more Zach's style. Screw conversation, it was all about the physical. The awareness that she'd been clear she wasn't into casual nagged in the back of his brain. While he hadn't come right out and said he didn't do relationships, he hadn't corrected her when she'd said she thought they wanted different things.

That's not the same thing.

He'd figured he could charm her into his bed. He was just surprised she turned around so quickly, and he didn't need the not-so-silent moral minority chiming in. When the hell did that part of his psyche decide to put in an appearance?

Zach wanted her. He was ready to suggest they leave and go to his place, but he knew better. Sam was being flirty, sure, but she wasn't there yet. He wanted, no, he needed her to be begging for him to touch her. Needed to know she wanted him as much as he wanted her.

They danced through the set and most of the next. At some point, Zach switched to water, the responsible driver part of his brain stepping in.

Eventually, the lights came up and the DJ called last round. Sam stretched and groaned dramatically. "I am going to feel this tomorrow."

"Worth it?" he asked.

She leaned on him and nodded. "Completely."

Sam shivered as they stepped into the cool night air. The

day had been sunny and warm, but the night had turned chilly, and neither of them had brought a jacket. Zach wrapped an arm around Sam's shoulders, then realized the height difference made it difficult to walk that way. He wasn't exactly warm, but Sam's outfit was a scrap of fabric and fringe that left her arms and legs bare.

"You want to wait inside while I get the car?"

She'd crossed her arms so she was hugging her own elbows. "I'll survive."

He didn't buy it.

"Well, unless you're planning on jogging the hundred or so yards to the car..." He tipped his head toward the club door, but Sam set off down the street. Zach caught up with her in less than two strides. He didn't stop to think or ask. He scooped her up, held her to his chest and crossed the street.

Sam shrieked and kicked her feet. "Are you serious?"

"You've met me, right?"

"This is so undignified." She crossed her arms over her chest again and shot him a pout, but she was shaking with laughter. He wanted to kiss the tip of her nose, but he didn't think she'd appreciate the gesture.

I wanna kiss a helluva lot more than her nose.

"You can't deny, this is faster. I apologize for not asking permission first."

At the car, he set her down gently, opened the door, and before she could protest, grabbed his brewery hoodie and tugged it over her head. It looked hilarious on her—baggy and oversized, the sleeves hanging well past her hands.

She flapped her arms like a penguin. "Fashion icon."

He laughed. "You're adorable. There's a seat heater button right on the side."

Sam tapped the button, then tipped her head back and her eyes closed.

He shut her door and came around to slide into the driver's seat.

"I had a wonderful time tonight. Thank you. That's a fun venue."

"Yeah, Metro Baltimore is always good. Great vibe for just hanging out." It wasn't a great place for hookups, but could be a solid choice for early dates. The low-key atmosphere and fact that it was just a spot to have a few drinks and dance hit the right note with some women. Not that he'd ever admit that to Sam.

She hummed softly and shifted like she was snuggling herself deeper into the seat. Sam tucked her legs under her and his hoodie swallowed her frame. As relaxed as she seemed, he wasn't surprised to see her dozing by the time they got to her place. The sleepy stage of tipsy had hit.

She sat up as he parked, rubbing her eyes and blinking like a tired cat.

"Thank you again for tonight," she said as she fumbled her door key from her bag and tried to peel his hoodie off at the same time.

"Keep the hoodie on or you'll freeze on the way up."

She waved her arms in the air, sending the over-long sleeves flapping, then dissolved into giggles.

Oh, still tipsy.

There was a time when he'd be suggesting they grab a snack, or bundle up, sit on the porch and make out. Anything to see if sleep or horny won. But now? Hell no. Sam wasn't drunk, but she was tipsy enough he wasn't confident in her decision making. She let her head fall back against the seat.

Fuck, she's beautiful.

Sam looked up at him, eyes soft. "You're very sweet."

He came around and opened her door. "Don't tell anyone. I've got a reputation to uphold."

"No, I mean it. You look like you're all tough, but you're the most considerate bad boy ever."

He helped her out of the car and bit his tongue. If that was how she saw him, he was doing something right.

Sam navigated the steps with no problem, so she wasn't too bad. At her front door, she turned to him. "I had a great time."

Zach took her hand and Sam stepped into his arms. She tipped her head up and back, then wound her arms behind his neck. Zach cupped her face in one hand. He didn't have to ask to know she was open to a kiss, but he'd guess that was all she was open to tonight. There had been a shift, sure, but not that big of one.

He hesitated. "May I kiss you?"

More of that old-fashioned romance stuff. He always got consent, but never in such a formal way. Judging by the way she smiled at him, it was the right choice.

"Yes, please."

Zach bent and brushed his lips over hers. Most of his first kisses were borderline feral things. Moments on the dance floor, in a back hallway, or pressed against the side of a car, or even a building.

Kissing Sam was different. Instead of a mad rush to press into her mouth, he took his time teasing until her lips opened to him. She was slow. Languorous. The scent of her perfume and the sound of her breathing wove into an intoxicating mix. It felt like his senses sharpened, and the night came alive with the rustle of trees in the wind and the scent of spring.

There was nothing slow about his body's response. His cock went hard in an instant, but he didn't push. Sam pressed against him, then let out a gasp and broke the kiss.

"Just kisses." Her eyes flicked downward, focusing below

his waist, then she looked back up at him with a smile. "Tonight."

There it is.

If he'd had any doubts about her desire, she'd just erased them. Which triggered a return of the nagging doubts. What kind of asshole pursues a woman he knows is looking for a relationship, when all he's into is sex?

"I get it."

She bit her lip and pulled in a slow breath, then opened her door. Halfway through, she paused and looked back at him. For half a second, he thought she'd changed her mind and was about to invite him in and he'd have to decide what to do about that.

"Will you text when you get home?"

"Of course."

He leaned down and kissed her forehead.

"Goodnight, Sam."

Her cheeks colored, but she smiled, then stepped inside. The door closed slowly, like she was reluctant to end the date. Zach felt the same. He wanted to push against that closing wall of wood and ask to come in. They could cuddle on the couch. No expectations of anything else.

When was the last time he did that?

Halfway down the steps, he realized she hadn't returned his hoodie. He laughed all the way to his car. He'd worn the thing on the ride home Friday night, then again that morning when he'd run some errands. Zach climbed into his car and started it up.

One thing he knew about women? Most of them had a thing for a man's shirt. Didn't matter if it was a sweatshirt, a hoodie, a sweater, or a flannel. Hell, even a t-shirt. They'd claim it was because they were softer, or that the oversize shirt was cozier. Both might be true, but he knew damn good and well scent played a part. He'd been working Friday night, but in the morning, he'd been freshly showered. Guaranteed it smelled like him in a good way.

Sam had looked awfully cute in the big hoodie. Zach's cock throbbed as he pulled up at home. Inside, he went straight for the shower. He hadn't jacked off two days in a row since high school. If he was horny, he'd find someone to fuck.

Except I don't want someone. I want Sam.

Oh man, I'm fucked.

CHAPTER 7

*S*omething's not right.

Sam blinked in the bright light pouring in through the open blinds. The open living room blinds. She sat up slowly, wincing as the sunlight hit her square in the eyes. Her purse hung neatly on its usual hook by the front door. The platform sandals from last night sat in a jumble, as if she'd kicked them off without much thought.

She shoved the throw blanket off and swung her legs off the couch. Pink fuzzy socks met the hardwood.

I still smell him.

It was like she was surrounded by that unique scent of his. Like all the good things about a beach bonfire and none of the bad. She stood and made her way toward the bathroom. The fringe romper hung on the back of her bedroom chair.

Okay. So I got undressed. That's reassuring.

It didn't explain why she'd fallen asleep on the couch. She flicked on the bathroom light, flinching at the sudden brightness.

Oh, that's a look.

Zach's hoodie swallowed her. Navy blue, with the Cold Bottom logo half-faded across the chest, it draped almost to her knees and completely covered her arms. She raised her hands, blinking at the oversized sleeves like they might explain things.

The fabric was soft. Worn in a way that came only from years of use. And cozy. So warm she hadn't needed more than the throw blanket over her feet last night.

Right. I changed. Got in bed. Zach texted.

Pieces slid into place. She'd just finished brushing her teeth when her phone had buzzed. Zach texting that he'd made it home. She'd sent something back. Something light and flirty with a tired emoji. They'd gone back and forth a few times. He'd told her she looked like gold and magic. She'd told him his shirt looked like something off a rum label but somehow he made it hot. They'd said goodnight. She remembered turning out the light.

So how the hell did I end up on the couch?

She padded back to the living room, hoping something would clue her in. Her worn paperback copy of *Pride and Prejudice* sat on the couch and memory flooded in. She'd been in bed, but sleep hadn't come, so she'd moved couch to read, but gotten cold and grabbed Zach's hoodie. Sam ran her hands down the front, smoothing non-existent wrinkles.

God, I smell like him.

Heat crept up her neck and prickled at her ears. It was a scent that lingered. Whatever sorcerer's concoction of his cologne mixed with soap, warm skin, and sweat that somehow didn't smell gross. Or maybe it was just his body chemistry, and it was working overtime on her hormones.

She didn't want to read into it. Not the scent. Not the

hoodie. Definitely not the forehead kiss that still ghosted across her skin.

She lifted the hood and tucked her chin so her face was buried in the neck of the sweatshirt. In the silence of the morning, when she closed her eyes, it was like he was standing right in front of her. The giant Viking who smelled like summer nights and who had the most penetrating blue eyes she'd ever seen.

And who kisses like a dream.

"Oh no." She hadn't been able to sleep because her body had been at war with her brain.

Just kisses. Tonight.

That had been her line. Her boundary. She wasn't ashamed of it, but she was surprised how much she'd wanted to blur it.

If he'd asked, she would have said yes.

Good thing he didn't ask. Why didn't he ask?

She'd felt him get hard and seen the want in his eyes. Every time they danced. Every time he looked at her like she was the only person in the room.

And she'd wanted him, too. It would've been so easy to invite him in. To let him carry her inside, press her against the wall, peel that romper off and let it drop to the floor. He would have.

Somehow, she'd held to her boundary, and Zach hadn't questioned or pushed. That said something about him, like maybe she'd misjudged him.

God, she still wanted him.

She caught her reflection in the mirror by the door. She looked ridiculous. And happy.

"Okay," she said out loud. Her voice cracked, and she cleared her throat. "Okay."

She turned into the kitchen and put on the kettle,

suddenly craving something warm and grounding like tea. Coffee did not sound good today.

Sam leaned against the counter while the water heated, tugging the sleeves of Zach's hoodie over her hands again. She should wash it and drop it off at the brewery or put it in a tote bag like it was a library book and give it back to him at the next Books and Brews.

Oh no. Oh no no no no. Oh my god.

Pulling on Zach's sweatshirt had been a mistake. Yes, it had warmed her up, but it had also surrounded her with him. Last night, on the couch, she'd laid back and made herself come more than once. She hadn't even bothered to get a toy. Just thoughts of Zach.

The hoodie's got to go.

Sam pulled off the sweatshirt, determined to wash it right away. It was the polite thing to do when you'd borrowed someone's sweatshirt. It would also make sure that she didn't leave it smelling like some combination of the two of them. She hauled open the closet door and bent to stuff the sweatshirt into the washer tub, but the thing was still warm from her body and smelled like Zach, plus a little bit of her.

Sam bundled it in her arms and sank to the floor. This wasn't on her agenda for dating with purpose. Maybe she was wrong about Zach, but she doubted it. Ever since Preston, she'd been determined to avoid unfulfilling relationships. She wanted love and marriage. Kids, not so much. That was the foundation for her self-imposed rules for when she felt ready to date again.

Be clear from the beginning that she was interested only in pursuing a serious relationship with someone who had similar values and goals and compatible sexual desires and drive.

Now she was questioning if her rules couldn't use some refinement.

That was an awful lot of weight to put on an early relationship. Maybe it was okay to be a little less rigid. How were you supposed to figure out if someone was marriage material if you didn't even date them?

Sam might be looking for her Mr. Darcy, but that didn't mean she had to abide by antiquated relationship rules. Maybe she couldn't do casual, but she wasn't a naïve college kid anymore. She and Zach might not be on the same page about relationships, but they clicked well everywhere else. There was no reason to not see him again. He was nice. They got along well and she enjoyed spending time with him. Also, he was hot and whatever chemistry there was between them was off-the-charts amazing.

She'd guard her heart. Starting with the damn hoodie.

Sam got up, stuffed the thing into the washer, added her favorite scent beads and slammed the door. Washer started, she headed for the kitchen to finish making her tea, thoughts of Zach safely tucked away for now.

The washer was done by the time she finished her tea. Sam transferred the sweatshirt to the dryer and turned it on. She took her shower, dressed and got ready for work, then checked the shop email, and dealt with a few customer questions.

When the dryer buzzer went off, she folded the freshly laundered hoodie, dropped it into a reusable shopping bag, then hung that in the closet before slipping on her shoes and grabbing her keys and work bag. It was a perfect morning for the walk to work. Sun shining and birds singing.

"Hey, how was the date?" Carla sat perched behind the register, reading glasses balanced on her nose. She broke a roll of quarters then dumped them into the drawer. "Can we puh-lease go cashless? Who carries money?"

"Lots of folks," Sam replied. They'd had this discussion. They both preferred the idea of a cashless system, but after doing the research, realized they'd be limiting their business. "And the date was fine. I'll return the romper after I get it cleaned."

Carla's head snapped up and she shot Sam a wide-eyed look. "Please tell me there's a reason for that beyond getting sweaty on the dance floor."

"Sorry to disappoint." Sam flipped the sign over and unlocked the front door. Sundays were often busy, but rarely before noon. Carla wedged a hand onto her hip and waved the other in a 'tell me more' gesture.

"We danced. It was a fun night." There was no way Carla would let it go at that, but Sam didn't feel the need to regale her with all the details. Besides, she wasn't ready to hear her best friend telling her she needed to just get over herself and get laid.

"Uh-huh. And? You're leaving out some precious details here."

The bell over the door rang, saving Sam from further prodding. At least while they had customers in the shop.

"Hi, welcome to Shelf Indulgence." She greeted the group of women, then directed them to the romantic-suspense section. She knew what Carla's advice would be, and it was tempting, but she didn't need her friend pestering her about it.

The first group led to others, and Sam stayed busy until early afternoon. She was on the register, giving Carla a much-needed break during a slow moment, when her phone pinged with a text.

> What do you think about grabbing lunch sometime this week? I did promise to show you around the city. We're not far apart and this is a foodie town.

After the charged atmosphere of last night, lunch seemed safe. With the time constraint of having to get back to work, and being in broad daylight, maybe Zach wouldn't be so tempting.

As if.

> Sounds great. And I can return your hoodie.

> My what?

Maybe he didn't remember loaning her his sweatshirt. Three little dots appeared and she waited, staring at her phone as if she could make him text faster.

> Oh. That. No rush.

"Hi, I'd like this, but in the special edition with the sprayed edges." A paperback copy of Kayla's book landed on the counter, along with several other books.

"I'm sorry, we handled the first run and it sold out. I can point you to the author's website where she's taking orders for a second run."

Sam braced herself for the irritation. Most customers were happy to place special orders, but there were always a choice few who were pills.

"But my friend said they got their copy from the shop and you were taking orders here the other night."

Here we go.

"I apologize for the confusion. We ran the first pre-order campaign and that's what folks were picking up. When we sold out, Kayla set up a second print order. Our staff helped manage it during the event, but I can't place the order for you. I can point you to her online store."

There hadn't been time to discuss details and Kayla had

needed a solution. Sam crossed her fingers this customer would accept that answer. The woman scowled, her hands still splayed across the stack of paperbacks.

"Did you want to get the other books today?"

"What? No. Not with this kind of service." She pushed her hands against the stack, sending them scattering across the counter. Sam grabbed one before it slid off the edge and shook her head at the jangling bell as the woman shoved the shop door open.

"Wow. I love my special editions, but holy cow." The next customer stepped up and laid a stack of books down. Quietly. "Just these, please."

She leaned forward and glanced toward the door as if worried the earlier customer would reappear. "I ordered mine last night and there were folks getting upset then, too. How do you both deal with that attitude? I just don't understand it."

That broke the awkward tension that had descended with the unhappy customer and Sam laughed. "We're both teachers." She grabbed the barcode scanner and rang up the books, grateful that most of their clientele were eager to support indie businesses and indie authors. "Grumpy customers are nothing compared to teenagers."

By the time Becca came in for the afternoon, Sam had dealt with half a dozen people looking to get in on the second order. Most of them were nice about it. Still, retreating to the office with Carla was a welcome relief.

"On days like today, I hold on to one thought—I could be in a classroom. That never fails to make it all seem better." Carla had grabbed two coffees and handed one to Sam, then settled at her desk. "Two Books and Brews down, two more to go before we switch to monthly."

That meant two more Fridays of seeing Zach. Sam's stomach gave a little twinge thinking about not seeing him every week.

Which was exactly the kind of thing she did not need. Getting hung up on Zach was a bad idea. She felt that in her soul.

That's not all I feel.

She shoved those thoughts aside and tapped the keyboard to wake up her laptop. "Micah's books won't arrive until Thursday, so we're running a little tight. But those aren't special editions. They are bringing a bunch of swag—stickers, bookmarks, and some custom bookplates I think."

Carla nodded. "Becca and Stefan both said they can come in early on Friday, so we'll be free to focus on set up."

"Won't that leave us shorthanded at the event? We need all hands-on deck at those."

Carla flipped her phone and showed Sam a text thread. "Kate and Greg are both big fans of Micah's so they'll be here for Books and Brews."

Carla leaned forward and focused intently on Sam. "Speaking of which. Think we should request Zach again?"

Sam rolled her eyes and waved a hand. "You already know we went out. It's not like that's news. And we're going to have lunch sometime this week."

Why did I tell Carla about that?

Her friend's eyebrows rose and she smiled. "See, I knew there was something there."

There was something, that was certain. The trouble was, Sam wasn't sure that something was good for her in the long run.

ZACH—MONDAY, APRIL 27

Zach stood in the brewhouse, staring down into the half-barrel fermenter like it might give him answers.

It didn't.

All it did was bubble.

He stepped away and pulled off his hairnet. The scent of hops hung thick in the air, and Zach tried to shake himself out of the daze he'd been in since waking up. But his brain? It had chosen violence. Specifically, the violence of looping every single fucking second of Saturday's date on repeat.

Sam. In that fringed romper. Glitter on her shoulders. Hair up like she was one spilled drink away from letting it all down.

Sam. Laughing against him on the dance floor, close enough to ruin him.

Sam. Grinding on him when the beat dropped. Then her legs wrapped around his hips like she belonged there.

Sam. Lips glossy and parted when he kissed her goodnight and didn't take it further, even though everything in him had screamed to.

He hadn't expected restraint to feel like yearning, but that was where he lived now.

He wanted her. Still wanted her. Badly.

But it wasn't just her body anymore, not that he didn't think about that. It was her voice, her smartass remarks, the quiet confidence she wore like armor. It was the way she saw him, even when he worked damn hard not to be seen.

She was dangerous, and not in the fun, flirty, tequila-and-regret way. Sam was the kind of danger that came with roots. Permanence. The kind that wanted all of him, and would absolutely call him on his bullshit.

Which made him a dumbass for making lunch plans later this week.

No sex on the table. No promises. Just time. The real kind. The kind where you might have to talk about shit that mattered.

Zach sighed and turned back to the bench where the experimental IPA sat in two labeled tasting glasses.

He picked one up and gave it a swirl. Pale golden yellow, hazy, with a soft, snowy head that laced nicely around the glass. The nose hit him first. Pineapple and guava, but not sweet. There was depth there. A bloom of passionfruit. Bright hibiscus riding the citrus notes. It smelled like dancing with Sam felt.

Jesus, man. Pull it together.

He took a sip.

A hint of coconut. Smooth and light malt balance. It was creamy without being heavy; tropical without leaning candy sweet. Crisp. Summer-ready. Just like Sam.

Nope.

He took another sip.

Yep. Still just like Sam.

It was bright and surprising and made him want more before the first swallow finished.

Goddamn it.

He grabbed the other glass, muttering to himself as he headed for the back hallway, then upstairs. His mom would be in her office by now, working through inventory before the tasting room opened. He pushed open the door and found her at her desk, laptop open, brow furrowed.

"Hey," he said.

She looked up, half-smiling. "You have that look on your face."

"I always have a look."

"Mm-hmm. And this one says 'Mom, try my beer so I can avoid dealing with shit that's bugging me.' It's that or you've got your eye on a new woman and haven't figured out how to get in her pants yet."

She held out her hand and shrugged. "Come to think of it,

it's been years since I've seen that last look. Guess you improved your game."

"Jesus, Mom." Zach handed over the glass. He didn't need his mother analyzing his sex life. Or lack of it, lately.

She took the beer, gave it the professional once-over. Swirled. Sniffed. Sipped.

Her eyes lifted. "Huh."

"That a good 'huh'?"

"That's a very good huh." She set the glass down and bent to peer through the side as if inspecting for flaws. Which she probably was. Apparently satisfied, she picked it up again for another taste. "Citra hops?"

"Yeah. With mosaic and sabro, of course. All late-addition and dry hop. No fruit. It's all from the hops."

"I get pineapple on the nose, then guava. Passionfruit on the mid-palate. And is that honey malt?"

"Little bit. I wanted a little softness, subtle sweetness."

She gave a low whistle and went in for another sip. "This is dangerously drinkable."

"Only five percent," he said, leaning against the doorframe. He was ridiculously proud of that number. Bringing in a lower-alcohol beer that packed good flavor took skill.

"Well, well," she said, giving him a long look over her glass. "What's her name?"

Zach didn't answer right away. After a minute, he shrugged. "Haven't named the brew yet. It's a tropical IPA, but you of all people know that. For now, it's TropIPA Batch 3."

His mom tilted her head. "Zach."

He groaned and shifted on the doorframe, shoving his hands in his pants pocket and feeling like a teenager again.

"Her name is Sam."

A smile tugged at the corner of her mouth. "Sam from the bookshop?"

He nodded once.

She studied him for a beat. "It's a good beer. Clean. Thoughtful. Not what I expected from you."

Zach rolled his eyes. "Thanks, I guess?"

"No, I mean it," she said, and her expression softened. "It's layered. Balanced. It doesn't pretend to be something it's not, and it's got character. That's a sign of someone thinking beyond the tank. Brewing for experience, not ego."

She took another sip, smiled and nodded. "Let's give this one a trial with the staff. Then I'm thinking you do a batch to put with our early summer seasonals. Kegs and growlers only."

"Wow. That's..." Zach didn't have words. It had taken him a year to get her approval for Over the Barrel and she was giving the thumbs up on the summer IPA with one tasting.

Zach felt his ears heat.

His mom, who could wield a tasting note like a dagger, looked almost gentle. "You really like her."

He swallowed. Leave it to his mom to see things he didn't want to face himself. "I'm trying not to."

She nodded like she understood. "Maybe stop trying."

He left the office a minute later, empty glass in hand, the taste of guava and Sam lingering on his tongue.

By the time he got back to the brewhouse, amid the hissing tanks and the normal morning hum, all he could think about was the way Sam had looked at him when he kissed her, soft and unguarded and too damn close to home.

This was not what he'd signed up for. He was in deep. Too deep. And lunch this week was going to be a fresh kind of torture.

CHAPTER 8

Coming into the shop early on a Wednesday morning was not Sam's idea of a good time, but that was the joy of being the owner. Or one of the owners. The other one had an appointment to get to. Which meant Sam had to be there for the air conditioning repair tech who'd said he'd arrive between eight and noon.

She unlocked the door and went straight to the office, which at least had a tiny window AC unit. She cranked it to high then returned to the shop floor. Temperatures had soared Tuesday and the shop's main AC had moved the air, but it wasn't chilling it. She was crossing her fingers it was a quick, and not too expensive, fix.

Sam popped her earbuds in, turned on some music and focused on one of the little, never-ending tasks of running a bookshop—putting books back where they belonged. It always astounded her how a customer would pick up a book, then when they decided they weren't going to buy it, rather than put it on the counter, give it to a staff member, or leaving it on a table, they would stick it on some random shelf that wasn't even in the same section.

By ten, she'd restocked shelves, tidied the shop, and even cleaned the office refrigerator. Still no word from the AC repair tech. Her cell pinged and she scrambled to grab it only to see a text from Becca saying she was sick and not coming in. Sam switched gears to the usual opening routines—making sure there was change in the drawer, a stack of bags near the register, and put fresh supplies with the coffee machine.

Wednesdays were usually slow, but today she had half a dozen people in the shop within ten minutes of opening. And it didn't let up. And still no call from the repair tech. And she was supposed to meet Zach for lunch. She grabbed her phone again and sent a quick text to Stefan to see if he could make it in, then another to Carla, explaining the situation and telling her not to worry. Finally, she pulled up Zach's contact.

> I'm going to have to raincheck on lunch. AC died, waiting on repair guy. We're shorthanded and I have no shop coverage, so I'm buried.

She didn't like canceling their plans, but she didn't have much of a choice. Even if Stefan got here, he couldn't handle the shop on his own. Nor deal with the repair tech. And she had no idea how long Carla's appointment would go for. She tapped her phone at the first hint of a buzz.

> Sometimes it's like that. How about I bring food by instead? I'll keep out of your hair so you can work. I've got a game this afternoon, so can't stay late anyway.

That's unexpected.
She'd put Zach in the party boy category. Someone

pleasant to spend time with, when everything was good and fun and easy, but not the kind of person to be around when things got tough, or less fun. Maybe there was a lot more to him than she thought.

She'd never dated a man who, faced with a last-minute change like that, would roll with it and say, "no problem, we'll shift things to accommodate your need."

> If you're ok with that, great!

She didn't have time to check for a response. Stefan said he'd be in as soon as possible, Carla said she'd be at least another hour, maybe two, and another group of customers came through the door. When Stefan came in and took over the register, Sam hoped for time to catch her breath and check her messages, but the AC tech arrived and Sam took him out back to the big commercial unit.

Once she got him settled, she headed straight for the office, locked the door, leaned back against it, and took several deep breaths. The office door rattled behind her and a sharp knocking echoed near her head.

"Unless it's an emergency, I need a minute."

The knocking stopped and she let her head rest against the door.

"Let me in. I've got lunch."

Sam flung open the door to see Zach standing there with Cold Bottom bags dangling from his hands. His broad smile shifted as his eyes landed on hers, and he stepped into the room, then shut the door behind him.

"Sit." He pointed toward her desk then set the bags on the long table. "I'm guessing you didn't see my texts."

Sam shook her head as Zach looked around the room until he spotted the refrigerator, then stuffed a bag into it. He grabbed the remaining two and unloaded them onto the table.

"Come on. Eat." He pushed what looked like a wrapped sandwich her direction. "You didn't respond with what you wanted so I made a guess. There's also our chopped veggie salad."

Sam rolled her chair to the table, looked down at the food Zach had spread out, then back to him. "Thank you."

She couldn't manage words beyond that. He'd heard her need and taken action. She unwrapped the sandwich and laughed.

"Is this the grilled cheese with bacon and tomato?"

"Came off the griddle about a minute before I left the brewery."

Sam picked up the sandwich and bit into a piece of heaven. She was dimly aware of Zach opening his own food, and struck again by how comfortable it was just sharing space with him. Sometimes, she enjoyed talk during meals. Right now, she needed to eat. Zach seemed to understand that and kept silent.

Eventually, she wiped her hands and took a swallow of water. "I suppose I should give Stefan a break so he can go get lunch. And check on the repair tech."

Zach wiped his mouth and gave her a smile that had her considering shoving all the wrappers off the table and having him for dessert. *And where did that come from?*

"He's got a pit beef sandwich," Zach said. "The bag in the 'fridge has wings, mac-n-cheese, and those sausage bites you like. Figured you or Carla might get hungry later. Nobody's come knocking. Take a breath. Drink some more water."

The low, calm tones of his voice did something magical in her head. Or maybe it was getting food into her system. Her shoulders relaxed and she went from feeling stressed about everything to realizing it was all under control.

"Oh! I almost forgot." Sam jumped up and snagged the reusable shopping bag from her desk, then stopped and surveyed the table. "Hang on. You brought lunch, clean up's on me."

She tossed the trash and wiped the table, then slid the bag over to Zach.

"Your hoodie."

"You really didn't have to." He tugged the sweatshirt from the bag and his expression shifted, going from amusement to something almost dark, and very sexy looking. "You washed it."

Sam bit her lip. What had possessed her to add scent beads? Returning it washed was one thing. Returning it smelling like the sandalwood and lavender she used on her sheets was something else.

"Yeah. I uh... I fell asleep in it, so it seemed like the right thing to do." She wasn't about to admit what else she'd done while wearing it.

He slid the sweatshirt to the side and took her hand. His touch sent pleasant shivers up her arm and Sam's entire body clenched.

"I still have a promise to uphold—showing you around the city. And you have a raincheck to honor. How does Saturday sound? Like, afternoon into evening."

The jump in topic was a little surprising, but the idea of spending an afternoon with Zach sounded great. Never mind the nagging in her brain telling her he was trouble.

"Saturday sounds great. I'll have a little work in the morning, but I'm free any time after twelve."

The dark, dangerous look crossed his face again. His eyes

narrowed and his already pouty lips pursed. "I enjoyed kissing you after our date."

Another topic shift and this time, his voice alone had her skin prickling in the nicest way. Zach stood and Sam couldn't take her eyes off of him. Even in jeans and a t-shirt, he commanded attention. It wasn't just that he was tall, and well built, and had all that ink. There was something else about him.

Don't forget the piercings.

She flicked her eyes to his chest where the barbells made a clear imprint on his shirt.

I didn't imagine them. What else is pierced? Aside from his ears.

Her gaze traveled down, past the skull belt buckle to the bulge in his jeans that looked like it had been sculpted to attract attention. His hand landed on her shoulder and Sam sucked in air. She'd been staring at his crotch and hadn't noticed he'd moved and now stood right next to her.

Zach slid behind her and rested both hands on her shoulders. His thumbs dipped down between her shoulder blades while his fingers dug into the tight muscles on top.

Good grief his hands are huge. Is everything about him oversized?

Heat rose in her face and the room felt too warm, but Zach was working the tension out of her shoulders with smooth strokes. His thumbs sank into tense spots and Sam groaned as the muscles released.

"Oh, I know that feels good." He rolled over the spot again and the warmth spread over her whole body. Sam tipped her head forward as Zach's fingers travelled up to her neck, kneading away the stresses of the morning.

The buzzer on the back door sounded and Sam groaned.

She opened her eyes and looked up at Zach. Even from this angle, seeing him upside down, he was still handsome.

"That'll be the appliance tech."

Zach lifted his hands and Sam opened the office door just as the tech was about to knock.

"I figured out the problem, and I've got you kind of up and running, but it's a temporary fix. You wanna come take a look?"

Sam didn't want to. She wanted to sit back down and let Zach's fingers work magic over her entire body. But this wasn't just a job. Shelf Indulgence was half hers. She'd poured everything into the business and she was damn well going to do her best.

"Excuse me a minute." She waved at Zach then followed the tech outside. A minute turned into thirty as he explained everything at least twice, despite Sam saying she would talk with her business partner and they'd call tomorrow to schedule the full repair.

WHEN SHE CAME BACK INTO THE OFFICE, ZACH WAS standing near her desk, phone in hand and his hair mussed as if he'd run his fingers through it.

"I was just about to text you," he said, slipping the phone into his back pocket. "I've gotta run. Standing basketball game with fraternity brothers. Deke's car's in the shop, so he's meeting me here to carpool."

Sam arched a brow. "Fraternity brothers? Of course you were in a frat."

Probably the resident bad boy, too.

Zach grinned, looking unbothered. "Only the finest degenerates I've ever known. And hey, we raise a lot of money for charity now, so redemptive arc."

That forced a smile to her lips.

He held his arms out in invitation. "Come here."

Sam hesitated for half a second, just long enough to remind herself that anything physical with Zach was a very slippery slope, and then stepped into his embrace anyway.

His arms closed around her, warm and solid and strong. Her body relaxed instantly, as if it had been waiting for this exact contact. She laid her head on his chest, and Zach sighed, long and low, like the exhale came from somewhere deep inside him.

The moment was quiet and still, thick with something she didn't want to name.

He pulled back just enough to drop a kiss to her forehead. "See you Saturday," he said, voice low and rough.

He tipped his head down and Sam rose on her tiptoes. Zach's lips brushed hers and the office door banged open.

"Hey man, you said be here ASA...oh." A tall, broad-shouldered man skidded to a halt in the doorway, eyebrows raised and mouth twitching like he was trying very hard not to smirk. "Interrupting something?"

Zach groaned and slowly let go of Sam. "Deke, timing is a skill you clearly never developed."

"Listen, we're already running behind. Not my fault you're..." He looked past Zach and smiled at Sam. "Hi. I'm Deke Wallace. This menace is my brother from another mother. And sometimes an actual headache."

"Sam Crowley," she said, startled, but reaching out to shake his hand. "Nice to meet you."

"Oh, you're Sam." Deke gave Zach a look. "Huh. Okay. I get it now."

Zach shot him a glare. "Don't start."

"Not starting. Just observing." Deke turned back to Sam with a grin. "Pleasure. Truly."

Zach muttered something under his breath and nudged Deke toward the door. "We're gonna be late."

"Yeah, yeah. I'm moving. Just happy to meet the woman who's got you standing still for more than five minutes." Deke winked at Sam as Zach shoved him out the door.

"Sorry about him," Zach called over his shoulder, already halfway into the hall.

Sam leaned in the doorway, arms crossed, lips twitching with amusement. "Seems like a handful."

Deke turned around, walking backwards. "He's the handful, but he's family. And we get discounts on the beers after the game."

Zach groaned audibly and waved at Sam before pushing Deke out of the shop.

The door clicked shut behind them and the silence that followed seemed to echo louder than it should have. Sam sank into her desk chair.

She dropped her forehead to the cool wood in front of her and groaned.

The man was walking, talking sex appeal.

And had friends who joked with her on sight.

Zach seemed custom-tailored to get past every single one of her defense mechanisms like he'd been issued a blueprint. This was not going to be easy.

A cool breeze ruffled the hair on the back of her neck and Sam sat up. She rose and stuck her hand in front of the vent. *Cool air. Yay!*

"Zach said there was food in the fridge. And what are you doing?"

Sam sat back down and blinked. Lunch with Zach had scrambled her brain. It was like waking up from a dream.

"It's a long story, but yes, there's lunch for you."

While Carla put together a plate then stuck it in the

microwave, Sam told her all about the air conditioner, Becca calling out sick, and Zach bringing lunch.

"What a morning." Carla tossed her fork to her half-empty plate. "But tell me more about you and Zach. Because that man is sex on a stick. So was his friend. Damn."

Sam shook her head. "Not until you tell me what's going on with you. You had three appointments this week."

Carla shrugged and pushed her plate away with a sigh. "Emmy and I decided we want a baby, and since she's in her residency, I'll carry. We haven't told anyone because people can be assholes, y'know?"

Sam's first reaction was to congratulate her friend, but something in Carla's tone told her to hold off. Instead, she slid forward and took Carla's hand in hers. The tight smile she got in response confirmed everything wasn't sunshine and roses.

"Nothing's happened," Carla continued. "We found a great doctor. Ideal sperm donor. We've done two rounds of intrauterine insemination and..."

Carla shrugged and pulled in a deep breath. "Nothing. But it's not uncommon. Today, we decided we'll try one more cycle of IUI, then consider if we want to try IVF or look at adoption."

As someone with a take it or leave it attitude about having children, Sam couldn't identify with Carla's situation, but she knew her friend. Latina to the core and from a large family. Carla wanted kids.

"Yeah, I know." Carla squeezed Sam's hand. "My sisters get pregnant if their husbands look at them sideways. And they didn't want kids."

Sam slid out of her seat and wrapped her friend in a big hug. "I'm sorry, hon. I can only imagine how hard this must be for you."

She didn't tell Carla it would be okay. Or that they'd have

a baby when the time was right. There was nothing she could say to make it easier. The only thing she could do was be a friend.

"And you let me babble on about air conditioners and staff issues and Zach? Really?"

Carla shrugged. "I needed a break from thinking about trying to get pregnant. It's a lot, and I didn't want you fussing or worrying about me."

Sam released her and sat back. "Okay. Fair. When you're ready, tell me as much or as little as you want. I'm your friend and I love you, and I want to be here for you. Even if it's just to give you the peace of someone not asking a million invasive questions."

That brought a laugh out of Carla. "You have no idea how invasive. And I'm holding you to that. Which means right now what I need is distraction in the form of all the dirty details of a certain hot Viking and you."

Sam rolled her eyes and sighed. "It's going to be a short distraction. There's not much to tell."

ZACH

"Okay, I get the tiny comment." Deke stopped by Zach's car. "Surprised you're not on the bike today."

Deke shrugged and unlocked the doors. "Day got kinda scrambled. Figured it was better to have my gear with me in case I didn't make it back home. What, you bummed you don't get to wrap your arms around me and cuddle up?"

He blew a kiss at Deke then slid into the driver's seat and waited till his friend was buckled in before he pulled away from the curb.

"Fuck, it's gonna be tight." Zach whipped the car onto Falls Road and crossed his fingers he'd catch all green lights.

"Ty's running late, too. Some shit with work."

Zach broke a few speed limits, but they made it across town in record time and he pulled into a shaded spot near the basketball courts. The afternoon sunlight cast the cracked surface in shifting shadows.

"Huh. Empty." Deke shouldered the gear bag and Zach grabbed the cooler of waters. By the time he dropped the cooler in the corner, Deke was bouncing a ball in a loose rhythm, sinking lazy shots like he didn't have a care in the world.

"Not like Ty to be late." Zach caught the ball on the rebound and bounced it back and forth between his hands, the sound of it slapping against the pavement oddly gratifying.

Deke shrugged, then lunged for the ball. "Life's gotten crazy. Wedding planning. Work. Nicky's got him doing more cardio than he did back when he was training for marathons."

Zach chuckled as Deke took another shot and missed. "So basically she's trying to keep him alive long enough to say 'I do.'"

"Something like that. And to keep his ass from stress-eating three dozen donuts like last month."

A few more of the usual guys arrived and started warming up. Most former fraternity brothers, plus a few add-ons in the form of work colleagues and folks who wandered onto the court on a regular enough basis that they'd been absorbed into the rotation. There was the usual small talk: O's stats, beer recommendations, neighborhood parking gripes. The warm-up was easy, comfortable.

Then Ty jogged up, dropped his bag next to the cooler, and leaned over, hands on his knees.

"You ran here?" Zach eyed his friend's already sweaty shirt.

"Nicky's got my car, and I am not riding her scooter," he

puffed, breathless. "I was planning to walk. Supposed to be my half day and there's so much going on I can't think straight."

Ty tapped a button on his watch and straightened up. "Also, bite me. I just made a mile and a half in eight minutes."

Zach whistled, then bounced the ball to Ty. "You good?"

"No. Between wedding stuff and events and the museum, I've forgotten what free time is. Nicky and I were supposed to take a weekend away this month. Just disappear. Now Artscape's been rescheduled to July, she's got committee meetings stacked like Legos, and I've got press hits and pop-ups from now 'til August. We're probably gonna skip vacation and just extend the honeymoon."

Deke missed another shot and made a face. "That sucks, man. Charlie and I are on opposite schedules half the time. I've got nights and weekends off and she works weekends. My summer's free, but that's her busy season. Syncing calendars requires some intense negotiations."

Zach laughed, light but reflexive. "Chalk that up as one of many reasons I stick with being single. My calendar only has to make sense to me."

Even as Zach said it, his brain betrayed him.

A flash of Sam, legs tucked beneath her in his passenger seat, his hoodie pulled down over her knees and her head tipped back like she'd been doing it forever.

He'd thought, more than once, about asking her to meet him after the game. No agenda. Just to hang out. Find a bar with a patio, order drinks, and pretend it was summer already.

And what the fuck was that about? He didn't do relationship shit. He did parties and sex. An occasional plus one if it sounded fun. But Sam made the silence between moments feel easy.

That kind of ease, unhurried and unforced comfort, was

starting to feel suspiciously close to something he'd spent the better part of a decade avoiding.

Something like intimacy.

Something dangerously close to real.

Fuck, he wasn't ready for that. Not with Sam. Not with anyone. He wasn't built for long-term, no matter how good her laugh made him feel or how much he'd wanted to kiss her senseless outside her front door last night.

"She's cute, by the way."

Deke's voice snapped him out of the mental spiral. It sounded casual, but Zach caught the undercurrent. Deke never said shit just to say it. Especially not about women Zach was seeing.

"She's cute," Deke repeated, like it was a benign observation, not a loaded hand grenade.

Ty, lining up a shot at the basket, paused mid-motion. Turned slowly.

"You met her?" Ty asked, ball still in hand.

Ah, fuck. Zach hadn't thought this through. He'd figured he had a little more time before the peanut gallery started taking notes.

"The bookshop owner?" Ty added. "Sam?"

"Yeah," Deke replied, cool and unfazed. "This afternoon. Carpooled with Zach and he told me to meet him at the bookshop. They were kissing in the office. Kinda sweet, actually."

Zach groaned, low in his throat.

Ty tossed the ball to Deke, who caught it one-handed. "And...?"

Deke made a show of bouncing the ball between his legs a few times before answering. "And, I think our friend's in trouble."

Zach rolled his eyes so hard he was halfway to a concussion. "You two are unbearable."

But his voice lacked bite. Mostly because he'd been worrying about the same thing, and trying to avoid thinking about it too much.

"C'mon," he added, yanking the ball from Deke and sinking a shot with a little too much force. "Let's play. Before one of you starts quoting poetry about feelings."

Ty snorted. "We're not the ones playing house with the hot bookshop owner."

"She's not a bookshop owner," Zach muttered under his breath.

"She literally owns a bookshop," Deke said.

"I mean that's not all she is."

There was a beat of silence. Not the mocking kind Zach was used to from his friends, but the kind that meant they were both clocking the truth he hadn't acknowledged himself.

"Well damn," Ty said, slow and amused. "You are fucked."

Zach didn't have an answer to that. Any smartass response he gave would only dig the hole deeper.

One of the older fraternity brothers clapped Zach on the shoulder. "We gonna play, or are you guys having a therapy session?"

They jumped into a few rounds of 3x3—fast, sweaty, a lot shit-talky. Zach was in the zone by game two, driving hard into the paint, blocking shots, goading Deke with a grin. The trio won two out of three rounds and didn't feel too bad about the loss in the first.

Afterward, they piled into Zach's car for the ride back to Cold Bottom, their shirts sticking to their backs and looking forward to the promise of cold beers. But when they pulled into the narrow employee lot, Zach let out a quiet groan. The patio was crammed shoulder-to-shoulder, and the interior didn't look much better. The hum of conversation was loud even from a distance.

"Fuck. Forgot about the new happy hour promo," Zach muttered.

They pushed through the doors and Zach flagged down Reg, who looked as frazzled as expected. "How bad are you in the weeds?"

Reg gave him a look that could kill. "Happy hour, a darts club, and two convention groups. What d'ya think?"

"Godspeed, man." Zach clapped Reg on the shoulder. "Try not to start any fires." Half-laughing, he herded Ty and Deke toward the back hall.

Zach dug into his bag for the key ring and, after a second of trying to find the right key, gave up and tossed the whole thing to Deke. "Guess it's back to the old haunt. Blue key. You know the one. Grab a couple pitchers and some glasses from the barback. I'll check with Mitzy and see if we can raid the kitchen for anything."

Ty arched an eyebrow. "Mitzy's still speaking to you?"

"C'mon, I'm a charmer. She loves me," Zach shot back.

Mitzy was like the cool aunt who let you get away with murder, and she loved the old space even more than Zach did. She used to call it the "witchy bar" back in the early days. The dark beams, cozy nooks, and exposed brick made it feel like someone had grafted an Old-World pub onto a prohibition cellar.

Zach was a kid when his mom and stepdad opened Cold Bottom in the old brewhouse and taproom. He spent many nights doing his homework on a folding table crammed into a corner. After two years of hustle, Cold Bottom's new pilsner won at the Best of Craft Beer Awards, and that fall, the lavender saison claimed an award at the Great American Beer Festival.

Lynn Abell had done it again. Only this time, she was making award-winning beers at her own brewery. By the time Zach was in middle school, they had taken over the adjacent restaurant space, then expanded the brewhouse and built a new taproom. The old one was still used occasionally for small events and private bookings, but drifted into semi-retirement and eventually became Zach's domain. A place to hang with friends. Some of his best memories happened in that room.

Deke tossed the keys in the air and caught them with a grin. "Nostalgia time. Love it."

Zach smirked. "Don't break anything."

"No promises."

He watched them go, the old key ring catching the light as Deke twirled it between his fingers. Zach turned to the big kitchen and put on his best smile..

Mitzy would give him shit, but she'd come through. Always.

The taproom wasn't the most polished space they had, but it had soul. And it felt like the right place to be.

Mitzy spotted Zach the second he pushed through the kitchen doors.

"The Three Musketeers have arrived. You can grab crab pretzels, sausage rolls, and chips and dips—but you're making and serving, and staying the hell out of my way."

He gave her a grin and a dramatic bow. "As long as I don't have to make the dough."

She flicked her ever-present towel at him, delivering a stinging shot to his thigh. "Please. You couldn't shape a pretzel loop if your love life depended on it."

"Good thing it doesn't, then, huh?"

"Incurable smartass."

"Learned from the best."

It took no time to prep and heat the food. Zach threw

together some salads—something green to cancel out the carb overload—and stacked everything on a tray. Mitzy gave him a skeptical glance as he shifted the weight to one hand and balanced it with his shoulder.

"You sure you remember how to do that?"

"Muscle memory," he said. "Plus, I've got style."

She rolled her eyes but smiled, and he was out the door before she could change her mind about letting him raid the kitchen.

He nudged the tasting room door open with his hip and found Deke and Ty already halfway through their first round, parked at the old bar with their feet kicked up and their sweat mostly dried.

"Food's up," Zach announced. He bent at the knees and accomplished the small miracle of setting the tray down without dropping anything.

He poured himself a pint, then leaned against the counter. "So, Mr. Organized. What's got your briefs in a twist?"

Ty was mid-bite into a crab pretzel. He swallowed fast and swigged some beer. "Told you. Nicky and I are over committed. Wedding. Events. Teaching schedule. At this point, we'll be lucky to get three hours of uninterrupted time between now and the honeymoon."

Zach made a face. "Again. Why I don't do long-term."

"You've mentioned." Ty rolled his eyes. "At least seven times this week."

"I mean, Deke gets it." Zach snagged a sausage roll and broke it apart with his fingers. He knew better than to bite straight into the thing.

"Says who?" Deke grabbed a second pint. "With the right person? It's worth it. Even when it's hard to make the time."

Zach didn't answer right away. Mostly because he was chewing. But also because Deke had that look in his eye. The same look he'd had on the patio outside when he'd recognized the tall redhead who'd just walked in. He'd been all-in for Charlie then and hadn't even known it.

His friends had found something real. Zach was thrilled for them, but he didn't do real. Not like that. No matter how tempting Sam might be.

He downed half a glass of beer. Anything to keep from giving voice to the thoughts in his head.

"You're doing that thing again," Ty said from the side, voice casual but eyes sharp. He had the pitcher in his hand, but didn't pour. Just stood there, watching.

Zach slid his glass over for a refill. "What thing?"

"That zoning out like you're composing haikus about a woman."

Zach scoffed, pushing down the sting of truth in that jab. "Jesus."

Ty grinned, that same shit-eating smirk he'd had since undergrad. "What's the bookshop owner's name again?"

"Sam."

Her name came out reflexively. Like it lived in his head. Like it belonged to him. Like it mattered. Like she mattered.

Ty blinked. "Well, okay then." He whistled under his breath. "Didn't even hesitate."

Zach winced as soon as he realized what he'd done. "Fuck."

Deke raised one brow. "You okay there, man?"

Zach leaned onto the bar, palms flat, breathing deeper than he needed to. "Fine," he said. Too fast. Too sharp. "We went out once. More friends than anything."

Except that kiss. Even that he could blow off as friends with benefits. Sort of.

Ty poured, the sound of filling glasses loud in the quiet space. "Uh-huh," he said, voice drier than the Nevada desert.

"That's not counting you being at her shop today. Which, last I checked, today is Wednesday."

"And?" Zach shrugged and snagged his full glass back. "Last I checked it's legal to do shit on your day off."

Ty unlocked his phone. "Just saying. For a guy who claims it's nothing, you're acting like it's something."

Zach took a slow sip, keeping his expression unreadable. Deke wandered back toward them, grabbed his glass and leaned in like he was about to drop a bomb.

"You want to talk about it?" Deke asked. He said it lightly, but his tone landed with weight. Not teasing—real.

Zach let the silence stretch for a second, then another. Long enough to make it obvious he wasn't biting.

"Thought so," Deke muttered. "Look, man, I'm not saying you're suddenly Captain Commitment. I'm just saying you might want to be honest with yourself. That woman? She's not a fling. She doesn't read casual."

Zach set his glass down harder than necessary. "And what do I read like?"

Deke and Ty both went quiet. The bite of Zach's words hung between them.

Ty stepped in gently, voice low. "You have to ask? You used to read like you were just looking for fun. A distraction. Killing time. Lately?" He shrugged. "Something's changed. You're like a guy who wants to be found."

Zach barked out a laugh, sharp and bitter. "You sound like my therapist."

"You don't have a therapist."

"That's my point."

Deke snorted and shook his head. "You can deflect all you want. Just remember, some of us have done the fuckboy redemption arc, and the flipside is pretty fucking good. Even when it's hectic and stressful."

Zach looked between the two of them. "You assholes planning an intervention?"

"Nah," Ty said, spinning a paper coaster in his fingers. "We just like watching you squirm."

"Fuck both of you," Zach muttered, but he was smiling. Deep down, where he didn't like to look, and sure as hell wouldn't admit out loud, he felt it. Sam's name still sat on his tongue, warm and familiar.

Ty laid the coaster down with exaggerated care then pulled his phone from his pocket and tapped the screen.

"What are you—"

Ty opened Instagram. "Nicky's on the Artscape planning committee. Along with one of the DJs at Metro Baltimore. You know where this is going."

He pulled up a post and swiped through it slowly until he landed on the image that mattered.

There it was. Sam, laughing, legs wrapped around Zach's waist on the dance floor. Hair and the romper's golden fringe catching the light. Her smile. The way she reached for him like she'd done it a hundred times. Like she knew him.

Deke leaned in, whistled. "Damn. Very different than at the shop."

Zach tried to play it off, but a tight, uneasy feeling settled in his stomach.

Ty raised an eyebrow. "So what changed? Thought you weren't mixing business and pleasure. That she didn't do casual and you'd grown an unexpected set of morals."

Zach stared at the image a second longer, then hit the button to minimize it.

"Nothing's changed."

Except everything had.

"Told you, we went out. No, we didn't sleep together. No, I'm not in love. She's just fun."

Deke hummed a familiar bassline.

Ty started tapping out a rhythm on the bar before humming along to 'Another One Bites the Dust.'

Zach flipped them both off.

They laughed, but it didn't stop the sinking feeling in his chest. It wasn't about the teasing. He'd dished it out plenty when they had caught feelings. It was that he couldn't stop thinking about her. The way she listened. The way she looked at him like she saw past all his bullshit.

He knew what Sam meant when she said she didn't do casual. She meant she'd been hurt. That she wasn't going to risk that again unless it was real. Long term. Committed. He couldn't promise her that. He'd given up on that long ago and saw no reason to change his point of view.

Zach poured himself another beer. Watched the foam rise. Let the silence stretch.

He might not have answers yet, but he knew one thing: He wasn't ready to lose whatever this was.

Not yet.

CHAPTER 9

SAM—FRIDAY, MAY 1

"Sheila was not kidding about the bartender," the next customer said, not even looking at Sam as she dropped a stack of books on the counter. "I'd like to climb him like a tree."

Sam kept her expression carefully neutral. "Twenty-seven fifty," she said, swiping the card.

This wasn't the first time she'd overheard women openly lusting after Zach, and it wouldn't be the last. She couldn't blame them. Tonight he was wearing a fitted Cold Bottom polo shirt that should probably be illegal for the way it clung to his biceps and stretched across his chest. It didn't help that he wasn't wearing his usual bib apron, but one tied low on his hips. The tattoos only added fuel to the fantasy, snaking up his arm and disappearing under his sleeve like an invitation to get him out of his shirt.

And that was before he opened his mouth. Flirty, friendly, and funny. Zach behind a bar was walking, talking weaponized charm.

The woman accepted her bag with a distracted "thanks" and looked over her shoulder at the bar. She inhaled and tugged her neckline lower, maximizing the visible cleavage. Sam gave her most professional "thank you for coming to Shelf Indulgence" before rolling her eyes as soon as the customer's back was turned.

She'd also just handed out her last small bag. Fine. Good a time as any to take a breather.

"Hey Becca, I need to restock bags. You good to handle the register solo?"

Becca barely glanced up from the tablet. "I got it. Line's short. Go. Hydrate. Breathe."

Sam headed for the office, forcing herself not to glance toward the bar, but she didn't make it. A ripple of laughter rose from that side of the shop. Zach's unmistakable warm and low laugh with a hint of cockiness. Sam glanced over to see who brought that out of him. A tall blond leaned against the bar, her posture pure practiced seduction. The flirtatious tones carried, even in the busy space. Zach was pouring samples, lining up glasses with practiced flair, all charm and easy conversation.

He was good at this. She knew that. It was part of what made him great at these events. He might spend most of his time in the brewhouse, but he was a natural with people. He made everyone feel welcome. Special. Seen.

So why did seeing him doing his job twist her stomach in a knot?

Sam turned away and hurried to the office. She yanked the bag box off the shelf, uncaring that she'd dislodged the tidy stack, then made her way back through the shop. The crowd was thick, definitely their biggest Books & Brews yet. She'd expected the combined fantasy and romantasy night to pack them in, but clearly pairing contemporary romance with craft beers and a hot bartender was a winning combo.

Sam shoved the bags into the cabinet under the register and tried to avoid looking at the bar again. But the blond was still there. Worse, she'd been joined by a friend. The new woman had her phone out, angling it for a photo. Sam could guess what she was trying to capture: Zach, mid-pour, muscles flexed, chunky rings catching the light, probably some charming grin half-cocked on his face.

"I'm gonna walk the floor," Sam told Becca. "Trash duty."

Becca gave her a knowing look. "Need to clear your head?"

"Yup."

Sam grabbed a trash bag and disappeared into the maze of shelves, ducking into the quiet aisles at the shop's edges. She wasn't hiding. She was being productive. There were empty plastic cups that needed clearing. She scooped them up, along with used napkins and a discarded promo flyer, and tried to drown out the murmur of voices. Most were harmless.

Some weren't.

"—and did you see his arms? Like, hello, sir—"

"Right? I'd risk a book hangover for a night with him."

"He's the brewmaster at Cold Bottom. He can be my master any time."

Sam clutched the trash bag tighter. This was fine. Normal. Zach was objectively attractive, and obviously she wasn't the only one who'd noticed. It didn't matter. They weren't serious. They'd had one real date, and a goodnight kiss that had left Sam in a state all week.

There was no reason for her to feel like someone had a death grip on her insides. She was being ridiculous. Sam rounded the far corner then ducked into the front reading nook to avoid coming out near the bar and she stopped cold.

A couple stood by the wall, tangled in each other, whispering and laughing. Sam turned to leave, then took a closer look.

On the low table sat a small, square jewelry box, open and empty.

She glanced back at the couple. Sure enough, a sparkly rock sat on the woman's hand catching the overhead lights and sending rainbow prisms around the nook.

A proposal. In our bookshop.

A laugh bubbled up, soft and rolling. That kind of romance still existed in the world. Public proposals and spontaneous kisses and swoony declarations. This was why Shelf Indulgence carried so much romance, and why their entire grand opening month was dedicated to the genre.

She backed away, giving the couple privacy, then spun on her heel and took the shortest route away from the nook. She'd have to tell Carla about the proposal. Maybe the couple would announce it on social media. That would be great. She turned at the end of the aisle and there he was.

Zach was laughing with a new woman now. An attractive redhead with bright lipstick and confident curves leaned in close, phone in hand, and Sam could imagine what she was asking.

It was a selfie, a drink recommendation, or Zach's number.

Zach spotted her. His smile shifted, softening. His eyes locked on Sam's, just for a second. Then came the wink.

And that, that wink, was her undoing.

Sam turned fast and bolted toward the back, weaving through book tables, barely acknowledging the customers she passed. She didn't stop until she reached the office, closing and locking the door behind her.

Her hands were shaking. She had no reason to be jealous. She and Zach weren't a thing.

Yet.

There was the truth of it. No matter how much her brain said otherwise, some part of her hoped they'd become a thing. He wasn't just hot or charming. He was kind. Funny. Sharp. He saw her, and after their date on Saturday, and the way he'd come to her rescue with lunch on Wednesday, she'd begun to let herself believe there was something building between them.

Still, there was no reason to be jealous over him doing his job. Except she had the sense that Zach was the type to not let it end at casual flirting. No, he'd follow it up.

So, here she was. Locked in her office like a heartbroken teenager at her own event.

Sam sank into her desk chair and grabbed her phone. She texted Becca and Carla to say she was taking a quick break, then tossed the phone aside and leaned back in her chair.

She wasn't just into Zach; this was deep want. It wasn't about his flirtiness or his abs or even his laugh. She wanted the way he looked at her when she rambled about tropes. The way he listened. The way he touched her like she mattered.

And that meant only one thing.

She was in danger of falling for him.

Not good.

ZACH

"I'm sorry, I missed that." Zach turned back to Charlie Jones, who was still standing there with her phone in her hand. All he'd been thinking about was why Sam bolted.

"Trying to find a date for a get together. Never mind, you're working."

Zach waved a hand. "Yeah, sorry. You know how it is. And hey, I didn't know you were a romance reader."

He supposed it made sense; she was a wedding planner after all. Not like he'd talked reading habits with Deke's fiancé.

"I'm not. Well, not contemporary anyway. I like historical. But this is a sapphic fantasy. I'm on my way to a bachelorette party for a coworker and she loves this author, and had her eye on this book. She hasn't picked it up yet, so I figured it would make a good gift."

She held up a small Shelf Indulgence bag. "Anyway, I'll text dates. Have fun. I'm sure you're getting a lot of attention here." She looked at the crowd and shook her head. "More than usual, I mean," she called out over her shoulder as she walked away.

Zach didn't have time to blink before another woman stepped up to Charlie's vacated spot at the bar. He wiped the counter, and fixed the newcomer with a smile.

"You looking for a tasting?"

The moment the words left his mouth, he knew he'd hit the wrong note. A mildly flirty line often opened up great banter with customers, but sometimes people took it too seriously. The woman braced her elbows on the bar and leaned forward, displaying impressive cleavage.

"Are you on the menu?"

Whoa. He'd had folks come on to him before and people definitely could blur the lines a bit, but that was pretty direct.

"I am not, but I've got a selection of terrific beers if you wanna give those a shot."

Huh. Where'd that come from? He'd had offers before. Some he'd even acted on. Yeah, mixing business and pleasure was an iffy prospect, but he was less picky about it when it was a guest. Especially one who was up front about what they were looking for.

The gorgeous brunette with epic breasts stood across the counter from him, clearly flirting with intent, and all Zach could think about was Sam. They'd both been slammed all night, but he'd caught her looking at him and the small smiles she'd give. He'd been looking, too. And smiling when he caught her eye. It was the tamest across the room flirting he'd ever done, and it was oddly exciting.

"I'll skip the tasting. What have you got that's strong and bold, with a long finish?"

There might have been a time in Zach's life when that line would have made him laugh and suggest that he fit that bill. Tonight, he gave the requisite chuckle and reached for a can of Over the Barrel. He sat it on the bar without popping the top and launched into his spiel.

Halfway through, she laid a hand on his arm and Zach stopped mid-sentence, debating whether to roll with it and let her move on when she got tired of flirting, or if he needed to bring the interaction to an end. At the brewery, he had easy ways out. Here? At someone else's event? He was stuck.

In the past, he might have taken a break and seen what kind of mischief they could get up to in a back room somewhere.

Yeah, screw might. Would have. She's hot.

But he had no interest. No twitch of a physical response. No mental gymnastics about how to make it work. Nothing.

Weird.

Instead, all he could think was that he should go find Sam and make sure she was okay.

Weirder.

He slid his arm away, or tried to, but her fingers tightened and she leaned close enough he caught an intense perfume and more than a hint of alcohol. She was already tipsy. Big surprise.

"Hey Zach. I hate to bother you, but we're running low on waters." A weird request. Cold Bottom wasn't providing bottled water. That was on the host.

Carla reached over and slid the can closer to the woman. "On the house. I need to borrow this guy."

That did the trick. The woman picked up the beer and turned away.

"Thanks." Zach wiped up the wet spot the cold can had left on the bar. "There are lines you don't cross, from either side of the customer/worker experience, but tipsy folks seem to forget that."

Carla shrugged. "Plenty of sober folks, too. Have you seen..."

"Just before our flirty friend showed up. I'll go find her."

He didn't wait for an answer. If Carla had needed Sam, she'd have texted her, or gone looking herself. She wouldn't have come to Zach for help. Something else was up, and Zach was willing to bet he knew what.

He knocked on the office door but got no answer. He knocked again and leaned close to the door.

"Let me in."

The door clicked and opened, and Sam stood back to let him pass, then shut it behind him. Zach tried to gauge her mood. She didn't look angry, or like she'd been crying or anything like that. She just looked tired. He grabbed a spare chair and dropped it near her desk, then tugged her hand until she sat in her chair.

"What's going on?" He didn't see a need to dance around the matter.

"It's nothing. Just silly, and I'm fine."

She's a terrible liar.

Her eyes had flicked all over the room, never focusing on anything for long, and never making eye contact with him. He didn't do jealousy. Or insecurity. When women started down that path, it was a good sign things were ending. He could smooth things over and delay the inevitable, or remind them he'd never promised anything and speed things along.

Except we haven't even started. Nope. Not giving up here.

He reached out and curled his fingers around Sam's wrists, cupping her hands in his.

"Just because it's silly doesn't mean it's nothing, and I don't believe you're fine at all."

Sam tugged her hands away and he worried he'd gone too far. Maybe he'd misread her. Then she bit her lip and crossed her arms, keeping her eyes focused on the wall behind him.

Nope. Didn't misread shit. ·

"I mean, it is nothing, and I will be fine. This is your job. It's normal. It just... I don't know..."

It had been a busy night and he'd had a constant stream of women coming up for tastings. Most of them flirting.

"The redhead..."

Oh shit. Zach bit his tongue to keep from laughing. He cleared his throat and looked Sam straight in the eyes.

"You met Deke. The redhead is his girl. They got engaged last New Year's Eve. Charlie is gorgeous, and very friendly, and I can see how that might have looked."

He took the arms of her chair and pulled her closer, until her knees sat between his. "Yes, it's my job. Yes, banter is normal. But there are lines you don't cross."

Never mind that he'd crossed them in the past.

Sam's arms unfolded and she tipped her head to look at him.

"Like I said, it's nothing and I'm fine."

"Except you weren't," he replied. He tried to take her hands again, but she moved them away. He should have seen this coming. When he'd kissed her goodnight after their date, she'd made it clear that it was just kisses. She'd been equally clear that was a temporary boundary. He already knew she didn't date casually.

Here was the razor's edge. He wanted Sam. The desire to get her into bed and see if she was as buttoned up once her clothes came off was a near-constant distraction. He suspected she was much less inhibited behind closed doors. While he was willing to be evasive, or speak partial truths and commit sins of omission, he was less comfortable outright lying.

So far, he'd not told Sam any big lies. Just that he didn't see a problem with her boundaries, which wasn't entirely untrue. He didn't see a problem with them, aside from them being outside his normal habits.

If he wanted to continue seeing her, then he'd have to give her more than noncommittal vagueness and partial truths.

Why not give it a shot? Have a relationship.

If he was willing to try, he wouldn't be lying. And if that wasn't some major justification, he didn't know what was.

"Look, I can't promise there won't be flirting. Like you said, it's my job. What I can promise is that I'm not interested in other women."

Well, that's not a lie. At least for now.

Sam's eyes narrowed and her head tipped to the side. "Really?"

The sarcasm and disbelief hung heavy in that single word. He reached for her hands, and this time she let him.

"Really." The truth of it hit him like a punch. He could tell himself it was the thrill of the chase. Or the challenge. Both would be true, but there was more to it than that. And he had no intention of examining it too deeply right now.

"I enjoy your company," he continued. "You're an amazing kisser."

Her cheeks brightened with color and Zach tugged her hands until she slid closer and he scooped her into his lap.

"When you're ready, when you're sure, I'd like to find out everything else, as well." He brushed a lock of hair off her forehead. "Like how you taste, for starters."

Sam's chest rose and fell on a sharp gasp.

He propped a finger under her chin. Her skin was warm, soft as silk, and when he tilted her face up to his, her eyes were still shadowed with doubt from their conversation. She should have been second-guessing everything. Hell, he should have been second-guessing everything.

That entire talk had been a neon-lit warning flashing 'do not proceed.'

Instead, he leaned in and pressed his mouth to hers with deliberate gentleness. Not a tease. Not a test. Just a kiss. Sam's body relaxed on a sigh threaded with hesitation and longing. She shifted in his lap, her body nestling against his, the movement slow and instinctive. Her arms slipped around his neck like they belonged there, drawing him in, closer, deeper.

Zach wrapped one arm around her and pulled her flush against his chest. His other hand slid behind her head, fingers settling into the soft waves at her nape.

Kissing Sam was like skimming a fingertip across still water, only to find an undertow lurking beneath the calm. She kissed like someone who didn't know her own intensity, but who tried to keep things measured and ended up unraveling them both. There was heat beneath her control, a fierceness carefully boxed away that felt dangerously close to spilling free.

Zach let himself sink into it, into her, and the world around them went quiet.

This wasn't the kind of kiss that pushed toward sex. It wasn't frantic or edged with desperation. It was better. It was a soft, stubborn kind of connection that wrapped around his ribs and pulled tight.

And it scared the hell out of him.

Still, he didn't pull back.

Not when she felt like the kind of trouble he might be willing to risk.

Sam shifted until she was practically straddling his lap.

The only things separating them were layers of cotton and self-control, both of which were starting to feel thin and optional.

Zach deepened the kiss, his lips moving over hers in slow, deliberate strokes, coaxing more from her. Her hands slid into his hair, tugging slightly, and that tiny edge of aggression went straight to his cock. He responded with a low growl, tightening his hold around her waist.

Her body melted against his. Warm and soft and fitting perfectly into the planes of his chest, his thighs. Her breath hitched each time he tightened his grip and she trembled just a little when he dragged his lips down the column of her neck, pausing at the hollow of her throat to taste her skin with the edge of his tongue.

"Zach," she breathed, barely audible.

It wasn't a warning. It wasn't a protest.

It was permission. Or maybe a surrender.

His fingers slid beneath the hem of her top, finding bare skin at the small of her back. She arched into him as his palm pressed flat against her spine. God, she was warm. Every inch of her was heat and motion and temptation. Her hips rolled once, and his brain short-circuited.

He tilted his head and captured her mouth again, this time with a hunger he didn't bother masking. She met him with equal intensity, her fingers curling into his shoulders like she didn't trust herself not to fall, but she didn't want to stop.

Neither did he.

Her tongue traced his bottom lip and he opened for her, groaning into her mouth. This wasn't careful anymore. This was messy and wild, and he wanted to disappear into her until he forgot his own damn name.

His hand drifted lower, finding the curve of her hip, gripping just hard enough to feel her pulse quicken. Sam gasped and rocked forward, and fuck, he was going to lose it if this kept up.

He broke the kiss long enough to rest his forehead against hers, breath ragged. "Sam."

Her eyes were half-lidded, lips swollen, and her pupils blown wide. She looked dazed. Wrecked in the best possible way. And so fucking beautiful it made his chest ache.

She pressed another kiss to his mouth, soft this time, a whisper of what they'd just shared.

A loud crash from the hallway outside the office door shattered the moment.

They both froze.

Another thud, followed by the unmistakable sound of someone swearing and something metallic clattering to the floor.

Zach exhaled hard, dragging a hand over his face. "You've got to be kidding me."

Sam blinked, pulling back enough to glance toward the office door, her cheeks flushed, chest rising and falling with every uneven breath. "Was that—?"

"Probably a keg," Zach muttered, running a hand through his hair. "I swear sometimes it's like babysitting toddlers."

Sam slid off his lap slowly, tugging her shirt back into place with shaking hands. "Well. That was..."

"Yeah." He stood too, carefully adjusting himself and wishing he'd grabbed his bib apron. The waist apron would do little to hide the bulge in his pants. "That was."

They exchanged a look that was half apology, half disbelief. The tension hadn't vanished. It had just gone still, coiled tight and waiting.

Zach reached out, brushing her cheek with his knuckles. "I should probably go deal with whatever dumbassery just happened before someone breaks something."

Sam huffed a soft laugh. "It's my shop, I guess I should..."

Zach shook his head. "Guaranteed that was my crew. I got this. I'll text you later?"

She nodded, her smile quieter now but no less warm. "Yeah. That would be good."

He backed toward the door, half-dazed, then paused. "Sam?"

She looked up.

"I meant it. You're something else."

She tilted her head, that unreadable glint in her eye. "That makes two of us."

Zach grinned, then slipped out the door, still buzzing with the feel of her mouth on his. And the worry that, after that kiss, nothing between them was going to stay casual for long.

Which is a problem.

Maybe he could do the relationship thing. At least short term. Did that make him the world's biggest asshole? Maybe.

CHAPTER 10

The rumble of an engine broke the silence of the quiet street and Sam glanced at her phone. *Right on time.* She stuffed her lipstick in her bag, grabbed her leather jacket and zipped out the door. She was on the porch steps when Zach opened the gate.

"I would've come up and knocked." Zach crossed to her and held out his hand, palm open and easy. Sam hesitated only half a beat before slipping her fingers into his, and he gave her a gentle tug as they turned toward the street.

The contact was simple, nothing more than warm fingers linked through hers, but it grounded her more than she expected. His grip was confident, not possessive. Like he wasn't claiming her, just letting her know he was there.

She glanced up at him. "Why should you have to come all the way up just to turn around and leave?"

Zach glanced sideways, a crooked smile playing at the corner of his mouth. "Because it's the polite thing to do? I'm not a total slug."

133

"Oh, I see. So you're a partial slug. Got it." She nodded and squeezed his hand.

A glint of metal caught her eye as they reached the bottom of the stone steps. Parked at the curb was a gleaming silver motorcycle, sleek and aggressive, like something out of a movie. Sam slowed, her eyes widening as she took it in.

"Okay, wow," she said, low and appreciative. "That takes shiny to a whole new level. When you said motorcycle, I was expecting... I don't know what, I guess. Maybe black? Vintage? Moody anti-hero vibes. I didn't peg you for polished chrome."

Zach threw his head back and laughed, the sound rich and full and just a little bit wild in the soft, spring-scented air. "You're describing my old bike. Flat black. Very moody."

The laugh faded into a crooked grin as he glanced down at her. "What about me says anti-hero?"

Sam gave him an exaggerated once-over, taking her time. "Two words: shadow daddy? Come on. The scruff, the chiseled features? Okay, you're blond, not dark, but there's some shadowy past energy going on."

He arched a brow. "Shadowy past? Really?"

"Sure. Like, the kind of guy who's either running from something or toward something. Or maybe both."

Zach's grin faltered, just for a second. It was so quick she almost missed it. There was something in his expression then, like a memory brushing too close to the surface. A flicker of truth behind the joke.

Then he cocked his head and smiled. "If that's what gives me broody points, what does a gold-fringe romper and platform sandals say about you?"

She smirked. "That I commit to a theme."

He tugged her gently toward the bike. "You're not worried are you?"

Sam eyed the machine; her fingers still looped through his. "Nope. But I'm convinced you're using the bike as an excuse to get me wrapped around you in public."

Zach stepped closer, voice dropping just a notch. "That's not an excuse. That's basic physics. Besides, do I need an excuse?"

Sam laughed despite herself, the nerves in her stomach doing a slow somersault. Being around him was like standing too close to a fire. He was dangerous, hypnotic, and a little too easy to fall into. And she wasn't sure what minimum safe distance was yet.

She lifted an eyebrow. "So, you were going to knock on my door in that leather jacket and pretend you weren't trying to look hot?"

Zach's smile turned into a cocky grin. "I don't have to try."

He reached out, brushing a loose strand of hair behind her ear with a gentleness that caught her off guard. "But no. I was going to knock and say hi and be the kind of guy who goes to a woman's door because it's what you do. Just like I walked you to your door after our date. Even if I'm leaving five minutes later."

The sincerity of it slipped under her skin like sunlight after a storm. Nothing flashy, or that came across as fake or forced. Just Zach being Zach.

Sam looked away first. "See, there you go again. Looking like the modern rake but acting like a gentleman. I never imagined you being the type to play by the rules. I don't know what to do with that."

Zach stepped in, just enough to shorten the space between them and there was nothing gentlemanly about his expression. "You don't have to do anything with me that you don't want to."

She nodded, then squeezed his hand before letting go. "Don't crash."

"I try not to," he said, pulling a second helmet from the saddle bag. "I've got too much riding on it."

Sam blinked, stunned by the easy way he said it.

"I asked if you were okay taking the bike, I forgot to ask if you've been on one before."

Sam shrugged into her jacket and zipped it, then tucked her braid into the collar and grabbed the helmet Zach held out. *Of course it matches the bike.* "More than a few times. Though never on a Harley."

And never behind a man Zach's size. She tugged the helmet on, tightened the strap, then pulled on her gloves.

"You're in for a treat." He fastened his helmet and straddled the bike. Sam waited for him to say it was okay to get on. Zach reached back and flipped the passenger footpegs down then nodded to her.

"I even put the sissy bar on for you." His voice rose above the noise of the engine and he winked. "You'll have to go wide to clear the saddlebags. Hop up."

He patted the seat behind him then grabbed the handlebars and waited. Sam stepped close, braced one hand on Zach's shoulder and put a foot up on the peg. A deep breath and a quick push and she swung her leg between Zach and the passenger backrest, then settled onto the seat.

"That was smooth." Zach's hand landed on her knee, he squeezed, then let go and put the bike in gear. "Hold on."

He pulled away from the curb and the bike vibrated and hummed beneath her. Sam gripped Zach's sides tightly before remembering to loosen up. She'd been on sport bikes before, but this was a different feeling. It was like the bike was a living thing.

She dropped her faceplate down as they pulled onto the

main road and settled in for the ride. Talking while on a moving motorcycle and wearing a full-face helmet was an exercise in frustration.

"It's all city riding for the first part. We'll get on the highway when we head to lunch." Zach's voice in her ear surprised her and she was glad they were at a stoplight. "You can talk. It's an open channel."

An open what?

"So this thing has what, like Bluetooth?"

"Yep. Helmet to helmet. Beats yelling."

The light changed and Zach's muscles tightened. His thigh moved against hers as he shifted gears and his whole body tensed as he leaned into a turn. It was the most natural thing in the world to move with him, feeling his body flex and move even through the layers of leather and cotton.

"I love this strip of road." The words tumbled out unbidden. "It's so green. Like an oasis in the city."

Zach's chuckle vibrated in her ears. "Falls Road is a nice ride this time of year. Wait'll we get out of the city later."

Warm sun beat down on Sam's shoulders as Zach navigated the next turn. The hum of the engine first tickled her legs and butt, then settled into a pleasant buzz that she imagined would feel good under other circumstances.

Sam leaned closer to Zach, letting her chest brush his back and resting one hand on his thigh. He closed his fingers over hers and squeezed. At the next stoplight, he grabbed her hand and pulled her tighter against him, so she was pressed against his body and shifted forward on the seat. The light turned and Zach revved the engine as he took off.

"Oh!" The shift in position made the seat vibrations hit different spots. Another low chuckle sounded in her ears.

"There's a reason folks call a Harley the world's biggest vibrator."

The rise and fall of the engine as Zach slowed, then sped up wasn't enough to get her off, but it was definitely a pleasant sensation. A bump in the road drew a gasp from her and Sam clamped her lips shut to avoid moaning in Zach's ear.

It didn't help that, ever since the night of the disco, when she'd borrowed his hoodie, she'd taken to masturbating to thoughts of Zach's kisses any time she couldn't fall asleep. And now, feeling his body between her thighs, and the vibration of the bike hitting almost the right spot, she was getting far more aroused than seemed wise. But she didn't care.

The rest of the ride passed in a blur. At stoplights, Zach would touch her knee, squeeze her hand, or reach back and grip her thigh. That last nearly caused Sam to tell him to skip whatever they were about to do in favor of going to his place, her place, or any place where she could satisfy the demands of her body.

He pulled into a parking lot in front of a series of low, industrial buildings and stopped the bike.

"You good to dismount?"

Was he laughing? It sounded like he was laughing.

Sam braced herself and swung her leg over, thankful she managed to land on her feet without a wobble. She focused on tugging off her gloves and helmet, afraid that looking at him, watching him move, would be too much.

Zach pulled his helmet off and sure enough, his lips curled in a grin, but it wasn't laughter she saw on his face. His eyes were narrowed and his smile was more that of a man anticipating some tasty meal. He put both of their helmets on the bike then reached for her and Sam's brain gave up thinking. She stepped into his embrace.

Zach wrapped an arm around her waist and lifted until her toes were barely touching the ground. He bent his head. Too slow. Sam reached up and tangled her hands in his hair.

The moment his lips touched hers, Sam's world exploded. It didn't matter that they were standing in a parking lot in broad daylight. She wanted more of whatever this was.

His tongue slid between her lips and his beard tickled. She could only imagine what that would feel like between her legs. A loud ping came from Zach's pocket and he broke the kiss.

"That's our appointment time." He eased her back down and retrieved the helmets. "Let's go."

"You never said what we were doing."

Zach held the door and ushered Sam into a place that smelled of sawdust. Laughter punctuated with a steady 'thwock' sound echoed off the walls. Zach stepped up to the counter.

"We've got lanes for two."

Lanes? Bowling? This didn't seem like a bowling alley. Sam shook herself and looked around, then spotted the t-shirts on the wall behind the counter.

Ax throwing?

It took only a few minutes to get signed in and then she and Zach stepped into side-by-side lanes with targets at the end.

"Hey, I'm Connor and I'll be showing you the ropes and keeping things safe today. So let's get some basics." Connor demonstrated two techniques then had them try a practice throw.

Zach hit the target on his first try. Sam missed.

"You've done this before." Connor nodded at Zach, then turned to Sam. "I want you to take one big step forward. Good. Now, take the same stance, and when you throw, really hurl that thing hard."

Sam tried again and hit the target, but too low.

"Gymnast?" Connor retrieved the ax and handed it back to Sam. "You've got the upper body strength. So, raise the ax like you're gonna throw, but stop when your hands cover the target where you want it to land. That's where you release the handle. Try again."

Sam checked her feet, gripped the ax and tipped it behind her head, then stepped forward and flung it hard. It flipped through the air and sank into the first ring of the target.

"Nice!" Zach gave her a high five after she'd gone to retrieve her ax.

"Okay, we'll start with a warmup to get you both on target, then we'll play some games."

Zach made ax throwing look easy—he stood there almost lazily swinging the ax, then threw it one handed to land in the target every time.

"No fair. You've got experience. Try it with your other hand." Sam was hitting the target three out of four throws and getting closer to the bullseye each toss. Unless she missed entirely.

Zach shrugged and flipped the ax to his left hand and tossed it with casual ease. It thunked into the first ring of the target.

"I'm ambidextrous." He leaned in and kissed Sam lightly. "A fact you may appreciate down the road."

He moved back with a gesture for Sam to go ahead.

"How do I throw one-handed?"

Connor stepped up and demonstrated the grip and technique. Zach might be ambidextrous, but Sam was not.

"Don't forget to throw hard."

Connor backed away and Sam planted her feet, checked the target, then stepped and threw. The ax sank into the wood close to the bullseye.

"Yes!" Sam fist pumped in the air, then high fived Zach. "Okay. Let's do this game. What're the rules?"

Connor went over the rules for the first game—each one would take five throws and who ever had the highest score won that round. They'd play three rounds. Best two out of three won.

Zach won the first round by a wide margin, then Sam won the second, by a single point. He won the third, also by a single point. Connor modified the next game so Zach had to get exactly twenty-one points to win—if his throw took him over, it didn't count. Sam just had to get twenty-one or over to win. Sam was close, and her arm was getting tired, when Zach nailed the next throw, giving him the win.

"Winner buys drinks," he said as he tossed his ax into the bucket then shook Connor's hand. "Thanks man, that was fun."

He caught Sam's hand in his and led the way to the bar. "I won't drink, since I'm on the bike, but we can get something cold and wet, then late lunch."

They settled at the bar and both ordered iced tea, then Zach leaned in, draped his arm over the back of Sam's stool and smiled.

"You picked that up pretty quickly. Did you have fun?"

Sam pretended to think about it for a second, but burst into laughter. "I did. That was a blast, thank you."

"You've got good aim and a strong arm. Now I'm curious. Were you in gymnastics?"

She hadn't answered Connor when he asked, but she wasn't going to ignore Zach.

"Twelve years of it. I quit in high school. I wasn't good enough to do anything with it like major competitions or get a scholarship or anything, so it didn't make sense to keep going."

Zach made an appreciative face, then laid cash on the bar for the drinks.

"Shall we?" He led the way out. "Make sure you zip up. We're going on the highway this time."

In the parking lot, he took Sam in his arms again and kissed her—slow and easy. It was a direct opposite of their earlier kiss that was all demand and heated passion. This felt like he was savoring the experience. All too soon, he stopped and climbed on the bike.

Sam tugged on her helmet and got on behind him. His voice crackled in her ears as they pulled out.

"I'm guessing beam and floor, but not sure if you'd do vault or uneven bars."

Sam scooted forward to press herself against him. "Bars. I could do the vault, but it wasn't my best event."

In no time, they turned onto the highway ramp and Zach sped up. The rush of wind made Sam grateful Zach was blocking most of it. The bike's vibration from earlier seemed mellow in comparison to the high-intensity buzz now thrumming under her butt.

Zach squeezed her thigh, bringing her tighter against him. "Rock your hips forward."

ZACH

There was a subtle shift as Sam moved, then her gasp whispered through his helmet.

Fuck that's hot.

"Has anyone ever... you know... like this?"

The fact that she didn't say 'come' or 'orgasm' was equal parts funny and concerning, but he didn't want to think too hard on that.

"Ever? I'm sure someone has, but not that I've known. Either personally or from stories. From what I've gathered, it just feels good."

He gripped her thigh again. "Does it feel good?"

Her laugh rang a little breathy. "Yes. Yes it does."

He let go of her leg to speed up and navigate around a cluster of cars, and Sam's sharp intake of air when he twisted the throttle would have had him raging hard under any other circumstances.

"We've got about forty minutes," he said. "Should I distract you with conversation, or let you enjoy the ride?"

Her chest rose against his back and he heard the sigh in his ears. "Ummm... I don't know..."

He wasn't sure how good of a conversationalist he'd be with her making little humming and gasping sounds in his ears every few minutes. He hadn't been lying when he said he didn't know anyone who'd orgasmed from the bike. He had known a few women who got very aroused from it, and a greater number who might have, but were uncomfortable about it for some reason.

As buttoned up as Sam seemed, he was surprised she was in the former category. They hit some traffic and Zach downshifted, then changed lanes. Roadwork meant the pavement here wasn't as smooth, and the big bike jittered under him. In seconds, Sam's legs tightened on his hips and a muffled moan echoed in his ears.

He sped up as they cleared the traffic and her fingers clenched into his sides. He debated changing lanes, getting back to the smoother pavement, but he was enjoying the sounds Sam was making. So much so he was almost sad when their exit came up and he pulled off the highway. Ten minutes later, he turned down the narrow lane, maneuvered around the gate and pulled up in the shade of a big oak.

Sam slid off the bike and stretched, then pulled off the helmet. Her lips looked like she'd been biting them and her cheeks were flushed. Zach shut the bike down and swung his leg over, then peeled off his jacket.

"You can hang the helmet on the handlebars and just toss your jacket on the seat. You up for a walk? Maybe a hundred yards."

She nodded, then he opened the saddlebags and pulled out the small cooler and a blanket.

"Come on." Zach led the way down a short trail to a grassy bank overlooking a rocky stream. Zach set the cooler down and spread the blanket. "That's Big Gunpowder Creek. Are you hungry?"

He was, but not for food.

"You packed a picnic? For real? Here I was thinking you weren't the romantic type."

He wasn't. Not normally. He was, however, all about what got him into a woman's pants, and sometimes, that meant romance. It hadn't taken much to figure out that Sam was into the little gestures and loved old-fashioned expressions of interest and affection. If he'd had any doubts, all he had to do was note the pile of Jane Austen books on her desk.

"I have my moments."

Usually when I think it'll get me laid. Not that he expected that to happen this afternoon. This was just laying groundwork. He was playing the long game here.

They kicked off their shoes and then Sam surprised him by stepping close, rising up on her toes, then tugging him down the rest of the way. Her lips were soft and yielding under his. Zach gave up any pretense and wrapped his arms around her to cup her ass and lift. Her legs came around his hips and tightened. The downside of riding the bike—she was in jeans. A skirt would have been so much easier.

Screw this.

He knelt, still holding her to him, and Sam squeaked in

surprise, but didn't complain as he laid her back on the blanket. She shifted her legs higher, around his ribs, and moaned as he deepened the kiss. Her hands pressed against his chest, fingers raking over his nipple piercings and Zach let out an involuntary groan. Sam's eyes fluttered open and she did it again, this time watching his face as he shuddered.

"So, these and your ears. Anything else?"

Zach shifted to plant a kiss under her ear, then traveled down her neck. "You'll have to find out for yourself."

He kissed her neck, then along her exposed collarbone. Sam threw her head back, let out a low moan and arched her hips up. Zach cupped her ass as she ground against him. His cock might have been out of the equation while on the bike, but now it was wide awake and pulsing.

She arched again, hands tugging at his shirt, the sounds spilling from her lips a mix of arousal and frustration. Zach propped himself on one elbow and caught the neckline of her shirt between his fingers. "May I?"

"Yes!"

He didn't waste a breath. With practiced care, he unbuttoned her shirt, revealing a pink lace bra that barely contained her breasts. He kissed down her chest, tracing the edge of one delicate cup.

"Please..." The breathy plea hit him like a match to dry kindling.

Hooking a finger under one strap, he slid it off her shoulder, baring a dusky pink nipple. He brushed his thumb over the tight peak, and Sam trembled. Everything he knew of her said take your time, be gentle.

But her fingers in his hair and the way she arched into him said something different. He lowered his mouth and drew her nipple between his lips. Sam moaned, writhing beneath him.

He sucked harder, rewarded by her gasping breath. Then he let his teeth graze her skin.

"Oh yes, like that!"

A few more tugs and Zach had her shirt and bra off. One hand closed around a pert breast, rolling her nipple between his thumb and forefinger while his mouth worshiped the other, sucking and nibbling harder and harder as Sam's breaths turned to panting.

Her hands found his shirt, tugging, and Zach paused just long enough to yank it over his head before going back to plant kisses from her neck back down to her breasts. Then her fingers brushed against his nipple piercings. Zach sucked in air and lifted his head.

"Don't stop," she whispered. "Please don't stop."

Awww fuck.

He lowered his mouth to her other nipple as Sam rocked her hips, moving in rhythm. Zach slid a hand between them and worked at her belt. Her fingers joined his and she had the buckle undone in seconds. He popped the button, pulled down the zipper, and eased his hand along her belly, slipping under the edge of her jeans.

The feel of lace under his fingers sent a pulse of pleasure straight to Zach's cock. He'd bet good money her panties matched that barely-there bra.

"Yes, please." Sam rocked her hips, inviting him in, and his fingers slipped beneath the lace and over soft curls.

"Harder."

Her voice was breathy, but sure. Her fingers fisted in his hair, holding him to her chest, and Zach didn't hesitate. He closed his mouth over her nipple, sucking harder, his tongue flicking in time with the rhythm of her body. She arched with a moan, hips pressing closer as her free hand shoved at her pants, pushing them lower, giving him more room, more skin, more her.

Zach curled his fingers and found slick heat, the kind that made his blood pound and brain haze. He traced along her folds, already wet and swollen, teasing his way inward until he slid between them, parting her slowly. His thumb came to rest just above her clit, poised, teasing, waiting.

This had started as a good day. A motorcycle ride. A fun activity. A picnic. He'd thought he'd earn another kiss, maybe more if the mood was right. But this? This raw, intimate permission, her openness, the urgency, this was so much more than he'd imagined.

Guess she's not as buttoned up as I thought.

As if to prove the point, Sam pressed her hand over his, grinding against his fingers. Zach adjusted, giving her a firmer touch.

"Oh yes. That's... yes... more."

Her other hand found his chest, fingers flicking the barbells in his nipples, and Zach hissed through his teeth. *Shit.* She'd have him losing control if she kept that up.

Fine. Time to up the ante.

He gently nudged the hood of her clit back and skimmed the pad of his thumb over the exposed bud. Sam gasped, bit her lip, and tightened her grip on his chest.

Good thing I like it a little rough.

She was fire and passion, matching his every move with her own. Zach teased a finger along her entrance. She shifted again, wider, deeper, and he slid in.

Jesus, she was hot. Tight. So wet he glided in to the knuckle.

Her body welcomed him, clenched around him, begged for more without words. He gave it, adding a second finger, and her moan broke like a wave in his ear. Her hands scrambled at his shoulders now, pulling him closer. Her control unraveling beautifully in his arms.

When he slipped in a third finger, her breath hitched and her whole body trembled. The feeling of her walls crumbling. She was letting him in. Literally. Physically.

And that, more than the heat or friction, nearly undid him.

Sam rocked her hips, fucking his hand as he sucked on her nipples.

"I want to taste you."

He didn't care that they were sweaty, or lying half-dressed on a picnic blanket, or outside, or anything. All he cared about was getting her out of the rest of her clothes and making her come on his tongue.

Sam's eyes opened, locking on his. She didn't speak. Didn't blink. The beat stretched long enough that uncertainty flickered through him. Maybe he'd pushed too far. Maybe this was her boundary.

Then she shoved her pants down further, baring herself with unflinching ease.

Zach didn't hesitate. He stripped the rest of her clothes off, revealing toned legs and lacy pink panties that matched the bra she'd already lost. With most women, that would have been a green light, a sign they'd planned for sex. With Sam, it might just mean she liked matching. She seemed like the type to do that for herself.

She sat back, calm and unselfconscious. Her apparent trust rocked him and he knelt between her legs with something like reverence, spreading her knees gently with his hands.

Short, golden curls crowned her mons, and her soft, pink lips were already glistening. She smelled like sex and salt and heaven, and it went straight to his brain like fuel.

"I think you really liked the bike," he murmured, voice thick with arousal.

Sam giggled, soft and breathless, and widened her legs in invitation. The sound of her laugh paired with the heat in her gaze leveled him.

He pressed a hand to her chest, easing her down to the blanket before he lowered himself between her spread legs. Zach kissed his way up her thighs, slow and easy, savoring every tremble. By the time he reached the slick heat at her center, Sam was already quivering, fingers curled tight in the blanket, hips rocking gently toward his mouth.

So much for taking his time.

His restraint snapped like dry tinder. Zach gripped her hips and pulled her to him, sealing his mouth over her clit and the soft lips beneath it. He sucked hard, dragging a cry from her that made his cock throb painfully in his jeans.

Sam's hips lifted and writhed. Her fingers scrambled over the blanket until one hand found his hair, the other anchoring to her own thigh as if she needed to hold herself open for him.

Zach didn't ease up. He devoured her. Every moan, every gasp, every roll of her body against his mouth stoked the fire building inside him. He wanted her to revel in pleasure until it overwhelmed her.

He wanted to be the man who gave her that. Taking his time could wait. This time, he wanted to watch her come apart under his touch.

Zach focused in, isolating her clit with his mouth as he slid his fingers back inside her. Sam writhed beneath him, hips rolling, chasing every flick of his tongue. She ground against his face, gasping, the sounds of his mouth on her matching the rhythm of her breath.

Then he stopped.

A cry tore from her lips, part protest, part desperation. He moved to lie beside her and pulled her in for a kiss, deep, messy, full of everything he wanted from her.

"Ride my face," he murmured against her ear. "Like you did the bike. Grind that beautiful pussy on my mouth. Tell me what you need. Use my lips, my tongue, my beard, my chin. I want you to come for me like that."

Sam's breath hitched. Her eyes, wide, dark, and wanting, searched his. And then she moved.

Slow, deliberate.

She rolled to her knees and planted them near his shoulders, straddling his chest with a tremble of hesitation before she eased herself forward. Her bare thighs bracketed his head, her pussy hovering just above his mouth.

Then she lowered herself, slowly, precisely, until she brushed against his lips.

"Make me come," she said, voice low and gritty with need. "I like it all. Suck hard. A little teeth."

Zach growled softly, hands gripping her ass as she guided them there. Her fingers tangled in his hair, holding him in place as she began to rock.

Zach met her rhythm, mouth open and hungry. He sucked her clit into between his lips, then flicked with his tongue. She moaned, a rough, raw sound that made him harder than he thought possible. Her hips moved faster, more desperate, grinding against his mouth as her pleasure built.

He teased her again, intentionally soft, drawing a whimper of frustration.

"Harder," she gasped.

Zach smiled against her.

That was what he'd been waiting for.

Zach let his teeth graze the base of her clit just enough to make her gasp, then sucked her deeper into his mouth and pulled, tongue flicking hard and fast. Sam moaned, loud and unfiltered, grinding against his face like she couldn't get close enough.

He shifted, holding her clit captive between his lips then slipping his tongue beneath the hood to circle the swollen bud.

"Yes! Like that," she panted, her fingers locking tighter in his hair. "Just like that."

Zach knew better than to change anything. He he sucked, deep and relentless, and locked his arms around her hips to hold her still when her thighs started to shake.

Sam let out a strangled cry, her whole body tensing before she broke apart with a rush of wetness that soaked his beard. She came hard, shaking, gasping, and he didn't give her a second to recover.

Zach rolled her onto her back, mouth still slick with her taste, and slid three fingers deep into her soaked pussy. He pumped them slow at first, then faster, curling just right until Sam shattered again with a soundless scream, her nails digging into his shoulders.

She collapsed back on the blanket, chest heaving, eyes wide and stunned.

And then she laughed.

It started as a breathless chuckle and rolled into a full, warm, belly laugh. Zach blinked, momentarily unsure, until she reached for him, tangled her fingers in his hair again, and tugged him to her for a kiss.

"You and that bike," she murmured, still breathless, "are dangerous."

Zach grinned against her mouth. "Not sorry."

And in that moment, his body still thrumming, her laughter in his ears, he wasn't. Not even a little. He was more than a little worried, though.

Zach grabbed a napkin from the picnic supplies and wiped

his beard. Sam propped herself up on one elbow, her braid loosening into soft waves, cheeks flushed, lips kiss-swollen.

Her other lips are puffy too. Just not as much as I'd like.

Her gaze met his, and the teasing glint in her eye warmed something low in his gut.

"Do I get to return the favor?" she asked, voice still a little breathless. "Also... maybe we should talk safety?"

Shit. Forgetting that wasn't like him.

"I test quarterly. Always use condoms. No issues." He scratched the back of his neck. "Last partner was four months ago."

He winced slightly. Saying it like that made it sound like it was more recent than it felt. Worse, he used to count those gaps in weeks. Sometimes days.

Sam nodded, unbothered. "Almost two years for me. I got tested at my physical last summer, but I'm happy to test again if you'd prefer."

Two years? Jesus. No wonder she practically vibrated apart on the bike.

"Nah, you're good." He gave her a slow smile. "You can return the favor next time."

She pouted and he nearly caved. "I don't come from head, and I didn't bring a condom. I wasn't trying to assume anything. So, sex is a raincheck. But next time? You can do whatever you want."

She rolled her eyes and laughed. "Fine. Where's my shirt? I should probably get dressed."

He shrugged, leaning back on one hand. "We're on private land. Brewery owns it. No one's coming by."

Sam found her shirt and tugged it on, leaving it unbuttoned, an image so casually erotic it made Zach's mouth go dry.

How had she gone from buttoned-up bookworm to sex

goddess in the span of a few hours? No hesitation, no overthinking, happy to take what she wanted. Hell, she'd held his head in place and taken a seat like it was her goddamn throne.

His cock pulsed again just thinking about it. He needed to get his mind off that topic before he started wondering if going raw was an option.

"You hungry?"

"I could eat," she said, scooting toward the cooler. She glanced up with a sly grin. "And if I can't return the favor now, maybe round two?"

No surprise there.

Zach handed her a sandwich, grinning. "However many rounds you want. I'll eat that beautiful pussy until you beg me to stop."

Sam blinked once. Then slowly, deliberately, she set the sandwich back in the cooler.

"Well, when you put it like that..." She straddled his lap and kissed him, slow and deep. "How about we go back to the part where you were sucking my clit and finger fucking me at the same time?"

Zach growled low in his throat, flipped her onto her back, and kissed his way down her body as she spread for him again.

Yep. Sexy librarian. No, schoolteacher. Bookseller. Fucking goddess.

He was in so much trouble.

CHAPTER 11

SAM—SUNDAY, MAY 3

Sam gritted her teeth as she crossed the street. Once she was in the bookshop, she could sit down, though that might not be any easier. She pushed through the door and braced herself for Carla's smartass.

"I'm guessing you had fun because you are usually the early one."

And there it is.

"You might wanna go home and change into pants. We got books in today and we need to swap the decorations."

Sam groaned and propped herself on the stool behind the register. She'd forgotten it was time to prep for the next Books and Brews and it was historical romance, her favorite. She had a whole box of decor ready to go. She could do that in a skirt. Maybe. She'd tried putting pants on this morning. It had not been fun.

No, fun was yesterday.

She waved a hand at Carla. "I can do the decorations and

handle register if you can handle the unpacking. Get Becca to help maybe?"

Carla put down the books she was stocking and crossed to the counter. "Are you okay? You love unboxing. What's going on? Did something go wrong on your date with the Viking?"

Sam grabbed Carla's sleeve and bolted for the office, calling out to Becca that they'd be right back as she dragged her friend with her. Once the door was shut and locked, she sat, carefully, and laughed.

"Nothing went wrong. Kinda the opposite. He's..." What was he? All along, she'd been assuming Zach was a player, just a fuckboy. Only in it for the sex. And all along, he'd been showing her he was sweet, and nice. The whole date was romantic. Even the unconventional parts like the motorcycle ride and the ax throwing. *All very Zach.*

"We had fun. He planned a whole surprise thing. We went ax throwing."

Carla pulled up her chair and offered the tin of Peanut M&Ms she kept handy. Sam popped one in her mouth and chewed, trying to wrap her head around what had happened the day before.

"Ax throwing is fun. Emmy and I've done it. How's your arm?"

Sam's arm was the least of her worries. "Nowhere near as sore as the rest of me."

Carla froze, a candy piece slipping through her fingers and bouncing off the desk. "Okay, I want all the details because I'm on hormones to help me get pregnant and it's got me so horny it isn't funny. Did you fuck him? Oh my god, how was it?"

Sam swatted at the air, her eyes wide as she tried to shush her friend. "No! Not... oh my god, not sex-sex. I mean, not all the way. God, I feel like a teenager saying that."

Carla squinted. "That's gonna need a breakdown."

She retrieved the dropped candy, tossed it in the trash, and fished out another like she had all the time in the world to hear this juicy report. She popped it in her mouth and stared at Sam, expectant.

Sam fidgeted, then leaned closer, her voice low. "First, do we have anything here for chafed skin?"

Carla's eyebrows rose slowly. "That is definitely going to need more explanation."

She turned to her desk drawer, rifled around, and came up with a small tube of cream. "I use this under my boobs in the summer. It's magic."

Sam took it gingerly, then hesitated. "What about beard burn?"

Carla stared for a second, then burst into laughter. "Oh, I cannot wait to hear this story. Yeah. Use a damp paper towel first, then put it on. But not before you give me the details."

Sam clutched the tube and sighed. "It was just intense. Really intense. And amazing. And kind of terrifying."

Carla's expression softened. "Terrifying how?"

"It all happened so fast," Sam replied, voice barely above a whisper. "And I can't decide if that's exciting or terrible or wonderful or what."

Carla tilted her head, her tone gentling. "Is he a good guy?"

Sam nodded. "That's the thing. He is. Or at least, seems like he is. Or trying to be. And he's funny, and thoughtful, and... God, Carla, he sees me. Like, really sees me."

"And are you okay? With how fast this is moving?"

"I don't know." Sam glanced down at the tube in her hand. "All I know is I can still feel his mouth on me and I've got literal beard burns from how much I wanted it to never stop."

Carla whooped. "Okay, now that's a review."

Sam cracked a smile despite herself, but her stomach twisted. Lust was easy. Chemistry was obvious. But connection and commitment, those were the parts she needed. She still wasn't sure she and Zach had compatible goals, but she also wasn't sure she could stop.

"Well, we were on his motorcycle. Did you know those things are... ummm..."

Carla's eyebrows went even higher. "Yeah. I did. Kinda fun. But that doesn't explain beard burn."

Sam twirled the tube of lotion in her hands, kicking herself for bringing it up. But this was Carla. Her bestie. They'd been through stuck diaphragms, broken condoms, and more relationship troubles than anyone should ever have.

"So, watching him at axe throwing, and the kissing, and the motorcycle..." Sam paused, already feeling the flush creep up her neck. "I was kind of already gone. And then he sets up this sweet little picnic in a quiet, remote spot under a tree, next to a creek, the whole deal. And well..."

She trailed off, bracing herself as she took a breath.

"That man goes down like it's not just his job, but like his entire existence depends on it."

Carla dropped back in her chair, howling with laughter. She was wiping tears from her eyes before Sam could finish. "Jesus, finally. Good for you. You deserve a man who knows how to worship at the altar. And I need way more details on this date because I still don't get how that leads to beard burn."

A weak laugh escaped Sam's lips. "Four times."

Carla blinked. "Come again?"

"Oh I did. More times than I can count. We spent the entire afternoon on a picnic blanket and..." She waved her hand toward her crotch. "Four. Times."

"No penetration?" Carla leaned forward, her tone incredulous. "Did you at least blow him?"

"Do fingers count? And no, no blow job."

Carla sat back with a low whistle. "Holy shit. I'm guessing it was good?"

Sam gave a helpless little laugh. "You think we'd have kept going if it wasn't?"

Carla slapped her hand against the desk and grinned. "Well, he does seem the type to know what he's doing. What's he packing?"

Sam shrugged, heat crawling over her skin again. "I didn't find out. Not for sure. This all kind of just happened. He didn't have a condom, and I didn't either. And he was so chill about it. He said he'd wait."

Carla stared at her. "Wait. Like, for next time?"

Sam nodded, but something about the gesture didn't feel as certain as it should. "Yeah. I mean, I think so. We didn't make a plan or anything. It was just... I don't know. Natural, I guess."

She remembered the weight of his hands on her thighs, the way his voice had gone hoarse when he said he wanted to taste her, how he looked up at her like she was the end reward and not just a steppingstone to sex. Her.

And that was what scared her. Because if she got used to that, to him, and he left, she'd be shattered.

"He was amazing, Carla. He didn't rush me, didn't push, didn't expect anything back. He just..." She swallowed. "It was like he wanted me to feel good. Really, really good."

Carla's grin faded to something softer. "Okay, maybe you found your unicorn."

"I'm trying not to think like that, but..." Sam exhaled hard and leaned forward. "It was supposed to be flirting. I was trying to take it slow. See where things went. Not rush into anything."

Carla lifted a brow. "And?"

Sam dropped her head to the counter. "I might be falling for him."

There it was. Said out loud, it felt terrifying and irreversible.

"Well, I mean, if you're gonna fall, at least you landed on a guy who makes you come several times in a field."

Sam snorted. "That's what makes it so hard. He's not just hot. He's nice. And I think I'm already in too deep."

Carla offered up the candy jar. "Then maybe stop worrying about falling and just see where it goes."

Sam took another M&M with shaky fingers, and tried not to think about how much she already wanted more of Zach.

"So, that's why you're not in pants and would rather sit at the register than unload boxes." Carla shook her head. "Is it that bad? I mean, are you okay?"

Sam rolled her eyes. She felt like an idiot. She and Zach had eaten after round two, then he suggested dessert—her. That led to rounds three and four. Then she had to pull her jeans on over tender skin, and climb on the back of his motorcycle for the ride home. It had been a mix of agony and ecstasy for sure.

"I'm more than okay, but I am feeling stupid." She hiked her skirt and turned the inside of one thigh toward Carla. "It's just irritated and tender."

Carla covered her mouth, but it wasn't enough to hide the big grin. "Oh hon. I know the feeling. One of my exes had a beard, and it was heaven during, but after I thought I was going to die."

"Exactly!" Sam stood and snatched up the tube. "So, I'm

going to go take care of that. Then I'm going to get some decorating done and I'll work the register today. Deal?"

"Deal. When are you going out again?"

"Thursday. Our schedules don't align well this week."

"Well good, that gives you time to heal. You're gonna need it."

Sam left to the sound of Carla's laughter. In the bathroom, she pressed a cold, wet paper towel to her thighs then smoothed on the lotion. The relief was immediate and she made a mental note to stop on the way home for more.

Back in the shop, she cleared away all the contemporary romance decorations and pulled out the historical romances they'd be featuring this week. She could do this part in her sleep. Layers of fabric. Some lace. Candles. Quill pens and pots of ink. Dried flowers and stacks of love letters tied with ribbons.

Carla hadn't said it with words, but her face had. What happened with Zach was Old Sam behavior. College Sam. The kind of stuff she'd decided only led to heartache.

And that drove me to a boring relationship with a controlling man.

Still, she knew she needed to talk to Zach before things went further. As much as she tried to fight it, she was falling for him, and sex, for her, always came with deeper feelings.

Which is just great.

Sam let out a sigh and surveyed the pretty display. The new books nestled in with some favorite classics, including her forever book boyfriend, Mr. Darcy. She picked up the paperback of Pride and Prejudice and settled at the register, flipping through the pages.

She'd fallen in love with Austen in middle school and that led to a love of challenging romantic leads. She had no illusions of Darcy being a realistic character, especially in a modern world. And no desire to compare men in her life to fictional characters.

Still, I'm sure Mr. Darcy would have never stripped Elizabeth naked by a stream and gone down on her for hours.

Then again, maybe he would have.

No, she needed to keep herself firmly grounded in reality. She'd had her fill of trying to use her love to fix broken but exciting men, and more than her fill of one equally broken but at least stable man.

At least it only took one of those to learn my lesson.

Whatever this was with Zach, she'd protect herself. Or try to. She crossed her legs, then winced. But the minor discomfort didn't change the fact that her body still hummed with pleasure, and she'd woken this morning with thoughts of Zach in her brain. So much so that she'd used the handheld shower head to get off while remembering the feel of his beard tickling at her inner thighs, then brushing against softer parts.

Sam slammed the book down and stood. She needed to stop thinking about Zach and finish the display.

CHAPTER 12

ZACH—THURSDAY, MAY 7

Sam sat back, sipped her wine and looked around the apartment as if she was in another world. Zach didn't have women over often. He preferred going to their place because it was easier to leave. But he knew from conversations that Sam had a full-size bed, and there was no way that was happening.

And he was hoping something would happen tonight. He'd lost count of the number of times he'd jacked off since their date on Sunday.

"What's on your mind?" Zach scooped their plates and took them to the kitchen.

"You're full of surprises." Sam pointed at the empty plates in his hand.

"Because I can cook pasta without setting the place on fire?" He cleared the rest of the table and stuck everything in the sink to deal with later, then poured more wine.

"No, it's this space. It's not what I expected. You have a

stronger personality than..." She waved a hand around the room.

"You've got me there. It's close to work, was priced right and didn't require much thought. Furniture came from a showroom—easy, simple. At the time, I wasn't really living here. Just stopping by."

She looked around the living space then turned back to him, her eyebrows raised. "No books?"

"E-reader," he replied. "More portable. Anything else?"

Sam picked up her wine glass and rose, crossing to the far wall.

"These feel different." She ran her finger along the edge of a framed black and white photo—his favorite. The Cylburn Arboretum. The contrast had taken him forever to get right.

"You took these."

"Yeah." Zach stepped behind her and let his hand find her hip. "High school hobby I kept up through college."

"They're beautiful. Intentional. Which feels like a funny word to use about you."

He smiled against the curve of her neck. "Is that a bad thing?"

"No. A surprising thing."

Sam turned to face him, setting her glass down on the windowsill. Her hands settled against his chest, warm and steady.

"You've got pieces in the brewery as well."

"I do." Zach pressed his lips to her jaw. "You said there was something you wanted to talk about and I don't think it was a hobby I haven't pursued in years."

"I mentioned this before and I need to say it again. Make sure we're on the same page. I think after Sunday, it's clear that I want you. I want this. But I don't have sex casually. Not anymore."

Zach stilled then pulled back to search her face. She wasn't defensive or apologetic. She was just being honest.

"I get that." He'd been expecting this conversation for a while, especially after the hours they'd spent on that blanket in the grass. The way she'd responded to his touch then, he was certain they'd have sex tonight. The only possible hiccup was this moment right here.

"Help me out here," he continued. "What does 'casual' mean to you?"

He didn't have to tell her he only did casual. Unless she asked outright. He just had to dance within the lines she drew.

Still a dick move.

She bit her lip, a gesture that he'd already figured out meant she was thinking, and feeling a little vulnerable.

"I don't think I know the answer to that anymore. If I ever did. I thought I did, but I'm not so sure."

Part of him took a bit of pride in believing he was the cause for that uncertainty. Another part of him felt shitty for it. He stayed quiet and let her think.

"I guess, casual means sex with no feelings. No care. It's just sex. No relationship. No exclusivity."

She'd just described his stock in trade. He could respond with questions, get her to set the parameters, then find every way to stay in those boundaries without making any promises. That was his norm.

Which is shitty.

Why had he spent the last few months not dating if he was going to jump back into his old routines? Zach shoved the thought aside and kissed Sam on the forehead.

"I can work with that. What do you need?"

Sam tipped her head back, her eyes narrowed. "Well, are you seeing anyone else?"

He hated direct questions like that. They were hard to avoid, but this time he was in luck.

"Nope. No dates, no hookups, no kissing anyone but you since January. Scout's honor."

Sam arched an eyebrow. "Were you ever a scout?"

"Hell no. I hate uniforms." He paused, then leaned in to whisper in her ear. "But I imagine you'd look really hot in one."

Zach straightened and managed a serious expression. "For real, if exclusive is the price of entry, you've got it."

There he went, making a promise he'd never made before.

"That's my bare minimum."

He knew this would come. It always did. But it usually happened after sex, not before it.

How badly do I want her?

Zach took a deep breath as memories of Sam with her legs over his shoulders, her fists clenched in his hair, and her entire body arching as she cried out her orgasm to the springtime sky filled his head.

"I got that," he said. She'd set a boundary and he could agree to it or walk away. He'd never done exclusive before, but he saw no reason not to now. Sam was the only woman who'd interested him in four months. He might feel differently after they had sex, but for now, that was a boundary he could live with.

"I like you and I like what we seem to have. I'm willing to meet you where you are and see where this road takes us."

How bad? Pretty fucking bad, I guess.

Something in her eased. She pulled him down into a kiss that tasted like wine and relief, and then all the air between them turned electric.

His hands skimmed over the silken blouse she wore. His brain urged him to go slow, take his time, but his body responded with need. And Sam matched his urgency. She plucked at the buttons on his shirt, and when she stepped back to peel it from his shoulders, he slipped her blouse over her head. When Sam kissed him again, his cock went hard in an instant and all he could think of was how quickly he could get her into bed.

He scooped Sam up and carried her to his bedroom, then deposited her on the bed, still half dressed in a silky blue bra and slim fitting navy pants. He hooked a finger in her waistband and caught her gaze, silently seeking consent. Sam stretched, lifting her arms over her head and lifting her hips as Zach stripped the pants down her legs, revealing panties that matched her bra.

Fuck, she's amazing.

Sexy as the underwear was, he wanted her naked so he would be free to touch and kiss everywhere. He made quick work of getting her out of her bra and panties, then straightened and finished unbuttoning his jeans while Sam watched as if transfixed. When the last button came undone, he paused.

"Is this what you want?"

Sam flipped over and crawled to the edge of the bed, then hooked her thumbs in his jeans and pushed down. *Nothing like a woman who knows what she wants.*

"Oh, my." Sam blew out a sharp breath, then reached out and stroked a finger along his shaft before rubbing her thumb over the thick silver ring in his Prince Albert.

"Wait." She turned her head to the side then smiled. "You have a Jacob's Ladder, too?"

"Yeah." He lifted his cock so she could see the row of eight barbells that went from just under the head all the way down to the base.

"So, I have a favor to return." Sam swung her legs over the

side of his bed and her fingers wrapped around his cock. Or tried to. They didn't quite touch. Once again making him wonder if things were going to fit.

Then her tongue swirled over the head of his cock and Zach's brain disengaged. Sam made an art out of giving head. One hand squeezed at the base of his shaft and her other reached up and found his nipple piercings.

Fuck, that's amazing.

She gagged a little, but didn't stop, even as tears trickled from the corners of her eyes. She pulled back and took in a deep breath, then slid her lips down his shaft again, this time getting almost to the base before she gagged.

Zach coiled a hand in her hair. "Good girl. Now get on your back and let me taste that beautiful pussy."

Sam didn't waste any time. She scooched backward, but Zach grabbed her legs and pulled her to the edge of the bed.

"I didn't say you could go anywhere." He pushed her thighs apart and slid a finger between her already wet lips. He wasn't in the mood for patience or taking his time.

Sam moaned softly, and the sound brought a smile to Zach's lips. He didn't bother with a slow tease. Everything about her body language said she didn't want it, and neither did he. He pushed three fingers inside her, curling them up, seeking the spot that made her breath catch. Then he lowered his head and tasted her again, savoring the salt and sweetness of her.

Sam gasped and spread her legs wider, her fingers tangling in his hair like she was afraid he might stop.

"More," she whispered.

He added his pinkie, stretching her carefully. She was tight, and the heat around his hand was almost enough to undo him. But she didn't pull away. She moaned, arched, and pushed back, fucking herself on his hand as her clit pulsed against his tongue.

Zach sucked her clit between his lips, building to a harder and faster touch until she cried out, then covered her mouth with her hand. Her whole body trembled, and he felt the moment she let go. Her hips stuttered, her other hand clenched in his hair, and she came with a muffled cry that hit him straight in the chest.

She tugged on him, breathless and flushed. "Get up here, please."

Zach lifted his head and smiled, brushing his lips against the inside of her thigh before slipping his fingers free, slow and careful.

"Not yet," he murmured, voice heavy with need. "First, you don't need to be quiet. The walls here are thick."

He wasn't about to tell her he'd never had complaints; he suspected that would be the opposite of sexy to Sam. She'd been uninhibited at the picnic. When they were outside and she knew they were miles away from anyone. He wanted the same now.

"Make all the noise you want," he said. "Now, roll over for me. On all fours."

Sam didn't hesitate. She moved with a fluid urgency, flipping over, parting her knees, and dropping to her elbows. Her spine curved into a deep arch, her ass high, exposed and gorgeous. She looked over her shoulder, lips parted, eyes simmering with heat.

Zach paused a moment to take her in. This woman, tiny and fierce, restrained and wild. He ran his hand down her back, fingers smoothing over the fine tremors in her muscles.

Oh, she knows what's coming.

Zach bent and kissed the backs of her thighs, then the soft, round curve of her ass. Reverent. Hungry for her. He buried his face between her cheeks and nudged her chest lower with one firm hand, spreading her open so he could reach her clit.

God, he wanted her ass too. He wanted to taste every inch of her, but that could wait. This moment was about indulgence. Worship. He let his tongue flick and swirl, teasing the sensitive bundle of nerves in her clit with soft strokes. Every time she pushed back, every breathy moan that slipped from her lips, he matched with a slower stroke.

She wasn't passive. Sam gave as much as she took, meeting his rhythm, whispering his name like it was sacred. Each time she said it, it went straight to his chest, tightening something deeper than just arousal. She was still being quiet and he made it his goal to get her to shout. To lose control.

"Zach," she gasped, her voice wrecked and trembling. "Please. Fuck me."

"Not yet." He kept his voice low and soft. Her begging to be fucked was nearly his undoing, but that could wait. He slid his hands up her sides, then gently pulled her upright. "Not here."

He grabbed condoms and lube from the nightstand, then tugged her by the hand toward the living room, his steps unhurried. The anticipation was its own kind of foreplay.

The long, leather ottoman sat in front of the couch, wide and low. He'd learned early on it was practically built for sex. He lay down on it, arms open, and fixed her with a level gaze.

"We'll get there. Are you forgetting how much I love tasting you?"

Bright color flushed Sam's cheeks and she shook her head. "How could I forget that?"

Zach crooked his finger, a playful invitation. "So, bring that beautiful pussy over here and make yourself come on my face."

Sam tipped her head, studying him like a riddle she already

knew the answer to. Then, with a glint in her eye, she stepped to the end of the ottoman and turned, facing him as she straddled his head, her knees braced on either side of the bench.

She didn't settle all the way at first. Instead, she hovered just enough for the heat of her pussy to reach his lips, teasing him. Then she stretched out along his body, lying against his chest, arms sliding forward until her fingers gripped his cock.

The moment her hand closed on him, Zach flicked his tongue out, but Sam lifted her hips an inch out of reach.

"You said you wanted me to make myself come on your face." Her voice was low, sultry, but threaded with confidence. "So keep your mouth closed."

Zach's heart thudded hard and his cock leaped to attention. He hadn't expected her to respond like that. He'd assumed her softness meant she leaned submissive. Maybe not. Maybe she had layers he hadn't even begun to uncover. And hell, he liked that even more.

Her fingers gripped him firmly, stroking with increasing rhythm as she rolled her hips, grinding her slick pussy over his mouth and chin. Zach stayed still like she asked, lips sealed, letting her set the pace, letting her use him.

It was hot as fuck, and intimate in a way that surprised him. The feel of her skin against his, the heat of her breath against his body, the low sounds she made just for him as she moved. Her hand on his cock as she rode his face. It wasn't just sex. It was trust. It was need.

She reached between her legs to part her lips, exposing her clit, grinding faster. Her breath hitched, the tight tension in her thighs giving way to trembling.

This time when she came, it wasn't quiet. A cry tore from her throat, low and raw, followed by a wet rush that soaked his face. She collapsed forward, panting, cheek pressed to his belly.

Zach didn't waste the moment. He dragged his tongue along the seam of her pussy, up to her puckered ass, and gave it one slow, deliberate swipe.

Sam shivered. "Save that for next time."

He grinned and gave her ass cheek a light smack. "If you insist."

She pushed up, her body still flushed and glowing. Zach stroked her hip, then added another soft swat. "Now hop off, gorgeous. My turn."

SAM

Sam stood, letting her gaze drift down over Zach's body as he lay stretched across the narrow leather bench like a gift laid out for her. His muscles were cut and taut, the ink on his arms drawing her eye along the curves of his biceps. Shadows played over his skin as he breathed, slow and steady, his composure at odds with the heat smoldering between them.

The silver barbells in his nipples caught the light and glinted, twin flashes against golden skin. She'd seen nipple piercings before, dated men who thought they were edgy, but nothing about Zach felt like a performance. He wore them the way he carried himself: unapologetically, like everything about him had a story. A reason. A purpose.

Then her gaze dropped.

Oh that.

His dick was long, thick, and curved toward his stomach, and so hard the skin looked stretched tight. A drop of pre-cum glistened on the heavy silver ring in the head. She swallowed hard. The line of thick barbells underneath had bumped over her tongue and she could only imagine what they'd feel like during sex.

Her mouth went dry. Nipple piercings she'd seen. A

pierced peen? Never. But she liked it. Heat pooled low in her belly as she took a step closer.

"You going to just stare," he asked, his voice low and teasing, "or were you planning to move so I can get up?"

Sam laughed, realizing she was still straddling his head and she backed up a little. She couldn't tear her eyes away from his body. He was stunning. "I've never been so curious in my life."

"Good." Zach grinned, dark and lazy. "I plan to satisfy that curiosity."

Catnip. Absolute catnip.

No denying it, she had a thing for bad boys. Always had. And Zach? He was the worst kind: the kind that looked like sin but acted like a gentleman, then delivered the devil in the bedroom. The kind that could ruin her for anyone else if she wasn't careful.

Too bad they always turn out to be assholes, she reminded herself.

She shook the thought loose and moved back so Zach could stand. He scooped her in his arms as he rose, then turned and deposited her on the bench.

"Like I said," he murmured, voice dark with promise, "my turn."

He guided her until her ass was perched at the edge of the bench and Sam's heart kicked up as he tore open a condom and rolled it down, every smooth, practiced motion stoking the fire building low in her belly.

"Lie back," he said, kneeling between her legs and laying one hand on her hip. "Your pussy's mine now. You're going to take every inch of my cock."

His words should've made her bristle, but instead, a shiver rolled through her, electric and eager. Never mind that she'd already come hard enough to see stars. She wanted him. Wanted the stretch of him, the weight, the raw intimacy.

Sam leaned back, propping herself on her elbows, still clinging to a sliver of control. But then Zach hooked his arms under her knees and lifted her, spreading her wider. Her breath caught.

"Fucking gorgeous," he said, his voice rough.

He tapped the head of his dick against her mound, teasing, then pressed it lower until he was nudging her slick entrance. The pressure was maddening, thick, heavy, delicious. Even through the condom, she could feel the drag of his piercings, a contrast to the molten heat building inside her.

Her hands gripped the bench. Her heartbeat echoed in her ears. And when she looked up, Zach wasn't just smug confidence and bedroom charm. His eyes had gone dark with something deeper. Desire, sure. But something else too. Like she meant something.

Don't go getting attached, she warned herself.

But then he smirked, just a little crooked tug of his lips, and that thought was toast.

"You gonna behave?" he asked, fingers sliding in slow circles at the crease of her thighs.

Sam raised a brow, tension coiling through her entire body. "Do you really want a woman who behaves?"

He laughed, low and rough. "Fair point."

Then he pushed in.

Not all at once. Just enough. Inch by thick, stretching inch, and Sam's mouth dropped open on a soundless gasp. He was a lot. The kind of girth that made you rethink your choices, but her body opened for him like it had been waiting for just this thing.

Zach groaned, the sound guttural and low, and his hands tightened on her thighs. The piercings dragged against her inner walls; a heady mix of pressure and friction that made her see stars behind her closed eyes.

"Jesus—" she managed.

He pulled back almost completely, then drove into her hard enough to rip a cry from her lips.

"Say it," he growled, leaning over her now. One hand braced beside her head, the other pinning her hips down like he owned her pleasure. "Don't hold back. Tell me how good it feels. Tell me who's making you feel this way."

God, he was cocky. And good. Dangerous combination.

Sam gave a breathless laugh, her thighs trembling. "Someone's fishing for compliments."

"That wasn't an answer," he said, then thrust again.

This one was slower, deeper. She arched off the bench, moaning so loud it echoed. And everything else fell away. The past. Her doubts. Even her fear of falling. Because Zach? He wasn't playing games. At least not in that moment.

It wasn't just the way he moved, or his size, or the metal sparking sensation inside her. It was the way he watched her. Like she was the only thing that mattered in his world. Like he was memorizing every reaction, every flicker across her face. That was more dangerous than any line he could throw at her.

She reached for him, fingers tangling in his hair, tugging him down until their mouths collided. She kissed him like she was trying to take back control, like she wanted to show him how wrecked she already felt.

Zachs response was just as fierce. His hips never stopped, thrusts gaining rhythm and power. Then he broke the kiss to bite her lower lip. "You think you're in charge?"

She growled and clenched her thighs tighter around him, derailing his momentum just enough to knock him off balance.

Zach laughed, cupped a hand under her ass as stood, taking her with him.

"You wanna play like that?" Zach turned and settled onto

the bench with Sam in his lap, still impaled on his dick. "Take control. Take what you want, then it's my turn again."

Sam dug her fingers into his shoulders for leverage and rocked her hips, slow and grinding, milking every inch of him.

Zach moaned, head tipped back, chest heaving. "Fuck. That's hot."

The look on his face when she clenched around him was pure ruin. His hands gripped her thighs tight, steadying her, letting her take what she needed.

Sam sped up, finding the rhythm that had the tension building up to another orgasm. She'd lost count of how many times she'd come already.

"Ah, there it is. Give it to me, baby." Zach wrapped an arm behind her and bent her backward. Then his lips closed over a nipple and sucked. Sam cried out as the orgasm hit, but Zach didn't stop. His hands guided her hips, pulling her against him as the orgasm kept rolling as if it would never end.

When she collapsed against his broad chest, he chuckled then lifted her off of him. "On your knees on the bench."

Sam got on all fours, her legs still trembling as Zach stood behind her. He reached forward, caught a fistful of her hair and tugged until she lifted her arms from the bench.

"I said on your knees," he growled in her ear. "You like it rough. I know you do. I'm gonna fuck your tight little pussy from behind. How hard can I go?"

He kissed the skin under Sam's ear, still holding her hair tight in his fist. Her back was arched so her ass brushed his thighs.

"As hard as you want."

His low chuckle raised goosebumps on her skin. Whatever games she'd played in college were just that, games. Zach was something else entirely. And he was dangerous.

"That'd be a first," he said. His dick pressed against her

entrance and he took a few short strokes before thrusting in all the way in one sharp move. Sam cried out in pleasure.

His arms wrapped her body as he slowed for a few strokes, then he pulled back before driving into her hard and deep.

"Fuck yes!" The words tore from Sam's throat and Zach seemed to get the message. He pounded into her until their bodies slapped together. He sped up, then slowed down, taking long, smooth strokes and letting her catch her breath before he took it back to a relentless pace.

"God that is so good." Zach's next thrust lifted Sam from the bench, but his strong arms held her in place, keeping her safe. "Say it, Sam. Tell me how good it feels."

He slid one hand down her belly and found her clit. Sam sucked in a sharp breath as his fingers grazed the still swollen bud. Then he trapped her clit between his fingers and squeezed with each thrust. A cry escaped Sam's lips, her fingers dug into his thighs, and there was a spreading puddle between her knees.

"Just like that. I love it!"

Zach was like a fantasy lover come to life. He seemed to instinctively know how and where to touch her.

"You are so fucking wet." He murmured the words against her neck, then sank his teeth into her shoulder. One hand cupped her pussy, stroking her clit in time to his thrusts, and the other cupped one breast, rolling the nipple between his fingers.

"Can you take more?" Zach's breath caressed her ear. Sam didn't know how much more he could give, but she was willing to find out.

"Yes, please."

"Good girl." Zach pulled out and Sam had to clamp a hand over her mouth to stop herself from begging him to come back. He straddled the bench behind her, then gently tugged at her hips. "Get belly down on the bench and wrap your legs around me."

Sam glanced over her shoulder at him, uncertain what he had in mind.

"Just lie down, Sam." His hand glided over her back, easing her down to the bench. Sam let out a slow breath and rested her thighs on Zach's.

He grabbed her hips and lifted, then pulled her closer. The head of his dick pressed between her swollen pussy lips and Sam gasped. Zach shifted her again, guiding her until her chest rested on the bench and her hips rested in his lap. Then he pushed her legs wider apart and she felt like his dick somehow got bigger.

"Oh my god."

"Fuck, this is an amazing view." Zach moved, thrusting into her. She thought she'd taken all of him, but she was wrong. She let out a moan as he stroked hard and deep.

"You can take it," he crooned. "That's a good girl. This pretty little pussy looks so good stuffed full of my cock."

Sam moaned and grabbed the sides of the bench as Zach sped up. Whatever he was doing was intense, but felt amazing. With her legs spread wide and her ass in the air, she'd never felt so exposed.

"Slide a hand down and stroke your clit, baby."

Sam didn't think, she obeyed. Her pussy was dripping wet and her clit was swollen and sensitive. Tomorrow would be another walking funny day.

Zach's hand slid over her butt cheek, then stroked a finger from her pussy up to her ass.

"Do you want this?"

Zach pressed gently against her ass, slow circles of pressure designed to tease, not rush.

"Yes, please." She sighed, needy and breathless.

But his hand didn't move.

"Say it, Sam. I want to hear the words. Tell me what you want."

She dropped her forehead to the bench, every nerve on fire.

"Please," she whispered, her voice raspy and raw. "Please finger my ass."

"Good girl." Something wet and slippery glided over her ass, then Zach was pressing a finger in, slowly pushing until her muscles relaxed. Her body trembled and she groaned against the leather beneath her cheek.

"I thought you might like that. Let's go for more."

He kept up slow, steady strokes in her pussy as he added more lube then worked a second and a third finger into her ass. He shifted his legs until Sam's hips angled higher.

"You are so fucking amazing. So hungry for my cock."

As far as Sam was concerned, Zach was a revelation. Whatever he was doing, it went beyond technique. It was like he'd tuned himself to her frequency. After years of sex that ranged from forgettable to functional, being with Zach felt like waking up in a body she finally understood. Mind-blowing didn't begin to cover it.

"Hold on tight, baby."

Zach's rhythm shifted, his next thrust slamming into her with a sting that stole her breath. The fingers buried in her ass moved in sync, stretching her wide with every surge of his dick. It was overwhelming; too much and not enough all at once. He caught her hair, twisted it tight around his fist, and used the leverage to hold her still as he drove into her harder.

Sam cried out, arching into the pressure, desperate to take all of him, to feel every inch, every drag and push.

"Harder," she panted, the word falling from her lips over and over in a litany of need.

Zach gave a low, breathless laugh and released her hair, only to press his palm between her shoulder blades, pinning her to the bench. With that added anchor, he levered into her, thrust after thrust hitting deeper, harder, until it felt like he was rearranging her.

One arm was trapped beneath her body, her fingers still working her clit. He didn't slow, didn't falter. He just kept pounding into her, lifting her hips with every drive forward, until she couldn't speak. All she could do was gasp and moan and fall apart beneath him. Her body trembled, muscles locking as the orgasm built in her.

"I feel that," Zach growled against her ear, voice thick with strain as he leaned over her, pressing her open and full. "You're right there. Right on the fucking edge. Don't move. Hold it. Don't you dare come."

Sam's whole body trembled, her teeth sinking into her lower lip as if that alone could hold the wave at bay. She clenched, desperate to obey, but everything inside her was winding tighter, aching, burning. Every nerve buzzed like live wire.

Then he moved again, one arm looping beneath her chest, lifting her off the bench with stunning strength. She gasped, legs dangling, caught between his dick buried inside her, the fingers that hadn't let up in her ass, and the hand now flat against her sternum, grounding her, holding her safe.

Suspended. Split open. Exposed.

She was floating in it, somewhere beyond lust now, on the brink of something terrifyingly real. Like if she let go, she'd fall into him, not just into pleasure. That scared her more than anything.

But he was everywhere.

"That's it, baby," Zach murmured. "Let it go. I wanna hear you scream my name when you come. I want it all."

ROXANNE BLACKHALL

Her head fell forward, her breath ragged. Her muscles clenched, then trembled, then broke apart completely.

"Zach!" she cried out, the name tearing from her like truth. "Oh my god... Zach."

And still, he didn't stop.

"Fuck, yes," he snarled, voice wrecked. "That's what I wanted to hear."

He fucked her through the aftershocks, wild now, almost frenzied, as if her unraveling had undone him too. She didn't know whether to scream again or beg him to stop, because the next orgasm wasn't just coming, it was roaring through her, sharp and electric and devastating.

Then he drove in deep. One last, brutal thrust before he stilled. His whole body tensed behind her as he pulsed, buried inside.

"Fuuuuck," he groaned, low and filled with need. "You are so damn good."

Sam couldn't speak. Could barely breathe. Her limbs felt boneless, like he'd stolen the structure from her along with her reserve.

Zach eased her down gently, carefully. Slid out of her with care. Then, still breathless himself, he leaned in and pressed a kiss to her cheek. Unexpectedly soft. Tender.

"Don't move," he whispered. "I'll be right back."

Moving wasn't even an option. Her body was too spent. Her emotions too raw.

When he returned, the warm, damp cloth between her thighs made her flinch from overstimulation. But he was gentle, so gentle, cleaning her with quiet care. She blinked in stunned silence as he lifted her again, his arms strong and sure, and carried her through the apartment. The sound of the shower reached her before they entered the steamy bathroom.

He stepped under the water still holding her, skin to skin in a gentle caress.

"Let's get you cleaned up." His voice was as soft as his touch.

The rest blurred. She vaguely remembered him lowering her, soaping her skin, rinsing every inch, towel drying her like she was breakable. Like she mattered.

Then they were in bed, her back cradled against his chest, his body curved around hers. She should've pulled away. Should've reclaimed space, if not for her body, then for her heart. But she didn't.

Couldn't.

His arms wrapped around her middle, anchoring her.

"I'm hoping you're a morning sex kind of person," he murmured against the crown of her head, lips brushing her hair like a promise.

Sam swallowed, then managed a smirk as she wiggled her ass against him. "I am."

Zach's laugh rumbled against her spine. "Good," he said, voice thick and sleepy. "Get some sleep, baby. You're gonna need it."

But sleep didn't come easy.

Because wrapped in his arms, her body spent and every bit of resolve to date with purpose and intention shredded, Sam knew she was falling for another bad boy.

She only hoped this time, it was real.

CHAPTER 13

SAM—FRIDAY, MAY 8

The gate slammed shut behind her with a loud clang that echoed far louder than it had any right to. Sam winced, muttering under her breath as she hunched her shoulders and tried to make herself small, like she could slip past Carla's radar if she just moved fast enough.

Hard to do with an evil gate that seemed to have a personal vendetta. Or maybe it was judging her.

The morning air carried the scent of wet grass, old brick, and whatever flowers the neighbor had planted weeks before. Sam tiptoed up the walk, trying to blend into the quiet. As if showing up on her own porch in the same clothes she'd worn last night wasn't a neon sign blinking I got laid.

Her feet hadn't even hit the first step when Carla's front door creaked open.

"Coffee's already brewed and..." Carla's voice cut off mid-sentence. Then came the smirk. "Walk of shame, I see. This I've gotta hear."

Sam sighed and veered toward Carla's door. No use

pretending she'd just been on an early morning walk in a silk blouse and yesterday's mascara.

Carla would sniff out the truth like a bloodhound.

The hallway was cozy and smelled like butter and something bready. Sam dropped her bag against the wall, kicked off her shoes, one of which was dangerously close to giving her a blister, and padded into the kitchen.

Carla was already parked at the table, wrapped in an oversized cardigan, sipping coffee like she had nothing better to do than interrogate her best friend.

"Where's Emmy?" Sam asked as she grabbed a mug from the cabinet, then poured herself some much-needed caffeine. The second of the morning, and probably not the last if she had to relive everything that happened last night.

"Early surgery. Total knee replacement," Carla said around a mouthful of croissant. "Now spill. Why are you still in yesterday's clothes? Didn't plan to stay over?"

Sam sat gingerly in the kitchen chair and let out a breath. Her body ached. But it was the kind of soreness that came from good things. Mind-blowing things.

"I didn't want to assume. And sleeping over? That always feels like it changes the rules."

Carla arched an eyebrow. "You mean it makes things real."

"Exactly. In my head, spending the night equals serious. And I..." she waved her hand in the air then let out a sigh. She could hide from herself maybe, but not Carla. "I'm still trying to pretend it's not serious."

Carla dropped her croissant. "I thought you wanted serious."

"I do. With the right person." Sam wrapped her hands around the warm mug and stared into the swirl of cream. "But I've only known the guy four weeks. I don't know what kind of man he is when things get hard. When he's not trying to impress me. I'm not even sure he's capable of doing real. I can't let myself fall for him."

Carla took a sip of coffee and gave her a long look. "And yet you stayed over. How much sleeping got done?"

"Oh, I slept. I just got woken up early," Sam said, wincing. "For another marathon round."

"You were hoping to avoid falling for him by not packing a toothbrush?"

"No." Sam laughed, low and self-conscious. "I knew we'd sleep together. I just... weren't you the one encouraging me to get laid? I was trying to trick my brain into holding back. Just letting things evolve into whatever they're going to be and not think of it as anything special."

Carla leaned back in her chair and crossed her arms. "Except it was."

Sam looked down at her mug and nodded. "Yeah. It was. And I don't know how to handle that."

A beat passed. Carla picked up her croissant and took another bite, chewing thoughtfully. "Judging by how slow you were moving, I'm guessing he did the job very, very well."

Sam cracked a smile.

Carla raised her mug and peered at her over the rim. "So. How is the Viking?"

Sam groaned and rested her forehead on the table. "Carla. I'm ruined."

"Oh shit." Carla grinned. "That good?"

Sam lifted her head slowly. "That everything. I'm not even mad about how sore I am. I'm walking like I rode a horse bareback for an entire day, and I would do it again. Wait, I did do it again. He woke me up at like five in the morning and..." She groaned. "You do not want to know what that man can do before coffee."

Carla fanned herself dramatically. "Oh, but I do. Details. Start with the dick. Don't skip ahead."

Sam covered her face with both hands but peeked through her fingers. "Okay, so, it's pierced."

Carla choked on her croissant. "Wait. Hold up. You didn't notice this when copping a feel? Zach the Viking has jewelry in his junk?"

"Several bits of jewelry," Sam said, laughing helplessly now. "And he knows exactly how to use them... it. Honestly, he knows how to use everything. His hands, his mouth, his— ugh, it was so much more than just sex. He was commanding. But gentle. Sweet, even."

Carla blinked. "Well, I'm glad to see he brought the real you out of whatever rock the stick in the mud had shoved you under."

Sam sighed and slumped back in her chair. "Carla, I felt safe. Afterward, he took care of me. He cleaned me up, carried me to the shower like I weighed nothing, washed my hair. Then wrapped me in the fluffiest towel ever. And when I thought that was it? He pulls me into bed and holds me all night like I'm not just some random hookup."

Carla was quiet for a second, which meant she was paying attention.

Sam stared down at her coffee. "I don't want to read into it. But he felt present. Like he wasn't holding anything back. And it's messing with my head because I know that type. And it never lasts. Guys like Zach? They're fun. They're hot. And they vanish when it stops being easy."

"Except he didn't vanish," Carla said softly.

"Yet."

"But you're bracing for it."

Sam nodded. "Because it's easier to assume he's temporary than let myself believe he could be different. I mean, he's got the whole look. Tattoos. Leather jacket. Piercings. That beard. But he doesn't talk about feelings or anything serious unless it's dirty talk. This has bad boy disaster written all over it."

"But you like him."

Sam exhaled through her nose. "I do. I really do. And I hate that I do."

Carla gave her a knowing look. "So what's the plan? Avoid him until the chemistry dies out?"

"You know I can't," Sam groaned. "Books and Brews is tonight. He's running the beer tasting again. Which means I get to stand there pretending I haven't seen him naked, and haven't begged him to make me come, and haven't fallen asleep wrapped around him like a koala."

"Sexy, clingy koala. Got it."

"Shut up."

Carla laughed and topped off their coffees. "Just wear that green dress. The one with that hugs everything and shows off that amazing figure. Plus, it screams 'I'm doing just fine without a man'. Which is probably why the stick in the mud hated it."

Sam narrowed her eyes. "I thought you were Team Get Laid?"

"I am. But I'm also Team Don't Scare the Shit Out of Yourself Over One Great Night. Just be your smart, sexy self. Flirt a little. See what he does."

Sam bit her lip, the nervous flutter starting up in her stomach again.

"And if he turns out to be different?" Carla asked, leveling her with a look. "If he is relationship material?"

Sam stared into her coffee cup for a long moment. "I can't even think about that. I'm screwed."

Carla raised her mug. "To being deliciously, terrifyingly screwed."

Sam clinked her mug against Carla's. "Cheers to that."

"Now get home and take a nap."

Sam wound up doing just that. Then a long, steamy shower, where she let the hot water pound over her skin like a cleansing ritual, as if she could wash away the leftover ache of pleasure, the memory of his hands, his mouth. The way he'd looked at her, like she was a surprise he hadn't expected but didn't want to let go of.

When the water ran cold, she wrapped herself in a towel and dug to the back of her closet. Her fingers landed on the green dress almost by instinct. She hadn't worn it in years.

It had been a reckless splurge. Vintage, pristine, and wholly unlike her usual style. Sage green with narrow stripes of deep, earthy brown. It was soft but structured, feminine with a bite. She'd found it during her student teaching year, back when she was still balancing lesson plans with Preston's growing list of complaints. He said she didn't dress up enough, so she'd tried. Bought the dress for his birthday dinner.

He'd hated it. Said it was too tight. Too much. Said it didn't look like her.

She'd smiled through dessert. Told herself she was being silly, sensitive. But when she'd gone home and hung the dress back up, she'd felt foolish. She never wore it again.

Until now.

Sam slipped it on slowly, a breath catching in her throat as she smoothed the fabric over her hips. It still fit. Perfectly. Her hands lingered at her sides, palms brushing the curve of her waist. The mirror reflected someone stronger now. Someone less interested in contorting herself to please a man who could never quite see her. Maybe the dress had always looked like her. Preston just hadn't known what he was looking at.

Did she dare wear it to work?

She hesitated, then lifted her chin. *Why the hell not.*

She found the right shoes, put on her makeup, and grabbed her things.

When she walked into the shop, Carla let out a long, appreciative whistle.

"I think that looks better on you now than it did back then."

Sam smiled, Carla was always a great hype woman. "I think I look better on me now than I did back then."

It didn't take long to get the store prepped for Books and Brews. Carla ordered in food for the team, and they gathered in the back office with takeout boxes scattered across the worktable.

"Event number four tonight," Carla said, pushing her empty plate away. "After this, it's down to once a month. Part of me's gonna miss the weekly chaos."

Sam nearly choked on a bite of roasted veggie wrap. She covered her mouth with her napkin and stared at Carla. "Seriously? I mean yeah, it's been great. But I'm running on fumes and caffeine. That part I won't miss."

Becca pointed her fork at the dream board hanging above the worktable. "So, the bookish speakeasy thing wouldn't be every day?"

Sam didn't need to look. The board had been her and Carla's shared obsession since college—images of low-lit book nooks, cozy lounges, mismatched chairs, and menus scribbled in chalk. A secret world, wrapped in pages and poured in glasses.

"That's its own business," she said. "Not an event. It'd be a second store. Smaller, curated. Ideally with a partner in food and drinks." She shrugged. "Books and Brews is about building community and bringing people into the shop. A little buzz. The speakeasy? That's about building escape."

Carla's phone vibrated and she glanced at the screen before silencing it. "Our brewery guys should be arriving any minute."

She gave Sam a look. Knowing and a little smug.

Becca smirked. "You and Zach seem to be getting along."

Sam didn't answer. She didn't have to. The rest of the staff tossed their trash and filed out, leaving her alone with Carla.

"Understatement," Carla muttered. She took a sip of her drink, then set it down and fixed Sam with a look. "Be flirty. Enjoy it."

Sam stared down at the ice in her cup. That wasn't the problem. The physical part was easy. Maybe too easy. Zach had made her feel wanted and worshipped in a way no one ever had before. It had been real. Undeniable. Addictive.

"I'm not worried about the flirty part." She finally spoke. "It's everything after that."

Carla reached out, her palm warm on Sam's arm. "You spent years with a man who dimmed your light. I'm not saying you need to go back to college-level chaos, but come on. Let yourself have some joy. Some goddamn fun."

"You're not wrong," Sam admitted.

Carla's tone softened. "You said you wanted to date with intention. I get that. But maybe you're clinging too hard to that intention part. It's like going into a first date with a financial report and five-year plan for the relationship. You don't even know if you want to be with someone long-term until you let yourself be with them in the moment."

Sam gave a half-laugh, half-sigh. "We've had this conversation before."

"And I'm gonna keep having it until you stop talking yourself out of good things."

Sam lifted her cup in mock-toast. "Thanks, Coach."

Carla smiled, but there was nothing teasing in her eyes.

"Just promise me you won't shut him out the second it starts to feel real."

Too late. Already halfway down the real ramp.

The buzzer over the back door sounded. Carla stood, brushing her hands on her thighs. "That's them."

She tossed Sam a look over her shoulder, half-smirk, half-warning, and swung the office door open. "Maybe what you need is a palette cleanser after the stick-in-the-mud. Just don't fall in love."

Sam stayed seated for a beat, her heart thudding a wild rhythm against her ribs. She tried to laugh it off, but her chest felt tight.

Right. Because that's exactly what won't happen with Zach.

She inhaled deep, squared her shoulders, and stepped into the hallway only to nearly collide with Zach, pushing a cart stacked with kegs, all easy confidence and that damn grin, like the morning after hadn't haunted her every breath.

"Holy shit. You look... wow."

Zach's gaze traveled over her, slow and deliberate, like he was replaying every inch of her bare skin from memory. A shiver slid down her spine, goosebumps prickling along her arms.

"Am I allowed to kiss you at work?"

Her heart stuttered. God, he looked good. Too good. Broad shoulders stretched the seams of his Cold Bottom shirt, those teasing lips, and those ice-blue eyes, always studying her, as if he was reading her thoughts.

She'd promised herself she could keep it light. Neat and safe. Last night, this morning, was supposed to live in a box, locked away where there was no danger to her heart.

But the look in his eyes? That look blew the box to pieces.

Sam stepped in, lifting her chin, voice low. "Yes. But keep it PG. Or at least PG-13."

His arm slid around her waist, firm and easy, pulling her just close enough to get every nerve on high alert. Then he dipped his head and kissed her, soft, warm, slow. A kiss that whispered want without taking. Gentle in a way that didn't match the hungry way he'd claimed her hours ago or the way he'd done unspeakable things to her body while he praised and encouraged her with filthy, perfect words.

This kiss was something else. Something dangerous. Sweet. Meaningful.

"Tame enough?" he murmured against her lips.

Sam nodded, but the breath caught in her throat. That one kiss had unraveled her more than all the wild pleasure before it. Her body still hummed from everything they'd done, still ached in the best possible way, but her pulse didn't care about restraint.

It wasn't her body she was worried about losing. It was her heart.

He smiled, eyes full of heat and promise. "Let me know when you'd like more." With one last brush of his lips against her nose, he gestured for her to go ahead of him down the hall.

Sam gathered herself and walked, heartbeat thudding too loud in her ears.

It was going to be a long night.

And if she wasn't careful, maybe a longer fall.

ZACH

Zach pushed the cart down the narrow hallway, trying like hell not to stare at Sam's ass as she walked ahead of him.

Tried and failed.

That damn dress. It clung to her body like it had been stitched by some mischievous goddess determined to shatter his self-control. Every time she moved, it shifted just enough to make him imagine peeling it off, slowly, like unwrapping a secret. Her hair was twisted up in some intricate knot that made his fingers ache to unravel it, to feel the weight of it slipping through his hands. She smelled like vanilla and something darker, something wicked, and she wore that soft, flushed glow that only came after being thoroughly, completely satisfied.

My doing.

And fuck if that didn't make it ten times hotter.

Even a single kiss, light and chaste, had him half hard, and half wondering what the hell he was doing here. And a hundred percent wondering if he could spirit her away after the event for another night of fun.

He navigated the shop and wheeled the cart to the Cold Bottom set up in front. Books and Brews. A Friday night gig he'd begrudgingly agreed to do, then discovered that he liked the vibe. Books, beer, music, people who didn't suck. Sure, the customers were even more prone to flirting than usual, but rarely out of hand.

And there was Sam. Jesus. Sam was—

Nope.

Don't go there.

She was fun. Hot. Surprisingly kinky under that bookish exterior. He hadn't expected that. Nothing about her had prepared him for that.

Maybe if she'd been wearing this dress.

She'd surprised him. Kept doing it, in ways he couldn't explain. And that was a problem.

Zach unloaded the cart at the pop-up bar and hurried to the back hall. He needed to regain control and that wasn't happening with Sam running around looking like a walking wet dream. He took a breath, leaned against the wall and pressed the heels of his hands to his eyes.

I am not a relationship guy.

He'd made the decision a long time ago. It was easier that way. No strings. No expectations. No 'where is this going' conversations. When they happened, that was when he bounced. Sex was fun. Women were fun. He was damn good at what he did. He knew how to listen, how to touch, how to leave a woman feeling like she'd just had her entire nervous system rewritten.

But beyond that? He didn't offer much. And he didn't pretend to.

Until now.

With Sam, he hadn't technically said he wanted more. He just hadn't said he didn't.

Which made him a coward. And maybe kind of a dick.

He let out a quiet groan and let his head thump against the wall, arms crossed. He hadn't touched anyone since January. That whole situation had been a dumpster fire. He could still hear the woman's voice in his head. *Who are you? Have we fucked?*

On the heels of that every woman he'd ever dated and the inevitable fight. Different women. Different words. Same meaning. *You never let me in. It's all surface with you. You're fun, but there's nothing real. You're an asshole. A dick. A jerk.*

They weren't wrong.

And here he was. Four months after his last whatever the fuck it was. Entangled in Sam's smile, her banter, the way she moaned when he...

Nope. Stop. Now.

He went to the bathroom and splashed cold water on his face. The face in the mirror looked no different. Same person. Nothing changed. *Bullshit.*

"You're fine. You're cool. You're not in trouble." All lies.

Zach gripped the side of the sink and blew out a breath. He could do this.

The shop was filling by the time he came back in. Sam was behind the register with Becca, laughing at something on a tablet, her cheeks flushed with warmth and command. Carla stood near the door with a stack of drink tickets and a welcoming grin.

Zach did what he always did. He pulled on his apron, flirted with customers, poured samples, gave a few too-generous refills to people who laughed at his jokes. The event buzzed with that perfect kind of energy—people loose but not drunk, engaged but not rowdy. Warm light. Good conversations. A sense that maybe something meaningful could happen between the pages and the pints.

And every time he looked up, his eyes found Sam.

It wasn't just the dress. Or her mouth. Or the memory of her legs wrapped tight around his hips and her fingers digging into the bench. It was the way she moved, effortless and magnetic, as if the air itself parted to make room for her. Like the world adjusted around her presence.

He wanted her. God, did he want her.

He caught her gaze as she leaned against the counter, sipping from a water bottle. She smiled, small, real, with a little tilt of her head like she was trying to read him.

Zach walked over, his gaze unapologetically slow. "You doing okay?"

Sam nodded and capped her water. "Event's going well."

"You're a walking distraction," he said, voice pitched low, meant only for her. "Hard to focus with you looking like that."

She rolled her eyes, but a smile curled her lips. "That's your line?"

He leaned in just enough to feel the heat coming from her skin. "Nah. My real line's not safe for work."

Then he winked. "I'll save it for later."

He reached out, brushing his fingers lightly against hers. Her lips parted on a tiny gasp and she shot him a wide-eyed look that was gone in a second.

"Behave." She said it under her breath. A gentle admonishment, but she didn't pull away.

I am fucked.

The idea of her pulling away made something in his chest clench. She wanted more. Eventually. Not tonight, not tomorrow, but she'd made that clear. And he didn't do more. Couldn't do more. Could he?

Zach stepped back before he could say something stupid. "Let me know if you need a refill."

"Always," she said, voice soft.

He turned before she could see whatever had flickered across his face.

Jesus. What am I doing?

He'd been down the relationship road once. Wasn't for him and he made no apologies for that. He didn't date women like Sam. Women who saw through his charm, who could outwit him without trying, who knew exactly what they wanted and had the guts to ask for it? Nope. They weren't for him.

So why couldn't he stop thinking about her?

Because some part of him wondered if this, whatever it was, could be different, and the rest of him was terrified it already was.

Later, after last call. After helping pack everything up, Zach hung back, not ready to leave. The shop had settled into the kind of quiet that only came after a good event. Leftover energy still buzzing just under the surface. Carla was gone, the rest of the staff had trickled out, and Zach had sent the Cold Bottom crew to unpack at the brewery. He stayed to help Sam, even though she hadn't asked.

She looked amazing. Still in that green dress, now with her hair falling a little messy, her lipstick mostly gone. She moved with the easy grace of someone tired but content.

God, she was beautiful.

And Zach felt like the floor kept shifting beneath his feet.

"You're good at this," he said, nodding at the cleared space, the twinkling lights still on the center display table. "The whole vibe. It works."

Sam smiled, eyes flicking toward him. "Thanks. It's a team effort, though. Couldn't do it without Carla."

"No, I mean... you. You make it feel like something people want to be part of."

She paused midway through putting a fresh trash bag in the bin and tilted her head. "Careful, your inner nice guy is showing."

He rubbed the back of his neck. "Yeah, well. It slips out sometimes."

The quiet returned. He wasn't sure how long they stood like that. Present. Breathing the same air and pretending it wasn't electric.

Finally, Sam straightened and reached for the folder of receipts next to the register. "So," she said lightly, too lightly, "what caused the slip tonight?"

Zach hesitated. This was the part where he needed to say something. Draw a line, make sure they both knew where this was heading, or not heading. He could tell her the truth. The whole truth. About his family. About why he couldn't be the guy she needed.

"I just want to be clear," he began, words slow, careful. "About what this is."

She didn't move. Not visibly. But the air changed again.

"Okay," she said. Quiet. Neutral. Too neutral.

"I like you, Sam. A lot. You're...God, you're kind of impossible to ignore. But I'm not... I haven't really done the whole relationship thing. Not in a long time. It's better to keep things simple."

Sam nodded, but didn't look at him. "I figured."

"I'm not saying I don't want this. Us." Zach gestured vaguely between them. "I just don't know what this is yet."

Sam exhaled, less frustration, more a bracing breath, like she was steadying herself. "I said I wanted to date with intention, not start a wedding registry. I haven't asked you to meet my parents." She paused. "Yet."

That word landed harder than he expected. She didn't know she'd already met his parents. His jaw flexed. The truth tugged at him again. Now would be the perfect time to say something. To tell her everything.

Instead, he rubbed a hand over his mouth, trying to scrub away the habit of keeping things close. "I'm just trying to not screw this up."

Her gaze finally met his, calm but unreadable. "You're not screwing anything up," she said. "At least not yet."

He huffed a dry laugh. "That yet's doing a lot of heavy lifting."

She gave him the smallest smile. "It usually does."

They were both hedging. Testing the weight of whatever this thing between them was. Still standing in it, neither ready to walk away.

She stepped a little closer, as if she was trying to bridge the space between honesty and risk. "I told you before, I don't do casual. Not since college. It's not in my nature. I'm not going to pretend I don't like being with you."

Zach's throat worked around a swallow. "That feeling is very mutual."

"Okay then," she said, and smiled. Not flirty. Not coy. Just warm and unguarded.

"Okay," he echoed, quieter now.

Then she kissed him. A soft brush of lips. Tentative, like she was testing the heat of something that might still burn her.

He kissed her back without hesitation. Slow. Grounding. This wasn't the wild, consuming kind of kiss they'd shared before. This kiss asked for nothing and offered everything.

When they pulled apart, her hands stayed on his chest, her fingers lightly curled in the fabric of his shirt like she wasn't ready to let go.

"So," she said gently, "we take it one step at a time?"

He nodded. "Yeah. One step at a time."

"Good," she murmured. "Because I don't want to stop seeing you. But I also don't want to feel like I'm walking toward a cliff's edge you already know you'll back away from."

That hit him hard. Right in the gut.

"I don't know where I'm going, Sam," he said, honest and quiet. "But for what it's worth, I'm still walking."

The softest smile played at her lips. "Okay then. Let's walk."

That brought a sigh of relief. He could do that. And maybe, just maybe, there was a way around that didn't require running away, or jumping off.

"Help me finish shutting this place down," Sam said, tossing the envelope into a wall safe in the office and slamming it shut. "Then I've got to get to sleep. Someone woke me up at an ungodly hour this morning."

Zach smirked as she locked the office door. He grabbed the trash bags piled in the back hall. "I don't remember you complaining at the time."

She shot him a look over her shoulder, half mock-scolding, half smiling, and he felt that familiar tug of desire low in his gut. But it wasn't just lust. Not entirely.

As he carried the bags out back, the night air hit him, cooler now, with the scent spring and a hint of impending rain. He stood there for a second longer than necessary, staring up at the night sky like it might offer answers.

They were past the point where he'd be shutting things down. Start being less available. Calling and texting less. Looking for the cleanest exit.

Nothing about this with Sam felt clean or temporary. And for the first time in years, he didn't know what he wanted. Not exactly. Not in the way he was used to.

He only knew one thing with any certainty.

He wanted Sam.

And wanting her wasn't simple.

He tossed the trash bags into the dumpster and let the lid fall shut, the sound echoing in the alley. Then he turned and headed back inside, toward soft lights still glowing in the shop.

Toward her.

CHAPTER 14

SAM—MONDAY, MAY 11

An acre of green felt stretched in front of her, the eight ball waiting like a challenge. Sam bent down to line up the shot. Zach had taken the first game. She'd come back swinging and won the second. Now it was down to this. Whoever sank the eight ball would win the night.

"Corner pocket," she murmured. It wasn't the best angle, but it was her safest play.

She adjusted her stance, narrowed her focus, and just as she exhaled, a warm hand slid up her back.

She gasped, her concentration breaking. Zach leaned in, beard brushing her cheek, his voice low and dark.

"Don't miss."

They had a bet. Loser owed the winner anything they wanted. She had ideas, and unless she was very wrong, so did he.

Sam snapped her cue back and tapped it against his thigh without looking. "Hey. No distractions."

Zach grinned but backed off, settling on a nearby stool. "Just adding a little pressure."

His gaze never left her. That knowing confidence. That smirk. She could feel it pressing into her spine like heat.

She inhaled again, bent low, and this time didn't let him get in her head. The cue struck true. The eight ball rolled, teetered on the lip of the pocket, giving her a moment's fear she'd gone too soft. Then it dropped.

Sam straightened and turned, slow and smug. "Boom."

"I don't know whether to be impressed or turned on." Zach's smile widened. "Guess I'm yours now."

Her smirk deepened. "Hmm. Yes, you are."

Oh how she wished that were true. No amount of telling herself to slow down had stopped the rolling tide of emotions. Telling herself it was too soon to feel this way had no impact.

All it took was him looking at her like he was right now. Some heady combination of lust and admiration. His kisses took her breath away.

When they were together, like now, Zach was all in. He didn't pick up his phone and text anyone else. He was kind, sweet, attentive. Then he'd switch gears and sweet gave way to the most delicious spice.

"Ready to go?" Zach backed her against the pool table, his arms pinning her in place. "Or do you want to chance best three out of five?"

Sam laughed and arched an eyebrow at him, pretending more bravado than she felt. "I'm already two up, all it would take is one more. I think you're trying to wiggle out of the bet."

Zach was good. She wasn't confident she could beat him again. She hooked a finger in his shirt collar and tugged him down to her level.

"Worried about what I might want from you?"

A slow smile spread across his face, then his eyes narrowed and he pressed himself closer, looming over her.

"I am very sure I can deliver anything you ask for." He kissed the corner of her mouth, then her ear, then her neck. "Can you say the same?"

Sam was sure he could deliver, so long as it was physical. She was less certain about anything emotional, and that was the problem.

"The original deal stands." She curled one hand in his hair and brought his head up for a kiss. The moment their lips touched, heat exploded throughout her body and Sam was ready to wrap herself around him right on the edge of the pool table in the middle of the bar.

Zach must have felt the same because he looped one arm around her and lifted her off her feet. He snagged her cue with his other hand and put it, and his, back on the rack, then scooped her purse and walked to the door, still carrying her.

Sam didn't bother to fight back or argue. There was nothing caveman like about it when Zach picked her up. Sometimes it was tender and caring. Sometimes, like now, it was a more primal thing. Like he wanted to be close to her, and get someplace more private as quickly as possible.

No arguments there.

Sam cupped his face in her hands and kissed him. Even the light rain outside couldn't quench the fire in her veins.

"Hurry," she whispered as he unlocked the car door and dropped her into the passenger seat. Zach clambered into the other side and tore off. His grip on her thigh communicated the tension he felt.

She reached over and slid her hand up his leg, then toward his crotch. A hard bulge stretched the front of his pants tight and Sam curled her fingers over him and squeezed. Zach hissed in a sharp breath and let out a little groan.

"How long is the drive?"

Zach shifted his body then leaned his seat back a little more, giving Sam greater access. "About fifteen minutes."

Enough time for her to tease. She undid his belt, then navigated the buttons until she freed his dick. Already hard and pulsing. She might doubt his heart, but never his body. His desire was clear and strong.

"Move your arm."

Zach lifted his arm out of the way and Sam turned, then leaned over so she could get her mouth around the head of his dick. He gripped the wheel with both hands and his entire body tensed.

"Oh, fucking hell. Wow." One of his hands landed on her head, not pushing, just holding gently. "Such a good girl."

She wrapped her fingers around the base of his dick and swirled her tongue over the head, playing with the heavy ring until Zach trembled under each stroke of her tongue.

"Goddammit, who knew you were such a naughty fucking minx." His breath came in short bursts and slow groans.

She didn't stop until he cleared his throat and took the hand off the back of her head. Sam sat up, wiping her mouth on her hand as they pulled into his parking garage. Zach was out of his door the second he parked. When he opened her door, his jeans were half buttoned and his belt still hung undone.

He braced his arms on the open door and shook his head. "You have me in a state. I should've known there was a sexy goddess hiding under that buttoned-up exterior. What is it you want Sam? What's your prize?"

He squatted in front of her and the look in his eyes was pure fire and sex. "Because if you don't tell me, I'm going to carry you all the way up to my place and fuck you senseless the second we get in the door. We might get more than our pants off."

He stood and Sam came face to face with his still hard dick making a clear outline in his jeans. She pushed out of her seat and forced him to back up.

"What if that's what I want?" She drew circles on his chest with a fingertip, teasing over his nipple piercings on each pass. "What if I want to tease you until show me just how much you bottle up?"

Sam reached up, grabbed his shoulders, then lifted her legs and wrapped them at his waist. Zach didn't flinch or stumble. He was like a tree she could climb. Sturdy. Solid. Strong. His hands cupped her ass. Sam sank her fingers into his hair.

"I want you to lose control."

A low growl sounded in Zach's throat and Sam threw her head back in laughter. Maybe she could break down his barriers like this. It was worth a try.

Zach turned and carried her into the building. He pinned her to the wall in the elevator and covered her face in kisses that didn't stop when they reached his floor. The gray-beige hall passed in a blur as Zach's long legs carried them quickly to his apartment.

Inside, he closed the door then pressed her against it, wedging himself tight against her body.

"Are you sure that's what you want?"

If he was able to ask that, he was still far too coherent for Sam. She reached between them, unbuttoned her shirt and unhooked her bra. Sam tangled her fingers back into Zach's hair and pulled his head down. She knew from experience that he loved giving pleasure.

His lips closed over a nipple, his touch gentle. Still restrained. She wanted him lost in passion. She held his head tight in her hands and demanded more. His beard seared her skin as he showered her nipples with kisses, licks, sucks, and bites.

"I want you sitting in a chair." Sam had an idea. She'd never done anything like it before, but she suspected Zach would like it.

He carried her to the dining area and sat in one of the sturdy wood chairs.

"What did you have in mind?"

Sam slid off his lap and smiled. "Put your hands under your thighs."

He tipped his head to the side and raised his eyebrows, but he complied.

"Strip club rules," she continued. "You are not allowed to touch unless I say so. Your hands stay put."

She unbuttoned his shirt and shoved it off his shoulders, trapping his arms against his sides. Zach's eyebrows went up even higher. Then Sam bent and undid the rest of his jeans.

"Lift your hips."

Zach lifted and Sam tugged until the jeans came down. She let them puddle around his ankles and left his shoes on. There was something sexy about Zach sitting like that, his hands trapped under his thighs, clothes askew, and that amazing body on display.

She locked her gaze on his and took off the rest of her clothes. Slowly. Seductively. Peeling off each layer until she was wearing only her panties. Silky, pink, and mostly see through. Those she kept on.

Sam knelt and stroked a finger over his dick.

"No touching," She reminded, then bent her head and took him into her mouth. She reached up with one hand to tease his nipple rings and used the other to stroke the base of his shaft. It took a little work, but she found the right angle and took his dick as far down her throat as she could.

Zach's groan was loud and ragged as she bobbed her head, setting up a smooth rhythm. His hips lifted to meet her and Sam flicked a finger on a nipple ring.

"Fuck, yes." One of Zach's hands slid out, then he clenched his fingers and stuffed it back under his leg. Sam took that as a cue to speed up. Her eyes watered and she fought her gag reflex as Zach thrust into her mouth.

She let him keep going until she tasted salt and musk, until Zach's moans were coming through gritted teeth and his dick pulsed against her tongue. Sam gripped the base of his dick, pulled her mouth off of him and sat back on her heels.

"Aw, fuck!" Zach collapsed into the chair, his breathing ragged. Sam didn't give him time to go beyond that. She straddled his hips and settled her panty-covered bits right on his hard dick. Then she rocked her hips until she found a spot that felt good.

Zach's mouth hung open and his chest heaved. His eyes drilled into hers. Sam leaned back, braced her hands on his knees and smiled at him.

"I want your mouth on my nipples. No hands."

"You're killing me." His voice shook, but he leaned forward, slowly taking one nipple into his mouth. Sam moaned and ground her hips faster. He was still being too gentle. Too tame.

"You know how I like it," she murmured. She grabbed his hair with one hand and held tight. "Harder. I want to feel your touch for days."

Zach growled against her skin, and his teeth grazed her nipple. That was more what Sam had in mind. She arched her back and rocked her hips, watching Zach for any sign it was uncomfortable. She wasn't sure about grinding against his piercings like that, but the sounds coming from him were all pleasure.

"Just like that," she said. "That's so good. Don't stop."

Her panties were soaked and Sam wanted him inside her, but she was determined to ride it out until Zach couldn't take any more and let out the beast she knew lurked under his tight control.

He switched to her other nipple, pulling it between his lips and lashing the tender bud with his tongue. His dick throbbed under her and Sam slid down. The barbells in his Jacob's ladder bounced over her clit, sending shockwaves of pleasure through her. She needed more. She needed to come.

She tugged Zach's hair until he looked up, his lips wet and smiling. Sam stood abruptly and looked around.

The table.

"Turn the chair and face the table. Then hands back under your thighs."

The look on Zach's face said he knew exactly what she had in mind. Once he was in place, Sam slid onto the table, draped her legs over his shoulders, and propped her hands behind her. She thought of all the filthy, sexy things Zach said during sex.

"No hands. Show me how much you like eating my pussy."

His mouth was on her before she laid all the way back. The thin panties were no barrier to Zach's lips and tongue. God, she'd be ruined for any man who came after. Zach had skills.

She reached down, caught his hair in one hand and pulled her panties aside with the other. She didn't have to say anything, Zach knew. He sucked her clit harder and Sam tightened her grip in his hair.

"Oh yes. Like that." She wanted to grind on his face. To feel his beard rasping against soft skin. She wanted to feel swollen and tender before his dick pushed into her.

Another hard lick slid under her clit hood and Sam lost her grip on the panties. Zach didn't miss a beat. He caught the thin fabric in his teeth and tore, then got his mouth back on her clit. Sam wrapped both hands around his head, holding him tight and still as she ground her pussy against his face.

"That's what I needed!"

Zach's body surged forward, pushing her back as he leaned into her, his mouth open wide, his beard prickling against her skin. His tongue worked her clit at a furious pace.

"Don't stop. Don't stop." Sam chanted the words, holding on to Zach's head for dear life as the tension built in her belly and legs. She was dimly aware that Zach had one hand around his dick and was stroking in time to the rhythm of her hips.

"Harder, please. Faster." She didn't know how he would manage it, but she knew Zach would deliver, and he did.

The orgasm broke over her like a shockwave, sending tremors to her toes and fingertips and bowing her back off the table as she cried out Zach's name. Before she had a chance to catch her breath, Zach stood in a rush.

His arms curled around her body and he hauled her off the table. Sam opened her eyes to see the thing she'd been trying to release.

Zach. Lost in a haze of passion and want.

He carried her to the bedroom, not putting her down until he got to the bed, then he fumbled a condom out, tore the wrapper and rolled it on. For a second, she worried he'd regained control, but when he looked back at her, his eyes were dark and hooded, and his mouth set in a determined line.

Oh, that is so sexy.

Zach gripped her panties and tore the hole wider. He had

her on her back with her legs over his shoulders in half a breath. Then his dick pressed into her. Hard and fast. There was no easing in. No slow strokes. Just intense pressure and a deep thrust, and Zach's rough growl as his body slammed into hers.

She reached for him, but he caught her hands and pinned them over her head as his hips pistoned into her. Sweat beaded on Zach's forehead and his muscles stood out in sharp ridges.

"Is this what you wanted?" He spoke through gritted teeth, his voice barely recognizable. It had Sam on the edge of another orgasm.

She threw her head back, exposing her throat as she gasped at another hard thrust.

"Yes! More!"

ZACH

Zach lowered his head and sank his teeth into the tender skin where shoulder met neck. Sam's moans raised in pitch and her hands clenched into fists. She'd pushed buttons he'd forgotten existed and he needed more. He needed all of her. Everything.

"Give me your ass," he growled against her neck. He slid one hand under her hips and pressed a finger against the tight hole. "I want my cock in your ass."

"Then take it." Her voice was a whisper that drove him harder than a shout. Zach let out another growl and rose to his knees, sliding her legs from his shoulders. He found the lube without looking, never taking his eyes off of her face.

He smoothed lube over his cock, then laid one thumb over her clit and slid a lubed finger into her ass. Sam sighed and spread her legs wider. He worked up to three fingers in, warming her up then positioned his cock and pushed forward.

Her eyes went wide and her mouth opened as the head

went in, but she let out a low moan of pleasure. Zach inched forward, even now, he knew he had to start slow.

Sam wrapped her legs around his hips and lifted herself, taking him deeper. A gasp escaped her lips, then she adjusted and did it again.

"Fuck my ass," she whispered. "Fuck my ass like you fuck my pussy."

Whatever shred of control Zach had left shattered at that. He grabbed her hips and thrust forward, plunging his cock all the way into her ass, before pulling back and doing it again. Sam's head tipped back. Her mouth opened on a cry of pure delight and that spurred Zach onward.

Her muscles clenched tight around his cock as he stroked into her, hard and deep. She cried out for more, for harder, faster, and Zach delivered. He rocked back on his heels, lifting her to rest on his thighs as he held her body and continued pounding into her.

Sam slid a hand down and stroked her clit, her fingers sliding along either side, pinching and gliding with each of his thrusts.

And still it wasn't enough for him. He pulled out and Sam gasped until he buried his face between her legs and sucked her clit into his mouth, teasing her to a fast, hard orgasm that soaked his face.

Zach pulled her to the end of his bed and knelt on the floor between her wide-spread thighs, then added more lube to his dick. Her chest and face were flushed and her breathing was fast. Her legs still shaking from the orgasm. Nothing had prepared him for this side of Sam.

He gripped her hips and slid her down until she was hanging off the end of the bed. His hands splayed across her body, holding her in place. She was tiny, but fierce.

"Zach, please." Sam lifted her legs, holding herself open

for him, trusting that he wouldn't let her fall off the bed. "Take my ass."

That was all the encouragement Zach needed. He thrust back into her in one stroke, leaning his body over hers so every thrust ground against her swollen clit while his dick pounded into her ass.

She came again in only a few strokes, but Zach didn't stop. He kept going, driving into her, feeling every twitch of her body. When she lifted her hips to meet his next thrust, he grabbed her hands and pinned them to the mattress on either side of her head.

Zach lowered himself, his body covering hers, arching his back so he could see her face.

"Look at me."

Sam's eyes opened and locked on his. He thrust once, hard and sharp. Her lips parted and she sucked in air. Her eyes fluttered closed.

"Don't you dare look away." He ground the words out while pressing his dick so deep in her ass his body ground against her swollen pussy. "Eyes on me. You've got another orgasm or two in there, then I'm going to fuck you hard and fast until I come deep in your cock hungry little ass. Got that?"

Sam practically purred beneath him. Sex goddess kitten, maybe.

"Got that?" He repeated with another hard thrust that made her suck in air.

"Yes, Zach."

That response went straight to his cock and Zach snarled. "Good fucking girl."

He clenched her hands in his and rocked against her, mimicking the way she'd grind her pussy on his face. Sam's eyes went wide, then she smiled and laughed. She seemed to love grinding herself over his beard, so he used his body to do the same. His cock buried in her ass had to be a bonus.

Fucking hell. That's so goddamn good.

"Oh god, yes. Right there. Oh right there."

Her hips bounced and rocked, her hands tugged against his, but he held her tight to the mattress and kept grinding into her.

"Zach!" His name came out as nearly a scream as Sam's whole body tensed, then shook and wetness cascaded down his thighs. Then Zach kept his word.

He levered himself up and pinned her legs wide apart, then fucked her ass, hard and fast. Until sweat dripped down his body. Until Sam was calling out his name, then nothing but gibberish as she came again. Until his arms shook with the effort of holding himself up. Until she had nothing left to give, and the only thing he had remaining was to come.

He roared her name as his cock throbbed, feeling like it would explode with the orgasm.

They both collapsed to the floor, his cock still buried in her ass as Sam wrapped herself around him and sagged against his chest.

What the fuck was that?

He had never let himself loose like that. Never. And hell, he loved anal, but didn't indulge often. Not many women could take him. Plus, anal was like an instant switch flip to 'serious relationship.' So, he only did it with women he knew were in it for the sex, and just the sex.

And that's not Sam. Shit.

His even bigger worry was that she could get him to let go. That he was free with her. The only fly in the ointment was that he wasn't a relationship guy. Everything else with Sam was beyond perfect. Scarily perfect.

He stroked the hair off her face and Sam smiled, tugging at heartstrings he didn't know he had.

"I don't want to move but we have to." He wasn't going soft yet, but it would happen. That or he'd get hard again, and he wasn't sure either of them would survive another round. She shifted as if to slide off, but he shook his head. He wasn't ready to break contact.

Instead, he cupped her ass and stood, still holding her against him. Still buried in her ass. Sam wrapped herself around him, laid her head down and sighed.

Fuck.

He'd known she was teetering on the edge. Sensed it. Whatever had happened today had tipped her over it. Up until now, he could half-ass things. Give vague answers. Make vague promises. Now? He could walk away and hurt her a little, or he could keep playing the game, knowing he'd hurt her a lot more later.

Or I could give it a shot. For real.

The fact that even thinking that didn't have his cock shriveling up was a little disturbing. He carried Sam to the bathroom and turned on the shower, then rested her ass against the bathroom counter while they waited for the water to warm up. She lifted her head and kissed him. Soft and tender and tasting like something meaningful.

"I'm trying to play it cool here, but you kind of make that impossible." Sam bit her lip then swallowed hard. It didn't take much thought to read between the lines on that one.

There was something humorous about having this conversation with his cock still hard, still filling her ass.

"I'm not good at this. Not good at relationships." He closed his eyes and nodded. Was he going to do this? "But you make me want to be better at it."

Sam's hands cradled his face, then her lips caressed his. Sweet and tender. "You seem to be doing okay so far."

She wiggled against him and fuck if his cock didn't twitch in response.

"Maybe a shower, then another round?"

Zach's eyes popped open. *Fuck, she's beautiful.*

"You think you can handle that?" He flexed his muscles, bouncing his cock in her ass.

"Oh, more of that? I don't know." She laughed and the sound was musical to his ears. "But you barely used my pussy."

She's gonna kill me, but what a way to go.

"I guarantee, after a shower, I will make sure to fill you up, use whatever you want used, make you come until you are exhausted, and fuck you until you beg me to stop."

Her smile lit up his world and Zach didn't know what to do with that. Then she grabbed his shoulders and rocked her hips, sliding her ass on his cock.

"Hmmm, maybe I could handle more."

"What have I unleashed?" Zach spun them to the shower and pinned her to the wall, out of the spray of water. "You sure about that?"

He levered himself into her, driving deeper into her ass. Sam cupped his face, her eyes half closed and her breath speeding up.

"Make me come, Zach. I need to ache from you."

"Careful what you ask for." He thrust into her harder. "I plan to deliver."

At what cost? Fuck. I am so screwed.

But Sam's legs around him and her cries in his ears wiped those thoughts away as he felt her body tensing, preparing to come again. Knowing he was taking her to those heights.

"Tell me." He ground the words out against her neck.

"You feel so good," she panted. "Oh my god, Zach. I love your dick in my ass."

Her words made him even harder, driving him to give her more, to fulfill her every need.

"Good," he growled. "You're gonna get a lot of it."

He'd deal with the consequences later. Zach cranked the water off, carried Sam back to the bathroom counter and found more lube.

They were going to need it.

CHAPTER 15

SAM—MONDAY, MAY 25

The morning light through Zach's apartment windows made everything feel soft, like a something out of a rom com, all golden beams and slow kisses. Sam curled her feet beneath her on the oversized chair, Zach's hoodie drowning her in warmth and the scent of him.

He was in the kitchen, bare-chested and barefoot, starting a pot of coffee like this was routine. Like they did this all the time.

And lately, they kind of did.

Her heart fluttered. The good kind. The dangerous kind. God, she liked this too much. The easy, domestic sort of intimacy that crept in when you weren't paying attention. She caught herself smiling like an idiot just watching him stir sugar into his cup.

She should've felt content. And she did, mostly. Zach was warm and thoughtful. He brought her snacks from the corner store near the brewery, remembered how she took her coffee and her tea, kept his playlist queued to the indie bands she liked. And when they touched, when they had sex, he made her feel like the only thing that mattered.

So, yeah. Content. Hopeful, even. But the ache still lingered.

Zach handed her a mug and Sam traced the rim with one finger, watching steam curl upward like a whisper. She hadn't met his friends. Not properly. Just Deke that one time at the bookshop. There had been no casual 'come hang out with the crew' invites. She hadn't met his family, either. She didn't even know their names.

And Zach's apartment? Gorgeous. Modern. Spotless. But aside from his artsy black and white photos, not a single personal touch. No clutter, no random mementos. Nothing that said anything about the person who lived there. Sometimes it felt like walking into a very high-end hotel room. Beautiful. But temporary.

She shook herself.

Stop it.

It was still new. People opened up on their own timeline. Maybe he was just private. Guarded. And wasn't that fine? Hadn't she told herself she would take it slow? That it was okay to see where it went?

Liar.

Sam exhaled slowly and let her head fall back against the chair. She wanted to believe he was just taking his time. That the way he touched her, fingers brushing her waist while she cooked, the way he kissed her forehead when he thought she was asleep, meant something. That he was learning how to be vulnerable.

But maybe he was just good at playing the part. Maybe she was once again falling too fast and wanting too much.

Nothing new.

She'd spent her first years of college accepting crumbs when what she wanted was the whole cake.

Zach settled next to her with his own coffee, his thigh pressing against hers. He smelled like soap and sugar. Her heart ached in a quiet, desperate way. He brushed a kiss to her cheek and slid an arm behind her shoulders.

And just like that, the moment passed.

She sipped her coffee and leaned into him. *This should be enough. This is good.*

Deep down, where she didn't like to look, Sam knew the truth.

She wasn't teetering anymore. She'd already taken the leap. And she had no idea if Zach was on his own edge, or backing away.

ZACH

Zach stood at the kitchen sink, drying the last of the dinner dishes while Sam curled up on the couch with a blanket and a book she'd pulled from her tote. Something painfully romantic, probably. She had a thing for old school historic romance. Stories filled with longing and slow burns culminating in sweet, tender expressions of love. Totally at odds with how she expressed herself in bed.

He liked that about her. That she wanted the soft and the sharp. That she was always a little more than you expected.

He watched her for a moment. Her legs tucked beneath her, her eyes skimming the page, her hair spilling over her shoulder in a messy braid he couldn't stop thinking about undoing.

Something twisted in his chest. Familiar and foreign at the same time.

Yeah, he was in trouble.

The kind of trouble he'd spent years avoiding. She'd spent the night last night. They'd had a lazy morning, sipping coffee on the couch before going to work. Then he'd called her out of the blue and suggested dinner at his place, and here they were. Again. It was a type of intimacy he wasn't used to, but part of him liked it.

He dried his hands, tossed the towel on the counter, and walked over to the couch, dropping down beside her. She looked up, one brow raised in question, and he leaned in and kissed her. Slow. Thorough. Like he could memorize her mouth. Her fingers slid into his hair, the book slipping off her lap.

It would've been easy to let it turn into something more. The way she responded to him? Fuck, it wrecked him sometimes. She didn't hold anything back. Not when she kissed. Not when she touched. Not when she came apart in his hands.

But tonight, Zach pulled back before it could spiral. Rested his forehead against hers instead.

"You're dangerous, you know that?"

Sam smiled, but it was soft and a little tentative. "Why's that?"

"Because I like this." He gestured between them. "Too much."

She blinked, her expression unreadable. "That's a bad thing?"

"No." *Yes. Maybe.* "It's...new."

He leaned back against the couch and let his arm fall across the backrest. She shifted to face him, blanket still wrapped around her, and laid a hand on his thigh. That tiny touch grounded him and set him on edge all at once.

He didn't know how to do this. The closeness. The

honesty. Letting someone into the places he kept locked up tight. But Sam was already there.

She'd slid right past every one of his defenses before he could reinforce the walls. And he hadn't even minded. Not at first. Not when it was all teasing and sex and heated glances across the room during her events.

Now it was long afternoons. Quiet dinners. Work mornings. And the best sex he'd had in his entire life. Sam matched him passion for passion. She was all things soft and sharp at the same time.

He still hadn't introduced her to anyone aside from the one time she accidentally met Deke. Still hadn't told her that Cold Bottom was his family's business.

Zach swallowed hard, guilt curdling in his stomach. He'd had so many chances to do that, but he hadn't.

He wasn't hiding her; he just hadn't figured out how to make her fit outside of their little bubble. His life, his world, it had always been partitioned. Tidy. Clean. He didn't let people see the whole picture because that meant handing them power.

He'd done that once. Got burned bad.

But Sam wasn't like that. Sam wasn't a game. She wasn't angling for anything but being a part of his life. All of his life.

So what the hell was his problem?

"I'm not good at the relationship thing," he said suddenly, the words spilling out like a confession.

Sam didn't flinch. Just tilted her head, patient. Curious. Kind.

"You've mentioned that," she said softly. "But I appreciate the reminder."

He huffed a laugh. "I'm trying. I just...I don't want to fuck it up."

She looked at him like she could see more than he wanted to show. "Then don't."

That simple. That clear.

He reached for her hand and twined their fingers together. Her palm was warm against his, her grip steady.

He wanted to tell her everything. About Cold Bottom. About his family. About the women before her, especially the one who taught him to be so closed off. But the words caught in his throat.

Instead, he kissed her again, less gentle this time. Letting the heat build. A promise without the words.

He'd get there. He had to.

But not tonight.

Tonight, he just wanted to feel her coming apart under his touch. Watch her fall asleep tangled in his arms while he figured out how to be the kind of man she already believed he could be.

Sam shoved the blanket aside, then climbed into his lap and the heat rose higher. There was nothing slow or relaxed about the way she tugged on his shirt, as if she couldn't get him undressed fast enough.

Tomorrow, maybe he'd start telling the truth.

Maybe.

CHAPTER 16

SAM—WEDNESDAY, MAY 27

Sam stood by the dresser, pulling her hair into a quick twist, a hair clip clamped between her lips. Her work dress hung a little crooked on the hanger behind her, waiting.

Zach was still in bed, sheets tangled low on his hips, one arm flung over his eyes as if he wanted to block out the sun that filtered through the blinds. She finished her hair and sat on the edge of the bed

"Do you have any clean hand towels?"

He groaned, lowered his arm and blinked in the light. "Check the dryer?"

She went into the hall, pulled open the dryer and extracted a fresh towel. It was domestic. Familiar. And it gave her hope.

Sam stepped back into the bedroom, hung the towel up and sat back on the edge of the bed. "Hey, I wanted to ask you something before I go to work."

Zach propped himself up, groggy but attentive. "Yeah?"

"So, the weekend of the next Books and Brews is my

222

mom's birthday. It's nothing formal, just a small thing that Saturday. Backyard, a few friends, cake. I was planning to take the train up late Friday night and I was thinking, if you're free, maybe you'd want to come?"

He was quiet for just a second too long. Then he ran a hand through his hair, grabbed his phone and looked at the calendar.

"Shit, I'm likely to be swamped. We're getting ready for summer roll out. I've got the new tropical IPA that's gotta be ready to launch."

"Oh." Sam reached for her dress and stepped into it slowly. "Right. Makes sense."

"I'd go if I could." He stood and came up behind her, zipping up the back of her dress without her asking. "Rain check?"

She nodded, smiling up at him over her shoulder. "Of course."

But something in her chest tightened. His words sounded like a promise, but they didn't have the ring of truth.

He kissed the side of her neck, slow and warm, and she let herself lean back into him just a second too long before stepping away to grab her bag.

"I've got plans with Carla tonight, and Thursday is a book club at the shop. I'll text."

Zach was already back in bed. She couldn't blame him. He'd had a long day, then spent hours making her come her brains out.

It should have been enough, but Sam felt the ache of something missing. She didn't have time think about that. Carla was taking the day off, so Sam had an extra busy day.

"C'mere." Zach crooked his finger and the urge to strip off her clothes and climb between the sheets with him was almost overwhelming. Sam leaned over and braced her hand on Zach's chest.

"Yes?"

He snaked his arms around her body and pulled her on top of him. "I hope everything's okay with Carla and Emmy. Do what you gotta do. You could come over after book club. I'll be up. And think about what you'd like this Friday night."

Sam didn't have to think about it. She knew. The only thing that could shut out the confusing thoughts clouding her brain.

"Hm, I'll call Thursday a maybe. Friday? That's easy," she replied as she slid her hand under the sheets to stroke his stiffening dick. "I want to ride that gorgeous face of yours until I come several times, then beg you to fuck my pussy and ass until I can't walk the next day."

Zach's dick pulsed in her hand and a slow grin spread on his face. "You really are a dream come true. It will be my pleasure to deliver. Now gimme a quick kiss and get outta here."

Sam kissed him lightly then hurried out the door.

The day went faster than it had any right to, and Sam was exhausted by the time she left. As much as she'd like to just go home and sleep, she had a promise to fulfill.

She didn't bother to knock on Carla's door, she just let herself in, kicked off her shoes and headed to the kitchen.

"I'm getting a coffee, you want anything?"

Sam opted for the pod coffee thing since it was faster and easier. She dropped in a hazelnut coffee and pushed the button.

"No, thanks. I have my giant vat of herbal tea."

Sam couldn't help but laugh. Carla was as much a caffeine addict as Sam, but had cut back while trying to get pregnant and she was hating it.

She poured milk into her coffee and headed to the living room. Sam settled into a spot on the couch and tried to read her friend's expression. No such luck.

"Well?"

"I did another round of IUI today," Carla announced. "Different donor. Now we cross our fingers."

Sam grabbed her friend's hand and squeezed. "Emmy at work?"

"Yeah, the life of a surgical resident." Carla curled her feet up under her and Sam flashed back to their college days, where they would sit on either end of the beat-up dorm couch, their feet touching, both focused on their homework.

"How are you feeling?"

After finding out about the struggles Carla had been going through, Sam had given it a few days, then confessed she was hurt that Carla hadn't told her sooner, but she understood. She promised she wouldn't ask or nag, but she wanted to be supportive in whatever way Carla and Emmy needed.

"I'm okay. Hopeful. I wanted you to know from the start this time," Carla said. "However it works out. This will be our last round of this. If I don't get pregnant, we'll try IVF. We even talked about delaying it until Emmy is done with her residency, but I'm thirty-two. It doesn't make sense to wait."

Sam grabbed her hands and squeezed. "You know I love you and I'm here for you. Whatever you need."

Carla raised an eyebrow. "What I need is for you to distract me from my drama and tell me what's going on with that gorgeous hunk of a man you're dating. You're at his place more than your own these days."

Sam laughed long and hard, until her eyes watered and she had to take a moment to catch her breath.

"If sexuality were a choice, I would not be dating men."

Carla looked up from her herbal tea, snorted. "As a bi woman, sometimes I wonder what I ever saw in men, too."

Sam huffed a laugh, but her smile felt forced.

"The sex is amazing," Sam said. "The time we spend together is always good. That should be enough, right?"

She put her coffee down and rubbed her temples. "I asked him to come to my mom's birthday. You know how that thing is. Low key. Backyard and burgers. And he had this whole bit about summer prep and a new beer, and how he had to be at the brewery."

Carla raised a brow. "First time you've invited him to meet the family?"

"Yeah."

"And?"

Sam shook her head slowly. "He didn't even think about it. Just, a two-second look at his calendar and 'I can't.' Like I should've known not to ask."

"You hurt?"

Sam didn't answer right away. She snatched up her mug again and stared at the steaming brew like it could tell her what she didn't want to admit.

"I don't know. I guess I keep thinking he'll open up more. That this thing between us is not just sex anymore. It can't be. Not with the way he touches me. Not with the way he looks at me."

Carla waited, quiet.

Sam took a deep breath before she continued. "I'm not even sure if his family knows I exist. I keep getting little glimpses into his life, but it's like I'm outside looking in. We're perfect together. Amazing. It's so good, so comfortable and normal and the sex. My god, the sex. I keep telling myself all of that is enough, but..."

"But it's not."

Sam swallowed hard. "I thought I was teetering. That I could still maybe get out if I had to. But I'm not teetering. I'm not falling. I've already fallen."

Carla's expression softened. "Have you told him any of this?"

Sam laughed bitterly. "No. Because I'm scared of what he'll say. Of what he won't say. And I don't want to break this thing we have. Not if there's still a chance he's getting there."

Carla leaned over and put her hand on Sam's knee. "You deserve someone who doesn't make you feel like a guest in their life."

"I know." Sam's voice cracked. "But I want him. I want what we have. Or what I think we could have."

"Then you've got to talk to him, Sam. Because wondering is going to eat you alive."

Sam nodded. But it felt like that edge again. The one she kept pretending she wasn't already past.

CHAPTER 17

ZACH—FRIDAY, MAY 29

The smell of coffee had barely filled the kitchen before Sam broke the quiet.

"Do you ever think about letting me into more of your life?" She wasn't accusatory. Not even serious, really. Just a gentle question tossed out as she bent to slip on her shoes.

Zach blinked, still halfway in a post-sleep haze, holding his mug midair. "You are in my life."

She'd stayed over more nights than not. Something he'd never allowed, let alone encouraged before. Sam was part of his routine now, but that wasn't what she meant, and he knew it.

Sam stood, slinging her bag over her shoulder as she crossed to the mirror. "I mean beyond your bed and your stovetop coffee." She paused. "Not that I'm knocking either."

He chuckled, but it caught in his throat. She was teasing. Mostly. This was the point he'd been dreading. When Sam needed more.

She came back over and leaned against the counter, arms

folded. "You've met my best friend. I'd like you to meet my parents. I know so much about you in some ways, but almost nothing in others. No stories from childhood, no messy ex drama. Not even a college roommate horror tale."

Zach set his coffee down and took a slow breath. He wasn't ready to let go of Sam. She was something special and what they had was amazing. The trouble was, he wasn't wired for what she needed.

"You want the one about the guy who used to brush his teeth in the shower while eating string cheese?" Maybe deflection would delay the inevitable. He could hope.

She rolled her eyes, but there was warmth behind it. "I'm not asking for your tax returns, Zach. I just want to feel like I'm part of your world. Not orbiting it."

He wanted to tell her she was already a huge part of it. That she took up way more space in his head than she should, that he'd caught himself looking at his bed Wednesday night and smiling like a dumbass just because he'd found one of her hairs on his pillow. But the words stuck.

"I'm trying," he said instead, quiet and honest. "This whole letting someone in thing? I don't know how to do that."

Sam nodded slowly, like this wasn't news to her. "I don't need everything all at once. Just something. Anything real."

She pulled him down for a kiss. Not goodbye. Not a brush. Something firmer, like she was anchoring them both to the moment. "Okay. I'll see you tonight?"

Zach nodded, grateful. "Yeah. I have a request to fulfill."

That got a bigger smile out of her. Sam headed out the door, and the joy of his morning disappeared with her.

Fuck. He downed his coffee and headed to the shower. The room still smelled of Sam, even though there were no traces of her otherwise. She didn't leave so much as a toothbrush.

Because I haven't encouraged it.

The one time she had left her toothbrush over, he'd returned it to her the next day, blaming it on his neat streak. She'd shrugged and tucked it in her purse, then never left another thing in his space.

Dick move on my part.

He'd make dinner tonight something special. Romantic.

That thought got him through the rest of the day, and the grocery shopping after he realized he didn't have any onions.

By the time Sam arrived, his place smelled like heaven in the form of garlic and butter. He'd set the table by the window and lit a candle. Uncorked a bottle of red wine.

"Wow. What's the occasion?" Sam asked, stepping in, arms full with her usual work tote bag, her overnight bag, and that wary smile she wore when she wasn't sure if she should be impressed or preparing for disaster.

"Being a domestic god. What else?" Zach took both bags from her, hung the work bag, then took her hand and led her to the bedroom where he dropped her overnight bag. "Take a minute to change. Get comfy."

He'd put on the linen pants he knew she liked and a plain t-shirt. She came out in five minutes in a flowy sundress. He poured a glass of wine and handed it to her.

Over dinner, she talked about a weird customer who claimed she could tell the ending of a book by sniffing the spine. He told her about the time Deke nearly broke his nose on the brewery's loading dock during their freshman year of college.

"We were high as fuck," Zach said with a laugh. "And drunk. And being stupid."

He paused. If he told the whole story, he'd have to explain everything. Zach took a swallow of wine. "I was working part time. Unloading deliveries. Stocking supplies. We weren't supposed to be sitting out there drinking shit booze and getting high. We must've tripped an alarm or something. Next thing we know, there's a cop car with its lights on pulling up."

Sam gasped and leaned forward, as if eager to hear the rest of the story.

"We're scared shitless of getting caught, so what do we do? We hide. Deke goes to jump off the loading dock and lands on one of the empty bottles we'd just tossed down there like the clueless fuckwits we were. And he faceplants into the dock."

"Oh no!" Sam's hands flew to her mouth and her eyes went wide.

"We made it behind the dumpster and sat there till the cop left. Deke split his lip and took some skin off his nose, but he was fine. The hard part was explaining how it had happened."

The real hard part had been dealing with his mom, who had just had security cameras installed and had a recording of the whole thing.

"It's a wonder any of us survive college." Sam leaned over and kissed him. "Dinner was excellent. Thank you."

After the dishes, they didn't make it to the bedroom right away. She kissed him over the sink. Soft, then deeper. Her hands slid under his shirt. His fingers found the curve of her back. She leaned into him; fit there like she belonged.

Zach pulled her dress over her head, trailed kisses down her chest, then lifted her onto the counter.

She gasped when he pushed her thighs apart. "Right here?"

"Right now," he murmured against her skin.

It wasn't frantic. Wasn't rushed. Just deliberate. Intimate. His mouth mapping every inch of her. Her hands buried in his hair, holding him like she was afraid he might disappear.

He brought her to the edge of orgasm, then eased up and

let her calm back down before doing it again. Then again, each time pushing her right to the brink before stopping.

She was shaking all over, gasping and clawing at the counter, his head, anything within reach. And Zach stopped again.

"Oh my god! Zach!" Sam twisted her fingers in his hair and pulled, hard, until he lifted his head to look at her. "Either make me come with your mouth or fuck me so I can come on your dick."

He stood and lifted her from the counter, then set her feet on the floor and took her hand. Zach led her to the bench in the living room, and lay down.

"Someone told me she wanted to ride my face until she came several times, then be made to beg for me to fuck her pussy and ass."

Sam's smile was sweet and delicious. She leaned down and placed a finger over his lips. "Close your mouth."

She straddled his head and lowered herself with exquisite care, then she rocked against him. She came almost instantly, a hard, shuddering release that had her whole body vibrating. But she didn't stop. She shifted and twisted her hands into his hair.

"Make me come again, Zach."

Sam held his head and lowered herself back down, pressing her wet lips against his mouth. This he could give her. He could worship her body. Make her shatter into a million pieces, then put her back together. Explore every hedonistic desire she had and make her fantasies come true. And he'd enjoy every moment of it.

But he couldn't give her the type of intimacy she needed.

He wished he could. Maybe he could learn. But until then, he would give her what he could.

SAM

Sam lost count of the number of orgasms she'd had. Her skin was red and tender from Zach's beard, and still she wanted more. Zach gripped her hips and slid her down his body as he sat up. He ran a hand over his dripping beard and smiled.

"Lemme get a towel, then I need to get busy making you beg to be fucked. Hop up. I want you on your back on the bench. I'll be right back."

Sam slid off of him and Zach stood. The moment he was out of the room, she arranged herself on the bench. He came back in moments, stripped naked and wiping his face on a fluffy towel. His eyes roamed her body and he smiled.

"We're going to start with massage." He set a small bottle of oil on the table and knelt between her legs. He dribbled oil on his hands, then his fingers smoothed over her thighs, along the crease of her hips, over her belly, and finally along the sides of her pussy.

"Spread your legs wider." He stroked his fingers everywhere except right where she wanted it, slowly ramping Sam back up to a state of need as if she hadn't just come her brains out.

"Do you want more, Sam?" Zach's voice was a caress. Low and sensual, sinking into her brain. "I won't go any further until you ask for it. If you want my cock in your pussy, you need to beg and make me really believe you want it that badly."

She'd told him she wanted this, but his words still sent shivers through her. He knew all the right buttons to push.

"I want you so hungry for my cock that you beg me to fuck you. I want you crying to be filled by my cock."

His thumbs stroked closer to her clit and Sam tensed,

hoping he'd slip. Aching for his touch. Then he moved away. Back to her thighs.

"When I believe you are desperate for my cock, I'll fuck that pretty little pussy, and I won't be gentle. You like it when I get rough and demanding, don't you?"

Sam gasped as his fingers stroked up to her breasts and skimmed her nipples. "Yes. I do."

He brushed her nipples again. "I know you do. I know how hard your come when I fuck you like that. And I know what else you want tonight."

His hands slid down her belly, over her hips, and his fingers traveled the insides of her thighs, pushing between her legs until he brushed over her ass.

"You're going to beg me to fuck your ass hard and deep."

His thumbs pressed just inches away from her clit and Sam broke.

"Please Zach, I need your dick in me."

He shook his head and went back the maddeningly slow strokes up her legs. "You can do better than that. I don't believe you really need it that badly."

Sam gave him her best pout and Zach laughed. He brushed her nipples, soft, then a little harder, then soft again. Her body shook and he did it again. Something like a sob came out of her mouth and Sam sucked in air.

"Please. Oh god, please Zach. Fuck my pussy. I need your dick filling me. I need you making me come."

Zach tipped his head the side and smiled. "Closer."

He lowered his head and ran his tongue over a nipple and Sam let out a long, low cry.

"ohmygodpleasefuckme." It came out as all one word. A harsh whisper that was almost another sob. Sam hitched a breath and tried again as his tongue made another lazy circle over her nipple. "Zaaach. I need. I want. Fill me up. Fuck me. Please. Oh god please."

He didn't say a word, and he moved so quickly Sam barely had time to register what was happening. Zach shoved her legs back and thrust into her pussy hard. He didn't take it slow or ease his way in and he didn't ramp up to a hard pace. He went from zero to full tilt in one thrust.

"Is this what you needed, Sam? You needed me pounding into you until you can't catch your breath?"

She couldn't answer. All she could do was nod. He held her hands over her head and drove himself into her until their bodies slammed together and every thrust pressed her harder and harder into the bench.

Sam came again, crying at the intensity of it. Zach swiped a thumb over her face and kissed her hard, still driving into her in a steady rhythm. Sam's breath hitched and her body tensed again.

"I need you in my ass, please." Sam got the words out in short gasps. "Will you please?"

Zach's expression turned dark and dangerous. He slid one arm under her and his fingers pressed into her ass, stretching her, warming her up. She felt the slickness of lube, then more fingers.

"Please Zach. I want your dick in my ass."

He slid out of her pussy, then the head of his dick replaced his fingers and he pushed forward until he buried himself in her. He took two slow strokes, then pinned her shoulders to the bench and fucked her harder than he ever had before.

The orgasm that rocked through her left her sobbing and shaking as Zach came with a roar. He didn't pull out. Instead he cradled her in his arms and stood, holding her as she trembled against him.

He carried her to the shower and washed them both, then

dried off, and took her into his bed where he wrapped her in his arms and held her as her body slowly came down.

When Sam caught her breath she planted a kiss on his chest. "Tonight was really good."

Zach kissed her forehead and chuckled. "I told you. Domestic god."

Maybe this was all she would ever have with Zach. He might never let her into all of his world, but there was trust and intimacy that went beyond anything she'd ever known.

She kissed his lips, wishing she could tell him all she felt, but fearing it would drive him away. No. She couldn't do that. Whatever was between them, whatever Zach's feelings, she was past falling. And she didn't care.

She kissed him again. Slow. Full of all the things she couldn't say.

Zach sighed and cradled her tighter, grounding her.

"I'm trying, Sam," he said quietly, his voice raw. "I really am. I want to be better at this. With you."

She curled into his side and allowed herself to hope.

CHAPTER 18

ZACH—MONDAY, JUNE 1

The brewhouse taproom echoed with friendly laughter and the long, reclaimed-wood table was littered with glasses and the remains of their dinner. And a pile of centerpiece concepts, including a six-inch disco ball vase. All of those courtesy Ty and Nicky, who were caught up in discussing wedding decor. The choice was down to iridescent glass vases filled with seasonal flowers or disco ball vases with plumes of colorful pampas grass and dried flowers. Deke lounged with his feet propped on an empty chair, looking like he'd prefer to avoid the topic. Charlie had her tablet out, ready to take notes or share images.

Zach leaned back, arms crossed, trying to seem invested in the flower debate while his mind strayed elsewhere.

Sam.

They'd spent the entire weekend together and he hadn't been itching to have his space back. Was this what it was like? A slow slide into domesticity?

She'd smiled that morning, soft and sleepy in his hoodie,

sipping her coffee, her hair still a jumbled mess. She'd kissed him like it was easy. Like she wanted more than just him naked. Like she saw past everything he wasn't saying.

A disco ball vase landed in his lap.

"We switched topics five minutes ago." Ty grabbed the pitcher and refilled their glasses. "So, serious question. Why haven't you brought Sam around?"

Zach raised an eyebrow. "How did we get from debating the merits of disco balls to that?"

Nicky snorted. "Don't dodge."

"I'm not dodging." Zach looked down at his freshly-filled glass. "I like her. A lot. She's..." He shook his head, at a loss. "Different."

Charlie's brows lifted. "Okay, so you like her. She likes you. What's the issue?"

Zach rubbed the back of his neck. "She's real. Like, wants-to-meet-your-parents real. Wants-to-know-all-of-you real."

Deke arched a brow. "Same question. What's the issue?"

"The issue is, she needs a guy who can give her that," Zach muttered. "I'm not that guy."

Ty leaned forward. "Bullshit."

Zach looked up sharply.

"You don't want to be that guy."

"What the fuck? It's not who I am. Never was."

"Oh, that's not true," Deke added, voice calm but cutting. "You're scared. You've been playing at casual for so long now that someone's asking you to show up for real, and you're scared."

Zach didn't say anything.

Charlie studied him over the rim of her glass. "Why do I get the feeling there's more to that?"

Zach exhaled. Fuck Deke. "Freshman year. This asshole and I were college roommates." He glared at Deke, who adopted an innocent look. *Fucker.* "I was seeing this girl. Thought I loved her. Thought she loved me. Then I found out she was only with me because of..." He waved his hand around the room. "She told her friends marrying me was her career goal and retirement plan all rolled into one."

Silence settled for a minute, then Nicky scowled and shook her head.

"It's never that simple."

Of course it's not. The rest was shit Zach kept locked away where he could pretend it never happened.

"After they broke up, she and her friends review bombed the brewery." Deke's voice was soft in the quiet room. Zach glared at him then looked away when Deke shrugged. "You don't get to avoid this shit forever, man. She blasted him on social media. Posted screen shots of their sexts. Big surprise, Zach's got a kinky streak."

"Bite me," Zach muttered, but he couldn't be mad at his friend. Not really. He didn't have to like having the skeletons in his closet dragged into the open, but Deke's heart was in the right place.

"Going after me was one thing." Zach sighed. Fuck it, the door was open, he might as well turn on the light. "It made the brewery look bad. I had to explain shit to my folks. My fucking grandparents saw a picture of my dick. It's why I'm not on social media."

"Jesus." Nicky looked disgusted. She'd been through something similar of her own.

"She wasn't the only one like that. Just the worst. After that, I kept things surface. No last names, let them think I just work here, no family ties. It was easier." Zach shrugged, eyes fixed on the condensation sliding down his glass. "The rest you know. Fuckboy extraordinaire."

"People change," Charlie said, tipping her head toward

Deke. She would know. They'd started out as a casual fling. Neither of them wanted a relationship.

"So what's changed for you?" Nicky leaned over and retrieved the disco ball that still sat in Zach's lap. "You're not usually conflicted."

Zach shoved a hand through his hair and laughed. "I never wanted this."

"Again, bullshit," Ty said quietly.

There was a time when Zach would've pushed back on that, but he'd seen both Ty and Deke when they fell in love. When they met the women who changed their lives.

"Fuck you." He had to say it. "Fine, I'm fucking confused and scared and all twisted up. Sam is…"

He threw his hands in the air and slouched in his seat. He didn't have words for everything Sam was. Stunning. Funny. Smart. She got him. She made him smile. He let out a low sigh.

"I don't know that I can be that guy." His voice felt small and quiet. "The guy she wants and needs. The guy she deserves. That's not me. I don't know how to be that."

There was the raw truth of it. The reality was, Sam made him want to be that guy, and he was terrified of fucking it up. He'd said as much to her, just not all the reasons why.

"I don't want to hurt her." That was true, but it was only part of the truth. Zach closed his eyes. "I'm afraid if I fuck it up, she'll leave. And…"

His gut wrenched just thinking about it.

"Life is risk. You can coast through the world, keeping yourself closed off and risking little. It's safer." Nicky tossed the disco ball vase back at him and Zach scrambled to catch it so it didn't hit the floor and shatter. "Fuck safe. Safe is boring."

The mirrored vase caught the light, sending sparkling

beams along the walls as he rolled it in his hands. Was he boring? Predictable, maybe. But boring?

"Not that my opinion matters in your wedding, but I think this is the right centerpiece." He spun the vase in his hand like a basketball and looked at Ty.

"You didn't propose to conventional." Zach turned his attention to Nicky and nodded to the iridescent vase. Pretty. But safe. "The flowers are one step up from basic, and Nicky, love you to death, but that is not you. This?" He tossed the mirrored vase back to her.

"That thing is you. Fucking brilliant, genius, wild chaos gremlin."

Nicky flipped him off, but she was laughing. "You're not wrong. Now you just need to decide who you are."

That's the hard part.

THAT EVENING, HIS PARENTS' HOUSE SMELLED LIKE thyme and garlic, a sure sign his mother had made one of his favorite dishes. Zach sat at the old farmhouse table, nursing a glass of white wine while his mom put the finishing touches on dinner and chatted about the upcoming summer releases.

"That tropical IPA still needs a name."

Zach groaned. His least favorite part about crafting a new beer. The Cold Bottom brand meant names that edged on punny, or had double meanings.

"I suppose Tropical IPA is out?" He knew it was, but he had to ask.

His stepdad refilled his wineglass, then leaned against the counter beside his mom.

"You know better," she said, glancing up from her salad tongs as Zach groaned again. "Come get a plate."

Conversation paused as everyone filled their plates and

gathered at the table. Chicken breasts swimming in a buttery sauce full of roasted garlic and sprinkled with fresh thyme. He didn't care what was served it was served with; the chicken was heaven.

"Fine. You don't want to talk beer names; we'll change the subject."

Oh, shit.

Zach braced himself for whatever was coming next. Anytime his mother started a conversation that way, it was not a good sign.

"Sam. She doesn't know you're our son, does she?"

Zach froze with his fork halfway to his mouth.

"No," he said. "She doesn't."

His mom's expression didn't change, but his stepdad let out a slow sigh and shook his head.

"We've met her," he said. "She's smart and funny. Good business sense."

"And she has opinions about barley like she's giving a TED Talk. I was impressed."

His mom saying something like that was high praise. It didn't change the fact that he wasn't ready to sit at his parents' table and discuss his sex life. Love life. Whatever.

"You think it would be a problem? That she wouldn't handle it?" She sipped her wine and eyed him over the rim of the glass.

Zach bristled. "It's not about handling it."

"Then what is it about?" His stepdad had always been the one to challenge Zach when he got evasive.

"Can we not do this?"

His mom's lips compressed, her chin tilted up and she sat her wine glass down. The sound of her exhale was sharp and cut deep into Zach's soul. She could express disappointment with the tiniest gesture. She didn't have to shout.

His stepdad was a different story. Always gentle. Always encouraging. But not one to sit silently through bullshit.

"Have you listened to the staff? Not the newer folks. I mean the ones who've been around for a while. Folks have noticed you and Sam." He paused and took a bite of chicken.

As a teen, that trick drove Zach nuts. Now he recognized it for what it was—his stepdad was giving things a chance to sink in. Zach could go off half-cocked, like he did too often as a kid, or he could use his brain.

"Is it a problem?" That couldn't be the case. The conversation would have started differently if it were.

"The only problem is that you're not bringing her over to meet us as your parents."

There it was.

"So, I'll ask again. Why?"

Zach set his fork down, suddenly not hungry.

"Like that's gone over well in the past? I don't want to be seen as the rich kid with connections. Or risk myself or the business. I'm...Fuck...I've got a few successful beers, and yeah, I think the new one is gonna kick ass. I'm just trying to be half as good as you." He waved a hand toward his mom.

"Sam sees me as the guy who works behind the bar and makes some beers. Not the son of one of her business partners. Don't mix business and pleasure, right?"

His stepdad laughed. Actually put his fork down, leaned back in his chair and laughed. His mom reached across the table and squeezed Zach's hand.

"First, you are on the way to being better than I was or ever will be."

Zach scoffed. His mom was a rock star brewmaster who'd helped launch a few indie brands into success then launched her own brewery that got rave reviews. He didn't know how he could compare.

"I'm serious," she continued. "That new beer? That's going in the competitions this year. It's better than Over the Barrel."

She took a slow breath and reached for her husband's hand. "And not to be crude but what in the hell do you think we are? We met at a beer festival when three of my brews had taken awards and he wanted to know why I was working for other people."

Zach knew that, or at least the individual details. He'd just never put the pieces together. Who wanted to think about how their parents went from friends to fucking? Not him, that was for sure.

"We were friends and business partners first," his stepdad added.

"Sam deserves the truth anyway," Lynn said, her voice gentle but firm. "You have to let go of the past hurts if you want to be with her, really be with her. You have to let her see all of you. Not just the pieces you feel are safe. Otherwise, there's no real honesty or trust."

"I don't know how to do that," Zach admitted, his voice barely above a whisper.

His mom gave him a look so full of love it almost hurt. "Then figure it out. Before she decides it's not worth waiting for."

Zach swallowed hard and stared down at his plate. The chicken was cooling, barely touched.

The truth clawed its way up his throat, but he had no idea how to go back and tell everything now.

CHAPTER 19

The filing cabinet stuck—again. Sam gave it a little jiggle and yanked the drawer open harder than she meant to. They had the next Books and Brews coming up in two days and she was behind on the admin duties. Partly because she'd spent the entire weekend with Zach. They'd both had a busy week, but he texted regularly. Still, her body was already craving more of him.

Maybe after Books and Brews.

She was usually tired but still buzzing after an event, and Zach's brand of relaxation seemed like the perfect thing.

Sam tucked the AC warranty into place then noticed a folder that was sticking up at an odd angle. Probably what contributed to the sticking drawer.

Speaking of Books and Brews.

Carla had taken care of the renewal contract with Cold Bottom, and she was notoriously sloppy about filing. Sam tugged the folder out and the pages went flying.

Aw, man!

She scooped up the sheets. Signed contracts for the first four events, and the latest for the monthly events. The top page signed by Carla like always, but it was the name beneath it that made her stomach go still.

Lynn Muir Abell—Owner, Cold Bottom Brewery

The page slipped from her fingers and fluttered to the floor.

Muir.

The name crawled up her spine like ice water. Zach's last name. She'd only heard it once, when he'd introduced himself at the first event. He'd never mentioned it after.

Neither had Carla.

That part wasn't surprising. Carla went by first names. Always. Even if she'd heard Zach's last name, it would have gone in one ear and out the other.

Sam's mind spun. She gathered the fallen pages, put everything back in the folder and filed it away properly.

Lynn. Zach's mom. The sharp, curious eyes. Bright blue and penetrating. The wry smile that lifted at one corner. The warmth that had felt so familiar.

Sam sat frozen for a moment, hands clenched on the open file drawer, her heart suddenly too loud in her ears.

No. No, this couldn't...It had to be a coincidence. People shared names all the time. Right?

Except Zach's smile. His eyes. The laugh. The way he commanded the Cold Bottom team, and took pride in everything they did. Like he owned it. Because maybe, in a way, he did.

"Oh my God," she whispered.

She slammed the drawer shut and grabbed her phone.

Hey. Can we talk?

She stared at the screen. The bubble didn't move. No dots. No response.

Of course. It was Wednesday. Basketball. She checked the time. He'd be at Cold Bottom by now, drinking and laughing with Ty and Deke like her world wasn't unraveling.

Sam's hand shook as she sat her phone down. The ache in her chest sharpened, calcifying into something jagged.

He'd said he wanted to try, but he hadn't even given her this. Sam grabbed her purse and hurried out of the office. She told Becca she had an errand to run. She didn't think, just got in her car and drove, hoping her whirling thoughts would settle into something she could make sense of. She glanced at her phone. Still no response from Zach. She told herself to wait, give him time, but her brain screamed for answers.

Nope. Not waiting.

She turned around and headed to Cold Bottom.

The bar smelled like citrus and yeast and late afternoon sun. A staff member behind the main taproom counter recognized Sam when she walked in and waved.

"Hey, Sam. Everything okay?"

No, everything wasn't okay. Everything was very much the opposite of okay. She pasted on her best customer service smile and called up the teacher voice that remained calm in the face of anything.

"Oh yeah, just needed to catch Zach and my phone's dead."

She hated to lie. Had never been good at it. But the employee nodded and smiled, sending a twinge of guilt through her.

"They're in the old brewhouse taproom. Down the hall to the end, then left at the barrel racks."

Sam thanked him and walked to the hall like her heart wasn't hammering and shattering at the same time. She passed the kitchen, where delicious smells and the noise of a busy shift wafted into the hall, then turned left.

The door at the end of the short hall was open and laughter spilled out. Deep voices in conversation. The sound of glasses hitting a table.

Am I really going to do this? Here? Now?

She should turn around. Leave. Have this conversation another time. Another round of laughter rolled out of the room and Sam stepped to the door.

Zach was leaned back in a chair, beer in hand, grinning at something. Deke was pouring beers, and a third man, lean and sandy haired with a tidy beard, she assumed was Ty, picked up a sausage roll.

All of them looked relaxed, like this was a regular moment in a regular week. The normalcy of it hit Sam like a slap, reminding her of the narrow part of Zach's life she got to see.

She swallowed hard. If she needed any more proof that she was not included in his world, it was right here in front of her.

Ty glanced up and caught her eye. He put the food down and his expression turned serious. "Hey, Zach."

Zach and Deke looked up, following Ty's gaze. Zach's smile dropped.

"Sorry to barge in," Sam said, voice even, measured. "But I don't think this can wait."

Ty and Deke exchanged a look, like some silent bro-telepathy thing. They stood in unison. Ty gave her a nod. "Nice to finally meet you, Sam. Sorry it's like this."

Deke clapped Zach on the shoulder, not gently. "Good luck, man."

And then they were gone. The door shut behind them with a soft *click*.

Zach stood slowly. "Hey, what's going on?"

She held up her phone. "I texted. No answer."

"I didn't see it yet, I..."

"You could have told me." Her voice cracked, just a little. "You had so many chances, Zach."

His brows drew together. "Told you what?"

"That your mother is my vendor, for one. Lynn Muir Abell. Same eyes. Same mouth. You never told me Cold Bottom was your family's business."

His jaw tightened. "It's not like that..."

"Then what is it like?" she asked, her voice rising. "Because I've been walking around like an idiot believing you were slow to open up and you just needed time. Trusting you when you said you were trying. I was trying to believe in this. In you. In us."

Zach didn't move. Didn't speak.

Sam shook her head. "You let me sit in business meetings with your mother, Zach. You knew I was pitching partnership plans and still never said a word."

"It wasn't about that," he said, low.

"It's always been about that!" she snapped. "You told me you were trying. You told me you wanted to let me in. And I believed you. Because I wanted to."

She crossed her arms, trying to keep herself from shaking.

"I've opened my entire life to you. I wanted you to meet my parents." She took a shaky breath, forcing herself to stay at least semi calm. She wanted to yell and scream and cry, but if she did that, she'd never get the words out.

"I asked you to let me in," she said. Better. Softer. Not on the ragged edge of crying. "The only friend of yours I've met is Deke, and that was unintentional. I asked about your parents. You never even told me their names. Now I know why."

Sam leaned against the wall and choked back the tears. Zach opened his mouth, but no words came out. Just silence. And in that silence, something inside her broke.

"You had so many opportunities, Zach." The calm voice had gotten easier. Like she was managing to stuff all the emotions away so they didn't overwhelm her.

"I never said I was looking for something serious," Zach said, low and flat, like a line he'd repeated in his head until it came out on autopilot.

"But you knew what I wanted. And you led me to believe that you were open to it. That you were trying."

He shifted, jaw tightening, eyes flicking away.

"Not saying something doesn't mean it's not deception," she added, voice quieter now, but sharp with the edge of grief. "You've been walking a line. Careful words. Half-truths. And I bought it because I wanted to believe you might be different."

Zach took a step toward her. "Sam..."

She stepped away and raised a hand, as if warding him off. If he touched her right now, she might crumble. "Don't."

He stopped, his expression a mix of emotions. Sadness. Regret.

Sam didn't care. She couldn't allow herself to care.

Her feet moved before her heart could catch up. Out the door, down the hallway, each step echoing like the thud of a closing chapter. She walked faster, pushing past the ache in her throat, the burn of unshed tears, the crushing realization that she'd been falling alone.

Because in the end, all Zach had given her were half-truths dressed like hope.

And she was done pretending that was enough.

ZACH

The sound of Sam's footsteps echoed down the hall like a countdown.

Then...nothing.

Just silence in the room. The only sounds came from the kitchen, distant and muffled. The hum of the air conditioner.

But no Sam. Once her footsteps had faded, the only trace of her was the lingering scent of her perfume. Not her voice. Not her laugh. Not her soft, measured breath. Just a hollow stillness that made Zach feel small. Crushed.

He stayed rooted, staring at the door like she might come back through it. She didn't.

His chest ached. There was nothing poetic about it. This was heartbreak, sharp and painful. Like something inside him had been wrenched out, leaving a bleeding hole that nothing could fill.

He pressed the heel of his palm to his chest, but it didn't help.

Sam was gone. And he'd let her go without saying a damn thing useful. Just more of his tired excuses.

"Fuck," he whispered. The word barely made it past his lips.

He didn't move when Ty and Deke came back in, their voices quiet. Careful.

Ty looked at him, then back at Deke. "You okay?"

Zach didn't answer. He couldn't.

"Man," Deke said, stepping forward like he might offer something, advice, maybe, or brotherly bullshit meant to fix things. But Zach shook his head, sharp.

"Not now." They froze. Zach's voice cracked. "I need you both to go."

Ty nodded. "Okay."

No arguments. No lectures. Just a long, measured look from Deke that hit harder than any punch he'd ever taken, and then they were gone.

Zach sat down at the old tasting bar like gravity had yanked him there. The stool groaned under him and he leaned on the bar, the worn wood cool against his forearms. He stared at the scuffed surface, at a knot in the grain that looked a little like an eye.

He'd been dumped before. Plenty of times. Once, in the middle of a brunch. Another time by voicemail. He'd had a woman throw her shoe at him in a parking lot. Another had posted a breakup playlist and named it after him.

This? This was worse.

Sam hadn't yelled. She hadn't cried. She'd just looked at him like he was a stranger. Like he'd already left her, and this was the point when she acknowledged it.

And maybe he had. Not all at once. But in slow, silent ways.

He thought he was protecting himself, keeping things light. Careful. Not too deep. Not too close. It had always worked before.

But with Sam?

She'd asked for things he thought he couldn't give. She asked for the truth, for him. Instead of trusting her the way she trusted him, he'd twisted it. He'd started out playing a game that he knew was fucked up and by the time he realized Sam was different, that he was different with her, it was too late.

He scrubbed his hands over his face, jaw tight, breath shallow.

The chance had been there. The one thing he'd sworn he never wanted, offered to him in a tiny package of sunshine and laughter. And he blew it.

Because he was too scared to let her see all of him. The real him. The one who still carried scars from a girl who smiled sweet and used his name like a ladder. The one who thought it was easier to keep women at a distance than risk being hurt like that again.

But Sam had seen him. Wanted him. Not caring about who he was, or where he'd been. She just wanted to be a part of his life.

Now she was gone, and the worst part was, he couldn't blame her.

Zach's head dropped forward onto the wood, the old bar pressing into his forehead like penance. The ache in his chest pulsed harder, sharper. And it hit him, bone deep.

I'm the problem.

Not Sam's expectations. Not her desires. Not her hope.

Him.

He'd built the wall. Cemented in place with charm and distance and just enough affection to keep her close while never letting her in. And she'd tried anyway. She'd shown up, again and again, with her whole damn heart in her hands.

And he'd let it drop.

He wanted to scream. To break something. Instead, he sat there, still and wrecked, surrounded by the scent of hops and wood polish and the ghost of her.

He didn't know how to fix this, but he'd rather spend the rest of his life trying than live a single goddamn day without her in it.

CHAPTER 20

S am stood behind the counter folding bookmarks with the kind of methodical precision she normally reserved for organizing spreadsheets or realigning crooked shelves. Fold. Press. Stack. Fold. Press. Stack. The repetitive motion didn't help. Not really. But it gave her hands something to do, and that was better than sitting still, staring into the nothing of her own thoughts.

She hadn't cried.

Not when she'd walked out of the old taproom and left Zach standing there in that room full of everything he hadn't said. Not the night after, when she'd laid in her bed trying not to feel the ache and emptiness. Not even yesterday, when Carla asked if she wanted to talk and she shook her head so hard it hurt.

Now, she was just numb.

There was a hollow ache just behind her breastbone, the kind that whispered if she let herself feel even a little, it would come rushing out like a wave she'd never survive. So she didn't feel. She folded. She smiled at customers. She nodded through staff questions. She pretended the bruising inside her hadn't spread.

A croissant landed on the counter next to her bookmarks.

Sam blinked.

Carla raised an eyebrow, her hands full with two takeaway coffee cups. "You've been folding the same three bookmarks for twenty minutes and you deserve one of the really amazing coffees from Common Grounds. Plus they had those pistachio croissants you like."

Sam glanced down. Sure enough, the corners of the bookmarks were soft, one already bent from overhandling. She exhaled slowly, pressing her thumb into the paper like pressure could make it sharper again. "I'm fine."

"You're not," Carla said, setting down one of the cups and nudging it toward her. "Here. Extra whipped cream. I even had them write *not broken, just resting* on the side. Thought you'd appreciate the humor."

Sam huffed a breath that might've been a laugh in better times.

Carla stepped around the counter, leaning against the register. "Go to your folks' now. I mean it. We've got enough staff for tonight's event. I know you're already packed for the weekend."

"I don't need to go early," Sam said, her voice raw even to her own ears. "It's just mom's birthday dinner."

Carla tilted her head. "I'm not suggesting. I'm telling. As your friend. Let someone who loves you more than anything feed you wine and carbs and rub your back while you cry."

"I haven't cried."

"I know." Carla's expression softened. "That's why I'm worried."

Sam looked away, eyes blurring, not with tears, but with

the effort it took to hold them back. "I don't want to ruin her birthday."

Carla thumped her palm on the counter until Sam looked at her. "This is your mother we're talking about. What were you planning to do, cancel?"

Sam had been considering just that, even though she knew it was the wrong thing to do.

"I fell," she whispered, casting her gaze back to the bookmarks spread on the counter. "Eyes wide open. I told myself not to, and I still did it. Again."

Carla's silence was kind, not pitying. When Sam glanced up, she saw understanding there. Frustration, too, but not at her.

Sam wanted to laugh. Or scream. Anything but tears. If she let those come, they might never stop.

Instead, she nodded, eyes burning, then snagged the coffee and pastry. "Thanks for these."

Carla touched her arm. "Go home."

Sam nodded. She cleaned up the bookmarks then went back to her apartment. Her mother didn't ask questions when Sam texted to see if it was okay to arrive hours earlier than planned.

She didn't say anything when she picked Sam up at the train station, suitcase in hand and shoulders hunched like she was expecting a fight. She just pulled her daughter into a quiet hug, drove her home and handed her a glass of wine.

The first sip burned going down.

That night, Sam curled up in her childhood bed, in her old room where her books filled the shelves and posters from her favorite Pride and Prejudice movie still hung on the wall. The familiar scent of old pine floorboards and her mother's favorite wood polish filling the air. In the safety of that space, she let herself shatter.

Not a pretty cry. Not the kind with mascara tears and one small hiccup of a sob.

Sam ugly cried.

Full-body wracking sobs that she muffled with her pillow, biting it to keep from screaming. She cried until her lungs and throat ached and her face was puffy, her sinuses stuffed and gross.

In the silences between crying bouts, she heard every whispered almost he'd given her, every bit of affection she'd mistaken for progress. And she would cry again, not just for him, but for the version of herself who'd hoped. Who'd trusted.

She had taken the leap off the cliff's edge, and Zach had turned away. He didn't leap with her, and he wasn't there to catch her.

ZACH—SATURDAY, JUNE 6

Zach sat on the edge of his bed, elbows on his knees, staring at the wall like it might blink first.

The apartment felt smaller than usual. Too quiet. Too clean. Like she'd never been there at all. He wished she'd been the type to leave little things, despite his thing with the damn toothbrush. But there was nothing. No sweater slung over the back of a chair, no book with a receipt or a dry leaf as a bookmark sitting on the nightstand. And there was no laughter echoing in the kitchen while she teased him about not having a kettle and boiling water in the microwave like a barbarian.

It had only been two days. Forty-eight hours since she walked out of the taproom, the sound of her footsteps the last thing he'd heard before the silence cracked open something hollow in his chest.

He hadn't stopped replaying it. The way her face shifted from confusion to realization to betrayal, each one hitting him harder than the last. The calmness in her voice when she apologized for barging in. It had been a warning bell that he'd missed. Worst of all, the look in her eyes when she turned and walked out. It wasn't just that she didn't trust him, it was like she didn't see him anymore.

He wanted to fix it, but he didn't know how.

That afternoon, his mom had pulled him aside at the brewery, her voice low and firm.

"Carla called and requested we send someone else to Books and Brews tonight," she said. "You stay away."

Zach hadn't argued. He had nothing to say. He couldn't have faced Sam anyway, not with the disappointment and hurt in her voice still ringing in his ears. He had driven past, torturing himself with the hopes of seeing her, but she hadn't been there. At least not that he could see through the window.

He got up and dressed on autopilot. Took the bike to work, walked like a zombie into the brewhouse, then came to an abrupt stop. His mom stood next to the vat of the tropical IPA. The one that still made him think of Sam.

"Since you haven't named this thing, and I know how much you hate that part, I've got some options for you. Choose one, or I will."

She dropped a clipboard on the counter and Zach pulled in a deep breath before picking it up.

"'Love in the Tropics.' Really?" He skimmed the list. Any other time, he might have found some of the names funny or clever.

"I'm fond of 'That Girl' because this is that perfect beer you reach for all summer."

Of course his mom would like that one. The names all

reflected her sense of humor, and maybe a willingness to poke at him for what his stubbornness had cost him.

"I'm partial to 'Sun Kissed Bliss' I guess." That was the least evocative name. The rest sent daggers into his heart.

"What about 'Love Potion No. IPA'? It's clever, but I'm not sure how I feel about it."

Zach shook his head and crossed his fingers that she'd just let it drop before she got to 'Passion Punch' and 'Summer Loving.'

"I'll get Jon's opinion on 'That Girl' and 'Sun Kissed Bliss.'" She narrowed her eyes and gave him a hard look. "You better off here, or at home? Because you look like crap and you'll get no sympathy from me over that."

"Yeah, I know. Thanks, Mom." *Fuck. This is gonna be hell.* He could list this as another reason to never introduce a woman to his parents, but he'd be fooling himself. His folks were loving and supportive, if a little hard on him when he was being a dick, or foolish.

He worked half the day, then quit when he realized he'd miscalculated a formula and was about to fuck up a new batch of pilsner, and he'd never hear the end of that. He cleaned up and left, but the last place he wanted to be was home.

He climbed on the bike, intent on going for a long ride, but he wound up stopping in front of Shelf Indulgence, hoping to catch a glimpse of Sam. He gripped the handlebars, watching a group of women go into the shop. But no sign of her.

"Oh, fuck. Yeah." He'd forgotten she was supposed to be in Connecticut for the weekend. For her mother's birthday. He pulled away and pointed the bike north, getting out of the city and onto open road where he could try to forget.

Sunday passed in fits of pacing and half-written texts he never sent. He didn't sleep much and ate even less. On

Monday, he pulled up to the bookshop before it opened, fingers tapping on the gas tank until his watch switched to ten.

He saw her through the glass. Her hair pulled back in a clip. Sleeves rolled up. She opened the door and greeted a customer, nodding and smiling, and it nearly broke him. She looked fine. Calm and steady. Like the world hadn't cracked open three days ago and swallowed something special.

He waited. Trying to convince himself to walk away like he'd always done in the past. He didn't do relationships.

Except he wanted to. With Sam

He pushed the door open and Sam looked up as the bell chimed. For half a second, her eyes widened, then her expression shifted into a polite smile. Cool and distant.

"Hey," she said, voice pleasant. Friendly. Like they were colleagues. Like he was a vendor dropping off a shipment.

"Hey," he replied, throat dry. "Can we talk?"

She glanced toward the register, then the back office. "I've got a lot on my plate today."

He nodded slowly. "Maybe later?"

Her expression didn't shift. "There's really nothing to talk about, Zach."

He swallowed hard. "I just...hate how we left things. I was hoping maybe we could..." He stopped, regrouped. "Maybe we could rebuild a friendship."

She tilted her head, just slightly. "Shelf Indulgence is tied to Cold Bottom for the next several months. I don't see any reason to end a good business partnership just because my relationship with the owner's son didn't work out."

It was a non-answer. Just like the ones he'd given her. Empty. Meaningless. There was no malice in her voice. No bitterness. And that made it worse.

Whatever emotions she was dealing with didn't matter.

That answer and her tone made it clear; she was done with him.

"I'm not trying to burn bridges," she added. "But I do need to move on with my life."

Her eyes flicked to his, and for a fraction of a second, he thought he saw it, the hurt tucked beneath the calm. But it disappeared before he could catch it.

"Right," he said quietly. "Of course."

Sam gave him a nod, then turned back to her stack of inventory forms like he wasn't the guy who used to trace every inch of her skin with his fingers, or whisper filthy things into the curve of her neck.

He stood there a second longer, then left. The bell above the door chimed once, as if marking the moment.

Outside, Zach blew out a breath and stared up at the cloudless sky. It was a beautiful day, full of the promise of summer to come, and he'd never felt more empty.

CHAPTER 21

SAM—WEDNESDAY, JUNE 17

The texts started the day after Zach came into the shop, then every couple of days, he'd send another. Just enough to remind her he was still out there. Still thinking about her. Still Zach.

A photo of a bookshelf in some little hole-in-the-wall café. A short audio clip of a song they'd once danced to in his living room. A meme so dumb she nearly laughed at the preview alone.

She never opened them. Just glanced at the previews on her lock screen, let her thumb hover. Then deleted.

Once, she blocked him.

Then unblocked him twenty minutes later.

It hurt too much to look, but it hurt more to imagine him stopping. That steady flow of a Zach-shaped presence, little pulses of memory and lost love, were like phantom touches. Ghosts of a thing she thought she had, flickering through her phone like maybe if she looked the right way, it would mean they weren't over.

But they were. She needed them to be. She couldn't live on hopes and wishes and empty promises. She needed something real.

She set the last of the new releases on the tiered display and stepped back. The shop was quiet in the pre-lunch lull. Sunlight streamed through the tall front windows, sparkling in the suncatchers and painting rainbow stripes across the hardwood. Becca was down the aisle by staff picks, trying to coax a wobbly stand-up sign into submission.

Sam rubbed at a smudge on the cover of *The Summer of Second Chances*. Not for her it wasn't.

Becca beckoned her over. "Do you think this is too cheesy?"

Sam blinked. "What?"

Becca gestured to the sign. "I added twinkle lights. I think I may have broken the cheese barrier."

"You think I'm going to complain about twinkle lights?" Sam let out a soft laugh. "Besides, it's summer. There is no limit to cheese."

Becca tilted her head. "You okay?"

Sam nodded. Automatically. Reflexively. "I'm fine."

Becca studied her a beat too long, but didn't push it.

They got back to work, arranging books and straightening table runners, taping down price tags and adjusting signage. But Sam's mind wouldn't stay still.

She knew what Zach would be doing today. It was a Wednesday. That meant basketball and beers.

He'd be on the court with the friends she'd barely met, then sitting in that room getting beer after. She'd only been in the space once and could picture it so clearly it made her chest ache. A full life Sam had only been allowed to peek into, never seeing the full picture.

Her phone buzzed in her back pocket. She didn't have to look. She already knew.

Zach.

She pulled it out anyway, screen lighting up with a preview. Just a picture this time. One of those hand-lettered sidewalk signs outside a coffee shop: *All good stories begin with "And then I met a barista..."*

She stared at it. Her thumb hovered.

Then she hit delete. The ache in her chest sharpened, then dulled. Like pressing on a bruise to see if it still hurt.

God, she'd done it again.

Fallen for the man with a fortress of walls around his heart. And she'd done it with her eyes open. She'd known. She'd warned herself. Every sign was there and she'd ignored them and taken the leap anyway. Straight into the fire. No Zach by her side.

She was surviving. It hurt, but she'd make it. She'd figure out how to heal her broken heart and move on. It would take time, but it would happen. She was in no rush.

She bent to adjust a stack of romance novels and lined up their spines with practiced precision, grounding herself in the order. In the familiarity. In the simple comfort of things that didn't lie.

"Shelf looks good," Becca said gently from behind her.

"Thanks," Sam murmured. "Just needs one more thing."

She pulled out the sign she'd designed that morning. Bright cardstock with looping script that read 'Hot Guys, Happy Endings'.

For a second, she hesitated. Zach was the fantasy book boyfriend, but there had been no happy ending for them.

She slid the sign into place.

Too bad life isn't like fiction.

CHAPTER 22

ZACH—FRIDAY, JULY 3

The bar was packed, expected on the Friday before a holiday weekend. A shoulder-to-shoulder wall of bodies filled the space. The kind of crowd Zach normally thrived in. Beer flowing, music humming low behind the buzz of conversation. It all screamed Cold Bottom at full throttle.

But tonight, it grated.

Zach slipped into the old taproom and shut the heavy door behind him, letting the cooler air and calm wrap around him like armor. Thankfully, they'd skipped the explosion of red, white, and blue this year. Nobody on staff felt particularly patriotic. But business was still business and a holiday weekend in summer meant folks wanted good food, good beer, and good times. Zach just wanted good quiet.

"Took you long enough." Ty scooped the tray of food from Zach's hands and set it on the table where Nicky, Deke, and Charlie all waited. Lounging like the world hadn't gone sideways a month ago.

It was just my world that went sideways.

"We thought you got swallowed by the line." Charlie unloaded the tray, sliding plates into the center of the table.

"Or ducked out to send another sad-boy text," Deke added, smirking.

Zach settled at the table, but didn't answer. He didn't have it in him to pretend tonight. He'd been tempted to drive by the bookshop. It was first Friday, that meant Books and Brews. The duty roster showed not just bar staff, but catering as well. Busy night.

"Why did you guys stop using this space?" Charlie was staring at the light fixtures like her brain was calculating what it would take to replace them with something more modern.

"College vibes?" Deke nodded toward the dart board that still hung on one wall.

"More like we grew up and were fit for polite company." Ty grabbed one of the sandwiches and slid it onto his plate.

"That and there were no women back here," Deke added. "Zach's not the only former fuckboy in the room. Just the last to give it up."

Zach pretended to ignore the jab. If he didn't respond to it, Deke would get bored and drop it.

"Which of you three had the most sex back here?" Charlie pointed at each of them with a fry. "Probably Zach, if for no reason other than convenience."

"No sex in the brewery." Zach leaned over and snagged the fry from Charlie's fingers then stuffed it in his mouth. "That was the rule."

Ty and Deke nodded in agreement. First, it had been a rule Zach's mom laid down, and he knew better than to push certain boundaries. Later, it would have risked exposing his connection to the brewery. It was safer not to. Eventually, they started hanging out in main rooms—

finding quiet spots on the patio, or keeping to the less busy sections.

"We only started coming back here again because the brewery's gotten busier, and at least back here, you can spread out all the wedding stuff." Zach pointed to the pile of fabric samples still on the old bar, and the disco ball that had taken up residence in the window.

"You ever think of fixing it back up?" Nicky leaned back and stared at the ceiling. "It's a good size and has a cool vibe. Business wise, it is kind of wasted space."

He'd had this conversation with his folks. Several times, in fact. The idea was on their radar, but not a priority.

"This space holds maybe seventy or eighty people tops. It's a drop in the bucket compared the rest of the building." He'd spent enough time doing the party rentals and events that he could cite the room capacity of every space Cold Bottom had from memory.

"Nicky's right about the vibe." Charlie waved her hand around the room. "All that exposed brick. The beams. Technically in the cellar, but there's light from the window up there."

Her eyes lit up and she bit her lip like there was something she was trying to wrap her head around.

"Two entrances, right? The alley and into the back of the brewery." Charlie laughed and sat back. "You've got a perfect speakeasy."

Zach sucked in a breath like he'd been gut punched. *Holy shit.* He'd seen the plans Sam and Carla had. Listened as Sam spoke of their dream of a bookish speakeasy. Shelves of banned and controversial books, moody lighting, vintage furniture, and themed cocktails.

"Yeah," he managed to croak the word out. "I guess we do."

It took no effort at all to imagine the renovation needed to outfit the room the way Sam wanted. It would work. He could picture her here. Leaning against the bar. Biting her lip to keep from smiling.

He missed her so fucking much his entire body ached with it, and he had no one to blame but himself.

The conversation shifted around him, something about Nicky's latest vendor screw-up, but Zach barely heard it until Charlie leaned forward, elbows on the table, and fixed him with a look that said Zach needed to brace himself because what she was about to say was going to hurt.

"You know she's not going to wait forever, right?"

Zach didn't answer. He didn't even want to think about it.

Charlie continued, voice even. "If you can't give her what she wants, let her go. I mean, really let her go. Quit sending her texts like she's still yours. You don't even know if she reads them."

Zach looked up, caught off guard. "She turned off read receipts."

"Can't imagine why," Charlie said, but she'd turned the sarcasm down to low. "So maybe stop trying to keep a foot in that door if you're not going to walk through it."

That landed harder than Zach expected.

Nicky, who'd been mostly quiet about Sam, spoke up from the other side of the table. "But if you can give her what she wants, then do it. All in. No hiding. No half-assing. And be ready to hear no. Because real love doesn't come with guarantees."

The silence that followed felt loaded. Deke took a long drink, then leaned forward. "We've all been dumbasses, man. You've just been dumb longer than most."

"Thanks. Here we go with the intervention thing again."

But there was no bite behind Zach's words. His friends weren't wrong.

He'd spent his whole life building walls. Hiding the Abell name, always waiting for the other shoe to drop, the ulterior motive to reveal itself. That old girlfriend, the one who'd played him like a game of chess just to get close to the family name and money, had left scars that shaped his entire personality. Every woman since, he'd kept at a distance. Fun to play with, but not playing for keeps.

Until Sam.

He'd let her closer than anyone. And she'd asked for the one thing he didn't know how to give—everything.

He thought back to the last thing his mom had said to him, earlier that week. Pulled him aside during a tasting and stared at him the way only mothers could, like she could see every secret written across his skin.

"You seemed happy for a while. When's the last time you let yourself feel that?"

And then his stepdad, that same day. Not as soft, but still kind. "You want to hide in the brewhouse forever, that's your call. But don't pretend you didn't lose something that mattered."

Zach had brushed them both off. Laughed. Changed the subject.

Tonight, in the space that had become his refuge, with the friends he trusted? The ache was dull and constant in his chest and his friends looked at him like he was the world's biggest fool. His laughter dried up.

For the first time, he looked and didn't just see the history. He saw the potential for a space that transported people and made them feel like they'd stepped back in time, or were living in a story.

Sam's bookish speakeasy.

The idea took hold and settled in his soul. A space that felt like Sam. Her magic and warmth.

"You've got that look on your face." Ty's voice cut into Zach's imagination and he shook himself.

"I'm just chilling." But he wasn't. His mind had gone down the road of how to make the space work.

"Nah, that's the face that says you've had a wild idea and you're trying to figure it out." Ty leaned back and laughed. "Nicky does the same thing when she's got a new art project in her head."

Zach set his beer down and stood, pacing the room, thoughts swirling in his head. The bookish speakeasy was a great idea, and he could make it possible for her.

"I need help."

Four sets of eyes fixed on him and Zach took a deep breath.

"I have an idea, and I need opinions to make sure I'm not...Fuck, I dunno."

He needed to make sure he was doing this for the right reasons. If he was going to offer the space, it had to be with no strings attached. It had to be Sam's space.

Maybe if he hadn't fucked up, he could have been a part of it. The whole thing could have been theirs. For the first time, Zach realized he wasn't afraid of forever with Sam. He was terrified of a forever without her.

"Just, hear me out."

No more half-assing. No more fear.

Just Sam. Or nothing.

CHAPTER 23

S am stood behind the register, her fingers idly tracing the grain of the countertop as Carla rang up a stack of paperbacks for one of their regulars. The bell over the door jingled as he left, a warm breeze drifting in behind him, and for a moment the shop felt perfectly still—sunlight slanting in through the front windows, dust motes dancing in the air like tiny sparks.

It had been forty-four days since she walked out away from Zach with her heart in shreds and her dignity barely intact.

Forty-four days of pretending. Of smiling at customers and replying to texts and getting out of bed in the morning like everything was fine. Of not crying, not cracking, not letting the grief drag her under.

It had almost worked, but today, something shifted.

Maybe it was the sunlight. Maybe it was the quiet between customers. Or maybe it was the dull, hollow ache in her chest finally making room for something else.

Not peace. Not forgiveness. Not yet.

But urgency.

She needed something to do. Something real. Something bigger than this ache that refused to let go of her ribs. And not just to keep busy, but to feel like she was building again. Moving forward instead of standing still.

"Hey," she said suddenly, turning toward the back table where Carla was updating the inventory spreadsheet. "You remember what we said we'd do if the shop ever started turning a real profit?"

Carla didn't look up from the screen. "Get matching tattoos and run away to Paris?"

"No," Sam said, cracking the first genuine smile she'd felt in weeks. "Well, maybe. But I meant the speakeasy."

That got her attention. Carla looked up, eyes sharp. "You're serious?"

"I think I am."

Sam pulled out the chair across from her and sat, heart kicking up in her chest and not from panic, for once, but purpose.

"Books and Brews is thriving. The event nights are packed; the new book clubs are doing well. Our banned book displays get more attention than half the influencer campaigns. And I'm still walking around like I've been gutted."

She paused, voice lowering. "I need something. We've built the foundation of our dream and I think we're ready. Have you been to Red Emma's? Their bookshop is amazing. We can do something similar, but our brand. Our vibe. Shelves filled with books people are trying to erase. Cocktails named after authors they're trying to ban."

Carla leaned back slowly, studying her. "You want to actually do this."

Sam nodded. "We've talked about it for years. Waiting for

the right time. Waiting until we had the bandwidth. But there's never going to be a perfect time. And with everything happening right now?" She gestured to the stack of books beside her, all titles that had appeared on censorship lists in more than a dozen states. "We need a place like this. A place that says we're not afraid of stories that make people uncomfortable."

Carla blinked once, then nodded, slow and certain. "I love the idea, but there's something you need to know. I've been waiting to share the news until we were sure everything was right."

"Oh, my god. Are you...?" Sam crossed her fingers. Carla and Emmy deserved every happiness.

"Pregnant," Carla said with a nod. "About seven weeks. We confirmed it last month, but it was too soon to share. I was planning to hold off saying anything for at least another month, but it might change how you feel about doing the speakeasy right now."

A laugh bubbled out of Sam before she could stop it, light and sudden and unsteady. It felt like a window cracking open in a room that had been closed too long.

For the first time in weeks, her smile didn't feel borrowed. She rushed to hug Carla, squeezing her friend and kissing her cheek.

"I am so happy for you! And I'll keep quiet." She crossed her lips, but couldn't stop the smile. Sure, Zach still haunted the edges of her head and heart. His laugh. His touch. His stupid smug face when he made her coffee or tea just right. But right now, in this moment, that ache was finally something she could hold in one hand, instead of drowning in it.

"I still want to work on it," Sam said, finally. "If you're okay with that. We don't have to do anything yet, but I can start the research. Running the numbers. Doing a business plan."

Sam wasn't whole yet, but it was a start. She couldn't rewrite the past, but she could build something new. Something that mattered. Something that lasted.

Something real.

CHAPTER 24

ZACH—JULY 29

Convincing Carla wouldn't be easy.

She'd protected Sam like a damn guard dog since the breakup, and she had every right and reason to. He'd hurt Sam. It didn't matter that it was his fear that caused it, that didn't make the bruise he'd left on her heart any smaller.

Carla agreed to meet him at brewery after closing. She walked in, arms crossed and her expression flat enough to make him sweat. "If this is some half-baked apology or another bullshit plea for forgiveness, don't waste my time. Or Sam's."

Zach didn't flinch. Not this time.

"It's not that," he said, then exhaled slowly. "Well. Okay, it is that. But not just that."

She raised an eyebrow.

"It's my grand gesture," he said.

That got her attention.

"I know I fucked up. And I know Sam doesn't owe me anything. But this...it's about more than trying to win her back. It's about giving her something she deserves. Something that was dreamed up long before she ever met me."

Carla narrowed her eyes, but the corners of her mouth twitched. "Did you use the phrase 'grand gesture' at me?"

"I did," he said. "Sam said you normally read romantasy, but I remember asking you about a book you were reading once. Not a fantasy at all. You called it your emotional support paperback. I listen when people talk to me."

She gave him a long look. "That book had a badass arson investigator heroine and a cinnamon roll hero. You are not a cinnamon roll, Zach."

He had no idea what a cinnamon roll was, but if he had to guess, he imagined it was the opposite of a shadow daddy.

"I'm working on it."

That made her snort.

"Okay, I'm listening."

"It's easier to show." He led the way to down the hall and opened the door. Carla walked in and Zach didn't have to say a word. She crossed to the middle of the room and turned in a circle.

"You have my attention."

By the time Zach explained everything, he had her blessing, and her promise to help.

Now he just had to not fuck things up again and hope Sam was open.

The next afternoon, Zach stood in the partially-renovated taproom, sweating. Not because of the heat, though it was pushing ninety outside, but because he was standing there, heart hammering, waiting for the woman he loved to walk through the door.

Loved.

He hadn't said it yet. Not out loud. Not even when he was

alone. But it was the truth, and it had been eating a hole in his chest for weeks.

This room was his way of showing it without crowding Sam.

The taproom looked nothing like it had before. He and his stepdad had cleaned and refinished the old bar, and fresh paint warmed the walls, soft cream and rich tones that made him think of Sam. The biggest project so far was the custom-built shelves lining most of the room. Each ready to be filled with banned books, rare editions, and whatever the hell else Sam wanted.

It was far from complete, the fireplace was still a mess, he hadn't replaced the light fixtures, and the kitchen needed to be gutted and redone from scratch. But it was a start.

He'd scoured vintage shops for a few pieces to set the mood. A thick rug in one corner. A set of mismatched chairs and a sturdy square table. Hints of what the room could become.

It wasn't perfect yet, but it was hers if she wanted it.

Footsteps echoed down the hall, then Carla's voice, cheerful and quick, and Sam's quieter reply. The door opened. Carla didn't come in.

Sam did.

She stopped in the threshold, blinking as her eyes adjusted to the low, golden light.

Zach stayed where he was, his hands shoved deep in his pockets so he wouldn't do something stupid. Like reach for her.

"Hi," he said.

Sam didn't speak. Just looked around, her expression unreadable. But she didn't leave.

"I wanted to show you this," Zach said, keeping his voice low. "I've been working on it since..." He had to stop and take a breath, then swallow past the lump in his throat. "Since I realized I didn't just let you go. I let go of everything that mattered."

Her lips compressed and her chest rose on a shuddering breath.

"This space—" He gestured around "—it's for you. For the speakeasy. For the dream you and Carla have had since college. You can call it what you want. Stock it how you want. Run events, pop-ups, late-night readings. Whatever you want."

Still, she said nothing. Zach took a deep breath and pressed on.

"It has two entrances. One from the brewery, and one from outside. Both are a little hidden. It's not a Cold Bottom brand, it's just the space, and a business partnership if you're interested. Your name. Your business. Your brand."

He exhaled hard, the words scraping his chest. That was the easy part.

"I know I hurt you," he said, his voice cracking. "And I'm sorry. I didn't mean to lie. No, fuck that. I justified it all to myself, and that was wrong. I was scared. Scared of letting you in. Scared of what it meant if I did. None of that is an excuse. I used my fear and my pain to keep you at a distance, and I am sorry."

He paused, swallowed, looked down.

"So, yeah. This is for you. No expectations. No strings. I just... I wanted to do something for you. To show you that I see you. I believe in you. And I'm so goddamn proud of you."

He almost said it. The words 'I love you' were right there. Tight in his throat, ready to burst out. But he bit them back. He needed to offer this without it being attached to him in that way. If she took the space and never looked back, he'd survive it. Bleed, maybe. But he'd survive.

SAM

The first thing Sam had noticed was the light.

It poured in through the high windows in golden waves, brushing over the exposed brick and warming the wide-plank floorboards. There was a feeling in the room. Something hushed and sacred. Hidden like some secret waiting to be discovered.

She turned, taking the room in, her breath catching in her throat.

The smell of new paint mingled with the woodsy scent of aged barrels and something floral, lavender maybe. The floor-to-ceiling shelves and a rolling ladder.

Her fingertips brushed over the back of a velvet chair, deep green and tufted, with scrolled wooden arms that looked like it belonged in an old study. A thick rug, rich with pattern and worn in just the right way, anchored the corner.

Zach stood near a gleaming wood bar tucked against the back wall and looking like he hadn't slept in days. A little scruffier than usual. Eyes darker, shadowed.

God, she'd missed him. And she hated that she had.

She hated that the ache she'd spent nearly two months trying to bury rose up in her throat just looking at him. Because of course he'd done this. Of course he'd built something perfect. For her.

He stood there, watching her take it all in, remaining quiet after the bomb he'd dropped.

Is there such a thing as a good bomb?

The room was atmospheric. Intimate. Exactly what she and Carla had dreamed about in college dorms and greasy diners and late-night planning sessions. A place for banned books, controversial stories, under-the-radar authors. A space for bookish rebellion disguised as a cozy community space.

She could already imagine the chalkboard menu—literary-themed cocktails, a rotating menu of small bites, paired tastings with book discussions. Her mouth twisted before she could stop it. She could also picture Zach, behind the bar, cocky as hell, all flirty banter and charm.

She closed her eyes and let out a sigh. Even here, even now, her heart knew what it wanted.

When she finally turned to face him, he didn't rush her. Just stood there, hands in his pockets, expression open and so damn vulnerable it made her ribs ache.

"I don't know what to say," she said quietly.

"You don't have to say anything," he said. "Whether I'm in your life or not. I wanted you to have this."

Tears pricked the corners of her eyes, but she didn't let them fall. Not yet. "You did all this for me?"

"I wanted to show you I believe in you," he said. "Not just in what we were. In what you are. What you're building."

Her chest felt too small. "You got Carla to help."

"With getting you here? Yes, and she made me work for it," he said, a small, rueful smile pulling at the corner of his mouth. "The rest? It's all from memory of what you talked about wanting."

Sam blinked hard, forcing the tears back. "Really?"

That he'd done that was mind blowing. He'd built something so perfect based on what he recalled from her rambling descriptions of this dream was something else entirely. He knew her. Understood her. There was more than just sex between them.

"I need to know everything." She gripped the back of the chair and pulled in a slow breath and kept her eyes on his face.

"No secrets," Zach replied, and the truth of his words rang in the room. "Not from you."

Sam dared to let a sliver of hope into her heart.

"This is beautiful."

"It's yours," he said.

She inhaled deeply, and looked around. There was still work to be done, but it was good. Better than good. And maybe, they could be, too.

"I want it. The space. The speakeasy. We're doing it."

Something passed through his expression, relief, disbelief, maybe a flicker of hope, but he didn't move toward her. He waited.

They would have to rebuild as well, but Zach had taken the first steps. Big ones, at that. "I guess you can come to the next Books and Brews. If you want. Our regulars miss their favorite Viking shadow daddy."

That made him laugh, soft and sweet. "Not a cinnamon roll, huh? And thank you."

She laughed, the sound bouncing off the walls. "You are most definitely not a cinnamon roll. Do I even want to know how you know that term?" She looked around the room again and tipped her head. "Okay, maybe there's a gooey center to you. But it's spicy, for sure."

This felt right. This felt like them, only better. Like walls had come down. Sam stepped forward then, closing the distance between them. Her fingers brushed his forearm. The contact sent a rush of feeling through her so sharp it hurt. She hadn't touched him in so long. Hadn't let herself imagine what it would feel like.

He pulled her into a hug slowly, like he was afraid she might vanish if he moved too fast. She sank into it. His arms came around her, strong and trembling at the same time.

The moment he closed his arms around her body, the last of her walls crumbled.

"I love you," he whispered into her hair.

Sam stilled. Her heart stopped and started again.

"What?"

He pulled back just enough to meet her eyes. "I love you. I want you in my life. All of it. Every piece. I know I don't deserve a second chance, but if you give me one..."

Her mouth found his before he could finish the sentence.

The kiss wasn't delicate. It was two months of longing and weeks of silence and a fire that had never gone out. He gripped her waist like she was an anchor. She wrapped her fingers in his shirt, tugging him closer until their bodies aligned and her world felt right again.

Clothes came off in a haze of breathless laughter and urgent hands as Sam backed him toward the square table she definitely had not had naughty thoughts about. They christened the table, the rug, and the bar, the air thick with heat and want and relief. It wasn't just sex. It was a homecoming. It was one body remembering another.

After, as they lay tangled on the rug, her head on his chest and the afternoon sun sliding across the floor, Sam traced the line of his beard with her fingertip. Not as tidy as his usual.

"I love you too," she whispered. "You infuriating, broody, emotionally stunted pain in the behind."

Zach laughed, holding her tighter.

"God, I missed you," he murmured.

"I missed me too, but I'm finding my way back."

She rolled and looked at the room, their room now, and smiled. "And I missed you. I missed us."

This was how new chapters started. With truth. With hope. With heat and heart and the belief that sometimes, when you dared to try again, love was a story that was worth writing twice.

EPILOGUE

T he next April

ZACH

The sun hung low over the ocean, spilling molten gold across the waves, and the breeze carried the scent of salt and frangipani flowers. The slow rhythm of the surf providing a perfect soundtrack.

Zach could not have crafted a more perfect day. It was like the universe was giving a thumbs up to his vacation plans. Jamaica was hot, but it was a welcome break from a chilly Baltimore spring.

Sam walked beside him barefoot, her sundress fluttering around her thighs. She tossed her head back in laughter, sending his heart soaring. Just like it always did.

A year ago, he'd been coasting through life. Chasing distractions. Dodging responsibility. Telling himself he didn't need more. Didn't want it. Then he'd met her at that first

Books and Brews. She challenged everything he thought he knew, wrecked every lie he'd told himself, and turned his world upside down.

He couldn't imagine a future without her in it.

They'd spent the last few days doing all the things they were too busy for at home—long naps, lazy mornings, sunrise sex, reading by the pool, drinking ridiculous cocktails with umbrellas. Zach even let her apply sunscreen to his ears without protest. Growth.

The ring in his pocket had been burning a hole in his thoughts for months.

He'd booked this trip quietly. No one knew. Not his parents, not his friends, not even Sam's business partner Carla. The only thing he'd shared was that they were taking a much-deserved week off.

Sam had been carrying an extra burden with Shelf Indulgence as Carla's pregnancy progressed. They were thrilled when she gave birth to a healthy baby girl in February. Zach's new beer, That Girl, claimed not one, but three awards and they'd been struggling to keep up with demand. Books and Brews was still going strong as a monthly event, and after nine months of planning and hard work, the bookish speakeasy was set to launch in the fall.

Life had been busy. He'd wanted a quiet moment with Sam. Just the two of them. A beach. A sunset. The spot he'd scouted earlier. A small stretch of sand tucked away in the shade of a copse of trees. The perfect spot.

He spread a blanket and Sam plopped down, stretching her legs, sighing like her whole soul had just relaxed. "This place is unreal."

"You're unreal," he said.

She laughed, rolling her eyes. "Cheesy."

"I'm a brewery owner. I live for cheese."

His heart stuttered as he settled onto the blanket next to her.

"Zach?" Her voice softened. The look on her face said she knew something was up.

"I had a whole speech," he said. "About the first time I saw you. About how I thought you'd be a challenge, then later, how I feared you'd wreck my life, and both are kinda true."

She blinked, her breath catching.

"I thought I knew what love looked like, and that I didn't want it. Turns out, I was wrong. Love looks like you. Bright laugh. Messy hair. Smarter than anyone else in the room."

Zach had to stop and regain some degree of self-control before he continued. "You tore my world apart, flipped it upside down, and complicated it in all the best ways. Your love is the only thing that matters to me."

He got to one knee and pulled out the ring. Simple. Classic. Like her.

"I love you, Sam. I trust you. I want to build a life with you. The brewery, the bookshop, the speakeasy, and whatever else we can imagine. So long as I have you, always."

He took her hands in his and swallowed hard. He was confident in her answer, but nerves still trickled along his spine.

"Will you marry me?"

SAM

Sam stared at him, chest tight, heart stretched wide. This man. This moment. This life they'd built from the wreckage of who they'd been a year ago. He took her breath away.

"Like there's a question?" She tugged his hands, needing his arms around her. Needing his kisses. "Yes, Zach! Yes."

He stood in a rush, scooping her into his arms and kissing

her as the sun set over the water. This was bliss. Whatever pains they'd been through seemed worth it to have the kind of happiness she'd known since they got back together last July.

Zach put her back down and slid the ring onto her finger with hands that trembled just a little. She kissed him again, slow and sure, then tucked herself into his side as they settled on the blanket.

The sky blazed orange and pink over the ocean. The kind of view that begged for promises.

"So..." she said after a while, tracing her fingers over the back of his hand. "Kids?"

Zach smiled, no hesitation. "Not for me."

Relief unfurled in her chest. "Me neither."

He turned toward her, brushing a thumb over her knuckles. "And pets?"

She laughed. "Absolutely not."

They both grinned. No surprises there. They were often so in sync that it was almost eerie.

She quieted, one tiny doubt nagging at her. "Will you be happy being monogamous? Like really happy? Will I be enough?"

The weight behind the question lingered. Not because she didn't trust him, but because marriage meant the rest of their lives. She didn't want anyone but Zach. Wanted to grow old with him, and she needed to know he felt the same.

His answer came without pause.

"It's been a change, but I don't miss that life. I don't need anyone else. You're it for me. You're more than enough. I wasn't exaggerating when I said you were a dream come true."

Zach cupped her face in his hands and kissed her gently. "I love you and you are my everything."

She leaned in and kissed him again. "Took you long enough to figure it out."

Sam breathed the moment in, the surf rolling like a breath, the ring a solid presence on her hand, her heart impossibly full.

"Think we'd get in trouble if we..." She cast her eyes at the overhanging branches, then down the empty beach.

"Worth the risk." His hand slid up her thigh and Sam lay back, spreading her legs for him.

There was no fear left. No doubt. Just the quiet certainty that whatever shape their life took, it would be real. Honest. Passionate. Theirs.

And that was everything.

---------- ♥ ----------

CHECK OUT BOOK 1 OF CHARM CITY CONNECTIONS

CHAPTER 1

NICKY—FRIDAY, MARCH 29

Nicky Bissett pushed through the glass doors into Ceremony Coffee and paused, trying to decide if she loved or hated the place. If the Apple store went into the cafe business, this is what it would look like. All clean lines, light wood, smooth surfaces, and no visible menu. The rich smell of heaven—or coffee, same thing—urged her on.

Splurging on a cuppa when job hunting and living on savings and whatever art pieces sold on her Etsy page wasn't the smartest choice, but Gramps was a tea drinker and there was no way she was doing an interview without her preferred caffeine-delivery mechanism.

Nicky approached what looked like the place to order and gave the person standing there her best smile. At least they had a name tag. Complete with their pronouns—they/them. Cool.

"Hi Jace. I've never been here before. Help?"

She braced for the cooler-than-you clerk to roll their eyes at the noob. Instead, she got a warm smile.

"Welcome." Jace pointed to a little easel on Nicky's left. "Menu's there. Or tell me what you want. Whatever pastries we've got are on display."

The rumbling of her stomach at the mention of pastries was a not-so-pleasant reminder she'd exited the house in a hurry this morning. Not the way she wanted to go to an interview.

The bell over the door jingled, pulling Nicky back to her caffeine need.

"What's good?"

"Everything. I'm fond of a flat white, but I'm betting that's not your style. You like it sweet, or less so?"

Nicky leaned over for a closer look at the pastries and caught sight of a polished tan leather shoe tapping behind her. She cast an eye back at Jace, who showed no signs of impatience.

"A little on the sweet side."

The shoe tap-tapped again. Nicky dared a quick glance over her shoulder. That shoe belonged to a pair of crisply pressed royal blue trousers.

Great. An impatient suit type.

"I'm thinking salted caramel latte with a vanilla coffee." The voice came from the cloud of steam by the espresso machines.

"Perfect! Thanks." Nicky straightened up and Jace typed in her coffee order.

"Gabe's our barista and they have a talent for making the right drink for people. Did you want a pastry?"

The unmistakable sound of shoe tapping penetrated Nicky's brain through the hum of conversations in the shop. She shot another look back. The edge of a camel overcoat, flung over the owner's arm, and long fingers that twitched in time with the toe tapping.

Nicky decided on a cinnamon roll, paid for her order, thanked Jace, grabbed her pastry and prepared to skirt past Mr. Impatient and wait for her coffee.

She turned and stopped in her tracks. The polished and pressed everything didn't end with the shoes and trousers. The man was so model perfect he could have been on the cover of a magazine.

He stepped past her, swiped his card, said something to Jace and called a hello to Gabe before turning a megawatt smile on Nicky, sending a little shiver of pleasure along her spine.

She had zero interest in getting to know yet another Joe Preppy, but there was no harm in admiring.

And there is a lot to admire.

Which she did, from the tips of those shoes to the top of his head. His rich buttery cream shirt looked so crisp it had to be starched, and a tie in swirling blue tones was in some complicated knot and centered with mathematic precision. Dude even had a pocket square—shades of gold and blue and red.

Lush sandy hair swept back from a strong brow and pale green eyes that were focused on Nicky with a look of amusement that said he'd caught her checking him out.

Feeling a little guilty for ogling, she squeaked an apology and hurried to the end of the counter to collect her coffee. She gave a nod of thanks to Gabe and turned to go. The faster she got away from those dangerous eyes and devastating smile, the better.

Something hard thwacked into her back and the unthinkable happened. Nicky's hand tightened on her cup, the lid popped off, and the hot vanilla-salted-caramel concoction sprayed down her top.

"Jeez lady, watch where you're going!"

A man in a rumpled suit and badly done tie hitched his backpack onto his shoulder. The same pack that had hit Nicky.

Coffee dripped down her hands, and her shirt clung to her chest. The smug expression on the man's face said he knew whose fault this was, but wouldn't admit it.

The buzz of conversation from the tables didn't stop. No one gasped or gawked. Except for Joe Preppy. He stood there with a worried look on his face, probably concerned he'd gotten coffee on his impeccable outfit.

She dropped her now empty cup onto the counter and glared at the man who'd caused the whole mess. He shifted his backpack and scoffed, turned away and walked toward the exit.

So much for Baltimore being Charm City. More like jerk city.

"Dude," she called after him. "Seriously?"

The guy flipped her off and shoved through the door.

She grabbed the napkins Joe Preppy offered and muttered a thank you before trying to mop herself up. It was only her shirt; she'd figure something out. She did not want to go home and change. Her grandfather would use it as an opportunity to get more jabs in.

"Are you okay?" Joe Preppy leaned in and spoke in soft tones. Up close, those eyes were mesmerizing.

Great. First hot guy I see in the city and I'm dripping latte.

"Oh, yeah. Twelve ounces of hot coffee to the chest is a great way to start the morning before a big interview." She needed to dial down the sarcasm. She held the handful of now soaked napkins up. "Thanks for these."

Gabe came over with a trash bag and an offer of more

napkins. They apologized for the rude customer before they started wiping the spill.

"I'm good, thanks. Rude dude isn't your fault. May I use the restroom?"

Jace handed her a towel. "It's down the hall."

Safely in the bathroom, Nicky cleaned up as best she could. Luckily, it was a chilly morning, and she had a button up cardigan in her bag that covered most of the coffee stain. Too bad she hadn't grabbed a scarf.

This would not ruin her day. She hadn't gone through the last several months of hell to move back to her grandfather's house for everything to go south like this.

She came out to find Joe Preppy leaning on the counter chatting with Gabe. A bag of cookies and two coffee cups at his elbow. His short, perfectly groomed beard seemed at odds with the preppy look. Okay, maybe Mr. Preppy had a wilder side.

"Thanks for the help there." She fumbled her wallet from her bag, ready to order another coffee, but he pushed a cup toward her.

"Gabe already made a fresh one." His voice was rich and deep, and lacked the distinctive Baltimore accent. He shot a smile at the barista then stood and the friendly grin didn't just transform into the megawatt beam from earlier. It became pure, panty-melting smolder.

Good grief, he's tall. Long and lean and hot AF. Nicky returned his smile.

"I don't know how much help I was. I should have stopped the guy and made him pay for the cleaning bill. But I can do this." He pulled a scarf from somewhere—big surprise, it coordinated with the rest of his outfit—and handed it to Nicky.

Oh great. On top of being drop dead gorgeous, he was the

savior type. Not her thing. The preppy Ivy League look more often than not went with a personality to match. Witness her grandfather and her ex-fiancé. No thanks. She was here to put her life back in order after that disaster of a relationship.

Her fingers closed on the soft and silken scarf. "Thank you, but I can't…"

Joe Preppy's lips curled into a half smile. "Please. You said you had a big interview. It shouldn't be ruined by a coffee shower." The half-smile cranked up to near blinding levels, and Nicky grinned in response. His deep voice somehow soothed her frayed nerves. "I'm guessing you're not from around here."

He was all legs, and that suit was so well tailored it should be a sin. There was the dash of cold water she needed. It didn't matter how hot he was. Finding a job and a place to live were her priorities. Men were not on her radar.

"Sort of. I spent my childhood here, but I've been in DC for years." She hauled in a deep breath. "You did the right thing. My battle to fight. That kind of jerk? Being him is its own punishment. Thanks for guarding my coffee."

The colorful scarf now spilling across her lap would cover what the cardigan couldn't. She sighed and looped it around her neck, trying not to get distracted by the scent of pepper and nutmeg.

"And thanks for this. See you around."

Nicky boogied for the door before she was tempted to stay and chat with hot Joe Preppy.

"Hold up." His voice stopped her in her tracks. She turned to find him waving a napkin at her.

TY

Bright blue eyes bored into his and Ty Lake forgot how to speak. He needed to get control of himself. It wasn't like he hadn't seen a pretty woman before; this one happened to be beyond pretty. She looked like an elf princess who'd stepped out of some Tolkienesque fantasy.

"You've got coffee on your boot." Ty pointed down and her gaze followed his finger. *Oh, screw this.* He knelt and swiped at the coffee splotch on a pair of well-worn but shiny yellow Doc Martens. *Where in the hell is she interviewing?*

"Oh." A nervous laugh sounded above his head. The utter ridiculousness of the scene clicked, and Ty stood.

"Nice boots. I'd hate to walk into the office with coffee all over my shoes."

As silly as he felt, it must have hit the right note for her because her laugh changed to something richer and throatier.

"I've got a lot to thank you for today." She held up her booted foot as if admiring the impromptu polish job. "I'd shake your hand, but..." She spread her arms wide—laden with a cup of coffee, a sparkly umbrella, and an eye-searingly bright yellow raincoat. Silver bangles jangled on her wrists and the turquoise streak in her hair matched the stone in her necklace. The same shade as her eyes, which were an uncanny blue.

She was out the door in a swirl of color and the world got a little less bright as she disappeared around the corner.

He'd come in early to have time to sit and enjoy his coffee before his day started, but now he didn't have time to hang around. Thanks to a pixie looking whirlwind in human form.

"Who, or maybe what, was that?" Ty gave a quick glance toward the door as Gabe slid a full drink carrier across the counter at him.

"Figured you'd be ready for these, and I dunno. First time I've seen her."

Ty grabbed the coffees and his bag of cookies and headed out, pausing at the door. "First, I thought MICA student, but..." He glanced down the street the way she'd gone. "She was headed the wrong way for that."

Jace came in wielding a mop and swiped at the last of the coffee spill. "She did mention an interview." They gave a one shoulder shrug as they dipped the mop into the bucket. "She seemed nice."

Jace was right. Even after getting hot coffee spilled down her front, on what was an important day, she'd been all smiles and charm. Ty pushed out the door and broke into a brisk walk.

At the Walters Art Museum, he swung through the front lobby, his footfalls echoing on the hard marble, and dropped the extra coffees and cookies with Bill, the morning guard. Ty waved at the crew staffing the information desk before hurrying out the back, then down the street to the rowhome that housed the museum offices.

He couldn't get the coffee shop woman out of his head. Which was ridiculous. He didn't go for the Bohemian type. She'd looked amazing, but where was she interviewing, dressed like that? What adult bought a bright yellow coat?

The same adult who wears bright yellow boots for a job interview.

Ty gathered his notes and headed to the director's office. Being late to a meeting with the notoriously particular doctor was not a good career move.

"Have a seat," Dr. Mason greeted as Ty walked through the door of the oak paneled office lined with books, framed photos of distinguished museum guests, and a surprising lack of art. He took the seat across from Mason.

"You're looking to leave development." Mason's tone of voice made it clear it wasn't a question. Ty had been clear from the beginning that he envisioned a career in museum work but he'd never told anyone here that it included leaving development.

"You've worked with Hopkins on repatriation research," Mason continued. "We have a divided board here. We've done quite a bit of work and about half in favor of more research, while the other half is content with what we've already done."

Ty already knew the board was split between traditionalists who avoided change, and a more progressive group seeking ways to keep the museum relevant to a younger crowd.

"I don't disagree, sir." *Where the hell is he going?*

"I'd like you to dig into our options from all angles—including PR and long-term cost-benefit analysis."

Wonderful. More work. Great start to the weekend. What Mason was proposing was a full-time job, one which was well above his pay grade.

"I know it's a lot, and it's outside your normal duties," Mason said, as if reading Ty's mind. "The work you do is impressive. Don't think it's gone unnoticed."

Dismissed. Without a chance for discussion and without Ty agreeing to take it on. Not that he'd refuse. It wasn't a title he could put on his CV, but the work would look good as he moved out of development toward his goal of a director-level position at a major museum.

Ty didn't have time to think about that today. His next meeting was in less than thirty minutes, and he still couldn't shake the image of the woman in the coffee shop.

AUTHOR'S NOTE

While this series is set in Baltimore, and features many famous institutions in the city, the people and specifics are fictional. It's not about real, behind-the-scenes details.

Why?

Because this is a work of fiction, not an insider's look at those places and events. Because they are the setting and framework for a story about people who do not exist and things that never happened.

I am a huge fan of all of the places mentioned in this story, and this whole series is something of a love letter to my adopted hometown.

Book 1 was drafted pre-pandemic and faced with the options of "fixing" it all, and the resulting changes to the narrative, or leaving them and letting this story exist outside of time, I chose the latter. Again, because this is a work of fiction and not a Baltimore tour book. Books 2 and 3 exist in that same world—outside of time.

Go to the link at the end and you'll find info on many of the places featured in the series—if they still exist, of course, sadly, many closed during the pandemic.

If you ever find yourself in Baltimore—look these places up. They're worth a visit!

In short, any negatives, or "inaccuracies" are entirely works of my imagination and there for the purpose of the story—they are not reflections of the amazing events, places, and people who make Baltimore what it is—a surprisingly wonderful, and very quirky, city that I am happy to call home.

www.RoxanneBlackhall.com/locations

ALSO BY ROXANNE BLACKHALL

Charm City Connections

Book 1 ~ Complementary Colors

Book 2 ~ Intersecting Paths

Book 3 ~ Brewed Awakening

Logan County Love Series

Book 1 ~ Rekindled

Book 2 ~ Scorched

Book 3 ~ Arrested

Bristol Park Series

Book 1 ~ Abbeydon Attraction

Book 2 ~ Abbeydon Academy

Book 3 ~ Abbeydon Abandon

ACKNOWLEDGMENTS

This series started out as a single title and somewhere along the way, it grew into three. And I'm so glad it did.

The list of folks to thank would fill an entire book on its own, and some of the amazing souls willing to answer my strange questions prefer to remain very, very private. Y'all know who you are.

To my Baltimore folks—especially Christa, Zoe, and Trey —thank you for helping this non-native get the right vibe to show off my adopted hometown.

For beer, breweries, and more science than I ever imagined went into making a drinkable brew—Joh, Michael, and Blaire. Plus a special shout out to Mr. Fitzgerald for helping me make my brewmasters feel real. Any errors are entirely mine.

My kids, Gabe and Marcie, are always on hand to help ensure my characters read like 20- and 30-somethings.

And a dizzying number of beta readers, editors, proofreaders, artists, designers, etc. You are so appreciated!

And always, my husband–my real-life romance hero!

This could not have happened without every single one of y'all!

ABOUT THE AUTHOR

Roxanne Blackhall writes steamy, emotionally gritty romances where strong women meet their match in broody, big-hearted men. A former magazine editor from San Diego, she now calls Baltimore home, where she spends her days crafting filthy banter and transformative sex scenes, and her nights cooking up decadent meals for friends, always with a glass of wine (or cup of coffee) in hand.

bsky.app/profile/roxyblackhall.bsky.social

facebook.com/roxanneblackhall

instagram.com/roxanneblackhall

threads.com/@roxanneblackhall

goodreads.com/Roxanne_Blackhall

tiktok.com/@roxanneblackhall